The WEDDING PARTY

TRACEY RICHARDSON

Bella
BOOKS
2011

First Bella Books Edition 2011

Printed in the United States of America on acid-free paper
First Edition

Editor: Katherine V. Forrest
Cover Designer: Linda Callaghan

ISBN: 978-1-59493-234-2

To the unbroken circle—no beginning and no end.

Acknowledgments

As always, thank you to all my readers—your encouragement inspires me so much. My gratitude and affection to Bella Books and all its talented and dedicated women. It has been a real honor and privilege to work with literary icon Katherine Forrest as my editor. Thanks to my fellow authors for your support, leadership and encouragement (you are a true family!). Cris S., as usual, I can always count on her unending help and encouragement. The love and support of my partner, Sandra, has given me the freedom to pursue the work I love. My everlasting thanks to my friends and family for their support and encouragement and for bringing joy to my life.

About the Author

Tracey Richardson is also the author of *The Candidate*, *Side Order of Love*, *No Rules of Engagement*, and *Blind Bet*. She was a Lambda Literary award finalist for *No Rules of Engagement* and has been a finalist several times over for Golden Crown Literary Society awards. Tracey's *Side Order of Love* also won first place in contemporary romance in the Rainbow Romance Writers awards for excellence. Tracey worked as a daily newspaper journalist for almost twenty-five years and now works from home as a freelance editor and writer. She lives in the Great Lakes region of central Ontario, Canada. Visit Tracey on Facebook and at www.traceyrichardson.net.

CHAPTER ONE

Dani (Chicago)

Never in her darkest thoughts had Dani Berringer imagined her life would take such a downward spiral. She was a spool unwinding, caught in a total freefall at the worst possible time—right before her wedding.

Crap! She liked that word and found herself saying it a lot, if only in her head. It was all-encompassing and captured the irony and shitty bleakness of her situation in one simple, useful word. She leaned heavily against the huge glass window, her gaze unblinking on the distant, gray expanse of Lake Michigan. It was an incredible view most days—the John Hancock building reaching into the Chicago skyline like a black arm raised in victory, the curvy line of North Lake Shore Drive hugging the lake, the patch of brown that was the sandy beach, and then the massive lake itself. The waters on this day were gray and turgid, typical for March, and blended perfectly with the sky and most of the surrounding buildings. Blended perfectly with her mood too, but unlike the endless horizon beyond the lake, Dani's world was closing in on her.

Jesus. She was going to miss this place. They both would. It was their dream home, this two-bedroom, sixteenth-floor condo a couple of blocks west of Michigan Avenue and Chicago's Magnificent Mile. It had been such a victory when they'd bought it eighteen months ago. The three-quarters-of-a-million-dollar mortgage and the five-hundred-dollar monthly condo fees were a bit of a stretch, but not beyond them. They'd made it work. Even with Shannon quitting her nursing job last fall, it was totally manageable on Dani's bloated salary.

Until now.

Dani took a deep breath, panic a knife in her gut. They could hold on for maybe four, five months after the wedding. Just long enough to sell and maybe walk away with a hundred grand in their pocket, if they were lucky. Their future, once a pristine and perfectly drawn map, was barren undiscovered territory now, full of unseen dangers. Well, it wasn't entirely unknown. The wedding next week would go ahead and Shannon would keep her appointment at the fertility clinic next month, because there was no way in *hell* Dani was going to see them sacrifice that. She would sell all her earthly possessions, steal if necessary, to ensure successful fertility treatments for Shannon. Having a baby was more important to Dani than anything she'd ever done, any possession she'd ever accumulated, any job title she'd earned.

At the bar she went to pour herself a scotch but stopped before any liquid hit the glass. These eighty-dollar bottles of single malt would have to stop. A lot of things would have to stop. Right after this wedding that was costing them a goddamned mint. *Christ!* Why hadn't they gone for something low-key, something simple, the way Shannon had wanted? Just a hall, nice and quiet, with a few of their closest friends. Or even a ceremony right here in their home. But no. Dani had to be the big shot. Dani had to line up a swanky ballroom at Las Vegas's MGM Grand Hotel for the wedding. Dani had pulled out her platinum Visa card and paid ahead for a lavish dinner and free bar for thirty of their closest friends and relatives. *Jesus*. Thirty grand, gone with the swipe of a piece of plastic. And that wasn't counting flights and the two-hundred-dollar a night room for a week. There were incidentals too, like the two-hundred-dollar boxes of Montecristo cigars, the Dom Perignon, the limo. She shook her head at her stupidity. Thirty grand worth of pride and vanity. Thirty grand they could really use right now.

She poured two fingers of scotch in the thick square glass, and wondered how much money she was about to pour down her throat . . . seven dollars maybe? She'd never thought about that kind of thing before, but now she did. Now the nickel and diming burrowed into her thoughts regularly, like a sliver under her skin she couldn't excise. She swirled the liquid slowly, took a tentative sip. The burning trail down her throat infused her with warmth and calm. A moment of sanity. The feeling wouldn't last, but she would hold onto it for as long as she could.

"Honey, do you think I should risk bringing my good jewelry?"

Shannon emerged from the bedroom, and the sight of her stilled Dani's heart, as it always did. After six years together, her sweetie still made her heart leap pleasurably into her throat. It was everything about Shannon, and not just her silky blond hair and gorgeous green eyes and her trim little body that fit so perfectly against Dani's. It was Shannon's generosity, intelligence, her sense of humor, the loving warmth in her that Dani admired so much. The right partner was supposed to make you a better person, and maybe that was true, she figured, because she tried so hard to be a better person for Shannon. Shannon deserved the best from her.

Dani grinned at her partner, her mood much lighter now. "Of course you should. It's Vegas, baby. Where else can you put on the dog?"

The little frown at the corner of Shannon's mouth was adorable. "I know, but I wouldn't want them to get stolen. Those pearl earrings that were my grandmother's are worth a small fortune now. And that diamond necklace you gave me for Christmas,

I don't even want to think about what you must have paid for that."

Neither do I, Dani thought and smiled through her sudden heartburn. It wasn't her sweet Shannon who had the champagne tastes, it was Dani. Dani was the one who'd felt the need to show off, the one who wanted to keep her woman looking good in brand-name clothes and Cartier jewelry. Shannon was perfectly happy in her jeans and T-shirts and worn down leather boots. It was Dani who'd insisted on the Anne Kleins, the Guccis, the Armanis, the Louis Vuittons in Shannon's closet. Dani was the one always flashing the bills and the patchwork of colorful credit cards in her wallet. Dani liked money, liked the trappings, and wanted the world to know she was a successful business executive who could take care of herself and her woman. And what the hell was wrong with that anyway? It wasn't like she was hurting anyone; she was simply enjoying life.

And they had been enjoying life and its finer things. Except now suddenly, they couldn't. She could no longer even swing half of it. They'd be back to living in a row house, clipping coupons, taking the El train. Shannon back to working shifts at the hospital, maybe even having to work while she was pregnant.

"Honey, are you okay? You look a little pale."

"I'm fine." Dani swallowed and forced a smile. She could cover pretty well for herself. "It's the greatest week of my life, darling. I'm more than fine."

Shannon was instantly at her side and up on her toes, planting a kiss on Dani's cheek. "Just making sure you're not getting cold feet on me."

That elicited a chuckle from Dani. "Never, my love." She kissed Shannon fully on the mouth, spun her around, dipped her. "You are the woman of my dreams, Shannon McCarthy, and if you think for one second that I'm backing out of our wedding, you can forget it. You're stuck with me."

Shannon giggled and squirmed in Dani's arms, pretending to free herself. "I see my lasso is firmly in place around your neck!"

Dani held her lover close. "You've got me hook, line and sinker, darlin'." There was nowhere else she would rather be than in Shannon's arms, and it made her instantly forget the wedding costs, the mortgage payments they wouldn't be able to make much longer, their rapidly shrinking bank account. There was true shelter in Shannon's arms and real peace. *Goddamn*! She was so gorgeous, stunningly so, and way out of Dani's league. She herself was rather plain with her ordinary brown hair and unspectacular blue eyes. She still couldn't believe her luck in snagging this woman. She'd hit the jackpot of her life, and really, any of her problems were nothing as long as she had this woman loving her.

"Since I already have you, sweetheart," Shannon whispered seductively in her ear, "I'd really like to *have* you right now."

Dani laughed, made a little growling noise. She was Wonder Woman and the Bionic Woman all rolled into one when Shannon talked to her like that; she could do anything, be anyone. "Guess this means we don't have to be celibate until the wedding, right?"

"Are you kidding me?" Shannon's green eyes scolded her. "That would be grounds for calling the wedding off, my dear."

"Well, we wouldn't want that, would we sweetie?"

"No, we wouldn't." Shannon poked her lightly in the chest. "So that means you'd better do me right now, my betrothed."

Dani picked Shannon up like a sack of potatoes and swung her over her shoulder, feeling every bit the barbarian about to carry her woman off to her cave. They both laughed all the way to the master bedroom, Dani nearly tripping over suitcases on the floor before she heaved Shannon onto the bed. Shannon, excited about the week, had been packing for days.

The cavewoman act was pure silliness, but there was nothing silly about the way Dani slowly and methodically began removing Shannon's clothes, softly trailing kisses on bare skin with each item of clothing shed. There were times when they went at it quick and hard, both too turned on for foreplay or even romance. Sometimes they didn't even bother to remove all their clothes. One's hands would jam down into the other's pants, a finger or two would slip in and they'd be off to the races. And sometimes right on the sofa or floor, one might yank down the other's pants and bury her head between her legs. Just like that. But this was not one of those hell-bent for quick release times. This was a time for going slow, for savoring every taste, every smell, every touch, every feeling.

Lovingly caressing Shannon's breasts, Dani looked at her lover with wonder. She didn't really deserve Shannon, but by some crazy karma, she'd landed her anyway. Every day, Dani tried never to let Shannon forget how much she loved and respected and needed her. She vowed to herself never to take their love for granted.

Dani stared into Shannon's eyes the entire time she made love to her. She loved seeing in those eyes how much Shannon loved her too. And in just over a week, their relationship would be solemnized. Not exactly legal, not in Nevada or Illinois, but they were tired of waiting. They would have their ceremony, their big wedding bash with all their friends, and in the summer they'd sneak off to Canada for a vacation and get legally married there.

"Oh, Dani!" Shannon was breathing hard, her eyes tightly clamping shut as spasms ripped through her body. "I love you baby," she murmured breathlessly, over and over as she basked in the waning ripples of orgasm.

Dani's heart swelled. She kissed Shannon's nose, her forehead, her eyelids. It wasn't that Shannon would cast her out or hate her if she knew the truth. Shannon loved her and she was the forgiving kind. She was also the kind of woman who would roll up her sleeves and say fine, let's do what we need to do to get on track. But Dani didn't want to look into those eyes and see disappointment. She didn't want to see her own failure reflected there, and she sure as hell didn't want pity. She didn't want Shannon to have to go back to work at the hospital again, just so they could claw their way back up again. They couldn't put off having a baby much longer either, not with Shannon's biological clock ticking. Somehow Dani would just have to navigate them out of this financial quagmire.

"You look deep in thought."

Dani smiled. She'd been good at covering things up the last few weeks; she needed more time. Lightly, she trailed a finger over Shannon's stomach. "I'm hoping in two or three months there'll be more of you to love."

Shannon reached down and stilled Dani's hand. Her voice was light but there was an edge of warning to it. "We'll see. No guarantees that it's going to take, remember?"

"I know, sweetie, I know. But I also know it's going to work. Just you wait."

"I'm not getting any younger, you know."

"Neither of us is. I'm so sorry you have to carry most of the load."

"Stop apologizing for that. You can't help that you had a faulty reproductive system."

"I know. Still . . ."

"Look, I'm fine with it. You know that."

Lately, whenever talk of having a baby came up, Shannon got a little edgy. It was nothing she could put her finger on, just a sense that Shannon was a little nervous. Which was fine. Who wouldn't be? There was the worry of trying to conceive for the first time at the age of thirty-eight—artificial insemination, potentially painful egg harvesting and in-vitro procedures. There were other worries too—a healthy pregnancy, raising a kid in the city, parenting issues. But they'd been over everything many times. Dani tried to lighten the mood. "First things first, my love. I need to make an honest woman of you before you bear my child."

"Ah, you are so chivalrous, Dani Berringer. That's exactly why I'm going to marry you. And I'm expecting you to ride into that ceremony on a white steed."

"Oh, yeah? What if I don't?"

Shannon rolled on top of Dani, pinning her arms above her head. It was a joke whenever she did this, because Dani outweighed her by probably thirty pounds and was far stronger. "I'm sure there are plenty of other hot dykes on white steeds riding around Vegas."

Dani threw her head back and laughed. "That I'd like to see!"

CHAPTER TWO

Claire

So much for getting a head start on packing. Claire Cooper glanced at the plain round wall clock in her office. It was after seven and she still had to eat dinner. And do laundry. And take her yellow Labrador retriever Tucker to doggie daycare. It was a list that wasn't getting any shorter while she continued to sit in her office. *Well, Claire, that's what you get for leaving everything to the last minute.*

Such procrastination and disorder were not typical, but it seemed to be a trend lately that her pregnant patients either popped their babies all at the same time, or developed a sudden complication. Keeping her late today was a worrisome case of third trimester bleeding, and since she was about to go away for more than a week, she didn't want to leave any of her patients stranded, especially this one. The whole week had been following the same script, one wrinkle after another.

"I thought you had a trip to Vegas to get ready for?" Maria, her longtime office nurse, peeked her head around the door. "Shouldn't you be home packing, or counting your bankroll for gambling or something?"

Maria was making fun of her and her conservative ways, which was nothing new. Claire was steady, predictable, boring. Certainly never one to gamble, unless you counted an occasional lottery ticket. Maria could tease her all she wanted but she had no intention of changing her ways and throwing caution to the wind. "Yes, that and washing my tight jeans and glittery tank tops for all the bars I'm going to cruise."

Maria snorted a laugh, her short red hair bobbing, and flopped down on one of the spare chairs in Claire's office. Maria was cute in a perky, youthful way. There had been a mild attraction between them once, months ago, but it had been very short-lived and quite innocent as far as those things go. A little chaste flirting had erupted one day after work over a rare drink in one of Chicago's lesbian bars. Without warning—in fact Claire had been digging around in her wallet for change to pay the tip— Maria had leaned over and kissed her. Right there in the booth as though they were lovers. It hadn't gone further, they didn't talk about it, and for days afterward they were both embarrassed and awkward around one another. It had downright frightened her to think that Maria might have a crush on her, and not because Maria wasn't cute and nice, but because Claire simply wasn't ready to date anyone. An office affair was the absolute worst, people often said, and she wanted nothing to do with it.

After she could no longer stand the tension between them, over a thick pile of lab reports one day she peered over her reading glasses and told Maria there was no chance of a relationship between them. She gave the perfunctory speech about how if she ever was ready to move on, Maria would be a wonderful choice. She took it well, even made a joke out of not bearing a torch for the unattainable Dr. Claire Cooper, and in an apologetic tone, divulged that she'd begun dating someone else anyway.

It had all worked out for the best. They went on smoothly as colleagues and friends, and Maria and her new girlfriend were now in the process of buying a house together. As for Claire, her life had remained solitary. Frozen dinners for one, long walks with her dog, early to bed with a good book. And the heart-wrenching, almost nightly dreams of the life she once had.

"You do know I would pay money to see you doing that!" Maria flashed one of those I-dare-you looks that Claire had come to know well in their six years of working together.

"Yeah, well, don't get your panties in a twist, cuz it ain't gonna happen. I'm not cruising any bars and I'm not gambling."

"Well, if by some miracle you change your mind, my spy will have her cell phone camera with her at all times." Maria's eyebrows danced with mischief. "I could make good money selling those kinds of photos around the hospital, you know."

Claire winced. Prentice Women's Hospital, like hospitals everywhere, was one giant gossip mill, and she was fairly certain that compromising photos of herself would fetch a handsome sum. In fact, Maria could probably retire on it. "Don't you dare! I should fire you for even thinking of it!"

"Oh, come on. You know you can't do without me around this place."

"True enough. But even if I was drunk enough or crazy enough to ever do something silly, which I am *not*, Shannon's hardly going to have time to be spying on me."

"Hey, who said anything about Shannon being my spy?" She winked at Claire to show she was just kidding. "You don't have to worry anyway, because you know what they say—what happens in Vegas stays in Vegas!"

Claire shook her head. "I somehow doubt that, but I can assure you, there will be nothing terribly exciting on my end that will be worthy of keeping secret."

"Well, I suppose I'll never know, but Claire, I really hope you have a great time at the wedding. Talk about puttin' on the ritz. And Vegas of all places!" Maria's eyes shone with mischief and envy. "If it were me going, I'd be camping out at the airport right now just to get a head start."

Claire stared out her fifth-floor window at the darkening

city, trying hard to keep a frown from further deepening the line between her eyes. She didn't share Maria's enthusiasm for Vegas. It wasn't that she was unhappy to go; Dani and Shannon's wedding was a wonderful motive for the trip and she loved them both. But she worried about Shannon. More precisely, she was worried about Shannon's secret. Worried that the secret would fester and grow like a cancer in the relationship if she didn't come clean with Dani before the wedding. It was always bad luck to start a marriage with secrets, wasn't it?

Ah, well. Whatever issues lay between Dani and Shannon weren't her problem. They were big girls, and it would be disastrous to stick her nose in. "I can think of about a million things better to do than sit around an airport, thank you very much," she grumbled to Maria.

"True. O'Hare is not exactly on my entertainment list." Maria heaved herself out of the chair. "Well, tell Shannon I wish her the very best! She's such a sweetheart."

"Yes she is, and I will."

"Good. Mind if I get out of here?"

"Jeez, of course not." Claire glanced at the clock again. "You should have been gone an hour ago. It *is* Friday night after all. Don't you and Karen have any plans?"

"Actually, Karen's visiting her folks in Milwaukee for the weekend. I was just going over a couple of records before I go home since I didn't have anyone to go home to." She sighed dramatically, which made Claire smile, then watched Maria stiffen awkwardly as if just remembering that Claire didn't have anyone to go home to either. "Listen, have a great time, okay? I mean that. And if anyone deserves a little fun, it's you."

"I'll try. And don't forget, I'll have my BlackBerry with me in case you need to reach me."

"I'll try not to have to call you. I know Dr. Bernstrom's covering for you, so don't worry about anything here. Just enjoy yourself. You deserve it."

At home, Claire put off the rest of her packing. The laundry was done, the dog situated, but that was all. She tried to will herself to finish, but didn't make it past the bottle of Merlot sitting on the counter. She poured a glass and sat in the wingback chair by the fireplace, taking solace in the ticking of the antique clock on the mantel. For months after Ann died, she spent hours at a time like this—sitting and drinking wine while time existed only in the movement of the clock's hands. The rhythmic tick-tock and the alcohol were the only things that helped her relax in those days, numbing her from the pervasive loneliness that had rooted into her soul and slowly taken over her life. It was a form of paralysis, the wine and the depression, and it had taken her a long time to pull herself out of it enough to reclaim her position as one of the best OB-GYNs in the city. The worst and blackest of those times were over now, thank God, but she still found comfort in disappearing like this once in a while. And being alone didn't bother her anymore. She'd even grown to like it.

Claire's eyes drifted to the framed picture on the wall of her and Ann in happy times. It was taken about a decade ago, during a camping trip in the Adirondacks, the two of them snuggled up together in matching heavy woolen sweaters, their smiles wide and easy and worry-free. She'd never been happier, never more complete as she'd been when that picture was taken. Everything about their life was easy, safe, nourishing. And then, three years ago, she'd never felt sadder or more hopeless. Such heights and such depths, a great soaring and plummeting that pushed her heart to almost unbearable extremes. Even though Ann's death hadn't been unexpected—the cancer wasn't survivable—Claire hadn't handled it very well, falling to pieces in every way imaginable. She still wasn't handling it all that marvelously, at least in terms of moving forward. Sideways yes, but not forward. Not yet. Oh, she'd tried to fling herself forward once, just over a year ago, at a medical conference in San Francisco. In her relentless search for something to ease her pain, she'd managed to momentarily convince herself that the answer lay in having a one-night stand. So she'd had sex with a very nice woman who had the quirkiest laugh and the kindest eyes Claire had ever seen. Her specialty was oncology, and she had exactly the right temperament for it, as far as Claire could see. They might have even gone on to be friends, but Claire had practically thrown up the next morning from the guilt of what she'd done, and couldn't bear to have anything more to do with the woman. She'd slunk away, guilty and ashamed, vowing never to be so reckless, so fallible, again. It was much safer being alone.

It was the memory of that trip, she told herself now, and her irresponsible sexual escapade that was at the root of her hesitation about Vegas. She sipped her wine, wishing she could just damned well stay home, but she had not been able to say no when Shannon asked her to stand up for her at the wedding. She would do anything for her best friend. Anything but get involved in the issue between her and Dani. *That* she would not do.

Claire closed her eyes, let the alcohol and the ticking of the clock lull her. Hell, what was the worst thing that could happen on this trip anyway? The wedding would be nice. Shannon and Dani would be fine. And she wasn't going to repeat her mistake of the one-night stand—of that she was damned sure. There was absolutely nothing to be afraid of, nothing to dread or worry about. Just go with the flow, that's what she'd do. And the upside was that there'd be so many people around her the entire time, she'd have no time to feel lonely. In fact, it couldn't hurt to get out of her shell for a change, to try life in different surroundings for a week or so. It might even be—dare she think it?—fun!

Claire finished her glass of wine. Her gut was poking at her again, that little warning beacon she got whenever something ominous was about to happen. She went in search of her ever-present bottle of Tums.

CHAPTER THREE

Jordan

Jordan Scott's trouble had begun in the ninth grade.

The trouble being girls. Then women. Any woman. Tall, short, black, white, Catholic, atheist, Protestant, older, younger, blonde, brunette, redhead, butch or femme and every variation in between. Yup, she'd pretty much sampled them all in the twenty-six years since her initiation into the wonderful world of loving women. If dating were equated to a smorgasbord, Jordan was an unapologetic glutton.

The initiation happened innocently enough, watching television one night with her younger brother's babysitter. Cathy was a fox; she'd be called a hottie now. *Whatever*. Fourteen-year-old Jordan was absolutely enthralled by Cathy's long blond hair, full pouty lips and spectacular tits bursting from a tight T-shirt, looking like ripe grapefruits in need of a good squeeze. Oh yeah, the squeezing had been fun!

Jordan rolled onto her back and stretched. The gray light of morning was beginning to peek through the blinds and spill in dim slashes across the bed. Why in the hell am I thinking about Cathy after all these years anyway, she wondered, snatching a glance at the sleeping form next to her. Krissy was blond and young, and yeah, her tits were damned luscious too, sprouting heavily from the long curvy vine that was her body. That must be why she was reminded of Cathy.

Jordan smiled at that night so long ago. Cathy had probably been about nineteen then, practically a woman of the world to the virginal Jordan, who'd done nothing beyond some intense kissing with boys up to that point. Jordan and Cathy were watching a horror movie on TV, the kind where you jump like your ass is on fire at all the scary parts and end up touching each other—legs, shoulders, hands, anything—for comfort and reassurance. When Cathy leaped into her lap and held on for dear life, Jordan had pretty much wet her panties on the spot.

It was an epiphany of the sweetest kind, the discovery of something new and decadent and deliciously forbidden. No one had ever made her wet like that before, and the effect was electrifying. Her world as she'd known it had washed away on the wave of her first real sexual hormones and that sexual high of Cathy in her lap with her arms around her, those soft full lips on hers and those firm hips crashing into her. Jordan didn't go near another boy after that, Cathy having sealed her fate with that first spontaneous orgasm in her pants. It was a high she had been chasing ever since.

That entire summer, Cathy had been amazing in bed. She was just the right kind of teacher—demanding and yet patient, attentive with just the right amount of assertiveness. She knew what she wanted from Jordan and how to elicit it. Knew what Jordan wanted too and how to make her beg for it. She had a lot to thank Cathy for. Cathy taught her how to be a good lover, the lessons having gone on until Cathy disappeared to college and life beyond. They never spoke again, but Jordan had never forgotten her.

Krissy stirred. Just as well that she was waking up, because

Jordan had a plane to catch in three hours. She needed to get moving.

"Hey," Jordan whispered a little coarsely. "Wake up."

Krissy stretched and slowly rubbed the sleep from her eyes. She smiled cat-like. "What's your hurry? I thought last night was just the warm-up."

They'd worn themselves out until well into the night. Or at least, Jordan was worn out. Then again, she was probably a good fifteen years Krissy's senior, and her body didn't bounce back the way it used to. "That was no warm-up," Jordan said dourly. *God!* Did Krissy have to be so bloody energetic and so blind to the fact that she just wanted to get up, grab a cup of coffee and get the hell on with her day? A day that didn't include Krissy. "I'm afraid that was pretty much the whole enchilada."

Krissy rolled her eyes and laughed as though Jordan had made a joke, the gesture providing an odd moment of déjà vu for Jordan. Krissy reminded her of someone. "All right, Jordan, fine. I just figured our date didn't have to end so soon." She stroked Jordan's forearm suggestively, draped a naked leg provocatively over the sheet.

Abruptly, Jordan pulled away. "I told you, I'm leaving for Vegas today. I have to head to the airport in about ninety minutes."

"Yes, and that's exactly why we should go another round." Her smile was sickly sweet and full of promise. "I won't see you for a couple of months. Maybe I'd like to leave you with something to remember me by."

Two months away might seem like some sort of looming disaster to Krissy, but Jordan looked forward to the change of scene. After the wedding, she would stay at her Vegas condo for a little rest and to dabble in some real estate work there. She'd never promised Krissy they would be seeing one another again after last night. Two dates and some hot sex did not make a relationship. Krissy reached for her again, her touch like a hot poker on Jordan's skin.

She pulled away again. "Don't worry, I'll remember you. It's me who will be the forgotten one in another day or two." Jordan tried to sound cheery, though in truth she couldn't wait to get Krissy out of her house and out of her life. "There must be a line of women waiting to get their nails into a hot young thing like you."

Krissy reluctantly sat up and swung her legs over the side of the bed. She slumped in defeat. "I doubt that. Besides, I don't want anyone else."

Jordan should have felt flattered. Krissy was not unlike dozens—hell, hundreds—of other women she had dated. Sure she was a good kid and all, but really, there was no room for her to be part of Jordan's life. If it was just a matter of an occasional date and some hot and heavy rolling around in the sack, Jordan was all for it. But Krissy had the hallmarks of being a high maintenance, demanding, I'm-in-love-with-you kind of girlfriend and very clingy, if her plaintiveness was any indication. It had been a blast, a brief sunburst, but now it was time to move on before the glow of the embers faded to black. It was no secret that Jordan didn't do relationships and all the expectations and the coupling behavior that went with it—picking out blinds, matching paint swatches, buying linen and discussing their thread count . . . *Jesus!* That shit was so not for her. She'd never advertised herself falsely to Krissy or anyone else, and she refused to feel guilty for enjoying a little uncomplicated sex from time to time.

Jordan hopped out of bed as if Krissy were holding a match against her skin. She wanted Krissy gone. Now. "You taking a shower here or at your dorm?"

"Throwing me out already, huh?" There was no humor in Krissy's words and certainly not in her tone. She was clearly pissed, which only heightened Jordan's impatience. Really, in the grand scheme of things, there was no reason for her to pull such a hissy fit. She was being childish. Getting all bent out of shape over nothing.

"Well, yeah, basically. I've got to get moving."

Krissy pouted for a long moment before asking in a challenging tone, "You going to e-mail me or phone me while you're away?"

Jordan picked up a robe from the back of a chair and slipped it on. "Probably not." She was nothing if not honest.

Krissy began pulling her clothes on, slowly at first, as if waiting for Jordan to change her mind and ask her to stay, before picking up her pace. "So that's it? Fuck me a couple of times and then break up with me?"

"Look, what do you want from me? And how can you break up with someone you're not even in a relationship with?"

Her bottom lip quivered before her expression hardened. *Great.* The girl was going to make a big federal case out of this. They were going to have to go through some kind of phony breakup dance first.

"Fine. Whatever," Krissy hissed. She stalked out of the bedroom, snatching up her purse on the way past the dining room table. At the door, she turned toward Jordan, her face red with indignation. "There's a couple of things you should know, Jordan." Her mouth curled into a cruel smile as she spat out the words. "I'm not a twenty-four-year-old graduate student like you thought. I'm a nineteen-year-old freshman. And the reason you keep looking at me funny, like you know me?" She laughed, and it was a bitter sound that sent a shiver down Jordan's spine. Krissy was clearly enjoying thrusting in the dagger. "You knew my mom a long time ago. Cathy Donahue."

Jordan's breath left her in a rush. *Cathy the babysitter?* Cathy who stole her virginity decades ago? Cathy who had been Krissy's age when they had that summer of secret sex? *Oh my God!* Jordan felt the blood drain from her face; it was probably collecting in her knees, which began to shake. But she wouldn't give Krissy the satisfaction of reacting. She said nothing, just trembled silently and let her stomach do crazy flips, wondering all the while if Krissy had planned to drop this bomb at some point or if it was simply an act of revenge for this morning's rejection. It was disingenuous and cruel to keep such secrets.

"She talked about you when you got to be this wealthy real estate person with your face on buses and billboards all over the

place. I wanted to see for myself what all the fuss was about."
That voice. That voice was so familiar now, so much like her
mother's.

Jordan's mouth had long ago gone dry. "Just get out,
Krissy."

Krissy laughed harshly, pleased with her little victory. "Fine.
I'll be sure to tell my mom you said hello."

Jordan leaned against the closed door, trying to coax her
breath back. *Christ*! She'd been fucking the daughter of her first
lover! What a crazy, sick, twisted circle jerk that was! Fuck me,
she thought. She didn't want to—couldn't—think too hard about
any of it right now. She had been juggling the balls in her life
just fine without stopping now for some useless navel gazing.
Business was good; in fact she was thriving professionally, and
in her personal life she was having a great old time, doing as she
pleased, seeing who she pleased, lovin' 'em and leavin' 'em. She
saw no reason to drop any of those balls now. She just wanted
to get on that damned airplane and leave this tiny nightmare
behind.

CHAPTER FOUR

Shannon

The airport was a roiling mass of humanity, but it was Saturday and it was damp and raw and the time of the year when many Chicagoans escape the dreary March weather for a while. Sunshine, warmth, palm trees—the perfect accompaniment to a wedding that Shannon would have been happy to have staged in Chicago. But if a lavish wedding in Vegas made Dani happy, then so be it. Her humble beginnings fueled her sometimes rabid need to spend money, and Shannon could not fault Dani for that. Money was Dani's drug, but most everyone had some kind of crutch or layer of armor against the world. Jordan had all her transient women. Claire's coping mechanism was to withdraw into herself. Shannon's crutch had often been her work. It still could be, if she hadn't given it up last fall so they could concentrate on getting pregnant. She continued to read all the medical journals, met weekly with her former nursing colleagues for coffee and volunteered at the hospital a couple of times a month. In her mind, she would always be a nurse, and she couldn't wait to get back to it one day. What she was growing more sure of was that her return to work would be sooner rather than later.

She sidestepped an energetic toddler crawling on the floor. The little girl gave her pause, especially when the big blue eyes looked inquisitively up at her. Her heart stuttered for a moment, but she would not allow herself to feel sad. Not now. Not this week. She hurried to her travel mates at the gate, glad for the diversion from thoughts of babies.

Shannon looked at the long faces of her friends. This would not do. She wanted—needed—a spark of joy right now. "What's with all the frowns, ladies? It's a wedding, not a funeral."

Dani clasped her hand and gave it a squeeze, her reassurance fading in her weak, accompanying smile. "Nothing to worry about, my love. Just storing up our energy for the week."

Claire added, "It's true. I have a feeling there won't be much rest for us after this plane ride."

"I suspect you're right." Shannon's gaze traveled to Jordan, who slouched in her chair looking anything but like the supercharged, carefree, party girl she usually resembled. She was closest with Dani, but Dani didn't seem to be noticing her funk. Something was most definitely going on in Jordan Scott's world. Shannon said pointedly to her, "Surely *you're* looking forward to a week-long party in Vegas. This should be like Christmas and New Year's all rolled into one for you!"

Shannon was teasing, but her words had a bite to them. She loved Jordan for who she was, but sometimes got a little impatient with the perennial college student act. Jordan was immensely successful in her real estate business, and she wouldn't be where she was in her profession without tremendous business acumen, hard work and a strong sense of responsibility. Unfortunately, she seemed to leave those traits behind at the office, because they certainly didn't extend to her love life. She had the playgirl role down to a fine art and women definitely flocked to her in droves. Her dark brown, almost black hair, her sky blue eyes and her exotic cheekbones were like some kind of chick magnet. Not to mention the seductive charm and the bulging wallet in her pocket. But Jordan was Jordan, and how she lived her life was her business. If the whoring around made her happy, well, who was it hurting? Certainly not her and Dani.

Jordan's smile fell short of convincing but her eyes brightened a little. "Trust me, the Strip isn't going to know what hit it when I get there." She yawned widely and stretched. The contrast between her words and her actions wasn't lost on Shannon. "I guess I had a bit of a rough night last night," she amended meekly.

Claire guffawed. "I thought you would have been storing up your energy instead of using it all up right before the trip. You look more like a pussy cat right now than a tiger!"

"Who said I used it all up? Are you kidding me? My tiger claws are already starting to come out. I'll be back in fine form in no time! A little nap on the plane and I'll be ready."

Claire shook her head sternly, the mother figure scolding a teenager. "Well, we'll just see about that. You should know by now that when you hit forty, the old body isn't the party machine it used to be."

"Speak for yourself, grandma."

Claire threw her head back and laughed. "Those are fighting words, Scott. Too bad I'm not going to take the bait."

"Maybe you should for once, Claire." Jordan's blue eyes were full of icy challenge.

Ouch, Shannon thought. It was true Claire was a little square. She didn't do anything to excess as far as Shannon knew, but the last three years—since Ann's death—Claire was more sober and isolated than Shannon figured was healthy. She hardly laughed anymore, and it was heartbreaking to see her so down, so disengaged. She was only forty-seven. She was still a very good-looking woman. Her short, sandy hair had only just begun graying at the temples, adding to her stately, calm demeanor. And while the frown line between her eyes sometimes gave away the churning inside, Claire's calming, intelligent brown eyes and serene smile were as reassuring as a warm hug. Shannon noticed the way women looked at Claire, how they tried to get close to her, but of course, they never could. Women swooned over the strong but sensitive types, and Claire could certainly have her pick of them. Whether or not she ever dated again, Shannon only wanted her friend to be happy. Maybe the trip would help pull her out of this pervasive disenchantment with life, make her see there was a world out there worth exploring and engaging in.

"Okay, ladies." Dani took the referee role. They were like a pack of siblings sometimes when they all got together, they'd all been friends so long. "No blood spilled before the wedding, at least."

Jordan laughed, springing to life a little. The spar with Claire seemed to have revived her. She settled back in her chair, her legs spread in that cocky, cowboy way she had about her that so many women seemed to find irresistible. "You women have to give me at least one night where you'll try to keep up with me. Seriously, it would do all you wet blankets a world of good!"

Dani grumbled. "Who you calling a wet blanket? There was a day, you know, when I—"

"Never mind, my dearest." Shannon clamped her hand over her lover's mouth. "We don't want to hear about your escapades, especially just days before you're to become permanently joined at the hip with me."

Dani gently removed Shannon's hand and covered it with kisses, the spontaneous affection melting Shannon's heart. "There is absolutely no place I'd rather be, my love."

They kissed tenderly, drawing the expected mild protests from Claire and Jordan.

"Get a room," Jordan teased, not meaning it.

Claire joined the act too. "Are we even going to see you two all week? Or are you going to hole up in your room the whole time, having newlywed sex?"

"Wait," Jordan protested. "Aren't you two supposed to be celibate all week until the wedding night? Not that I would know, but isn't that how it's supposed to work?"

"Celibate my ass," Dani shot back.

Shannon giggled, her mischievous streak asserting itself. She couldn't imagine she and Dani going a week without sex. "Okay, let's all make a pact. We all go celibate for the week or else we all have as much sex as we can."

Claire nearly choked on her coffee. Jordan whooped like a teenager.

"You know which one *I'm* voting for," Jordan supplied, grinning like a fool.

Dani winked. "Me too."

"Claire?" Shannon raised an eyebrow at her friend.

Claire's face was a mask of white. "You can't be serious. What are we, a bunch of undersexed college freshmen on spring break?"

"Yes!" Jordan replied. "Besides, you're single. What's holding you back?"

Claire went silent, sulking into her coffee cup, and Shannon felt compelled to come to her rescue. "Okay, look, I was only kidding, you guys. Forget I even brought it up."

Jordan rolled her eyes. "Speaking of college, what about your niece, Shannon? She's young and gotta be up for having a good time this week. I'm looking forward to having a playmate, since none of you all fit the bill!"

"Hey, no corrupting the kids," Shannon warned, but she was teasing. Amanda was far from being a child. She was a twenty-six-year-old University of Chicago graduate student. She'd been away studying at Stanford the last few years, returning to Chicago last fall to begin work on her PhD in art history. She was so busy studying and working that Shannon barely saw her, but as far as she knew, Amanda was not the partying type. She was a smart, sensible kid. Shannon had picked her to be a bridesmaid in part to rekindle their once close relationship.

"How come she's not joining us on the flight anyway?" Jordan asked.

"She had to work today. She's flying into Vegas tonight."

"God, I haven't seen little Amanda in years," Jordan said. "I probably won't even recognize her."

Dani stood and stretched. "She's not so little anymore. She's twenty-six now and a lot taller than me."

Jordan whistled. "Jeez, I feel old."

"You shouldn't," Claire sniped. "In fact, you should feel right at home with college students."

Jordan leveled a murderous look at her. "Well, if college kids are my milieu, then a nursing home is yours!"

"Whoa!" Shannon interjected. "Truce, you two?"

Claire smiled sweetly. "Don't worry. Jordan and I won't be jousting all week. As soon as she realizes her buffoonery, that is."

Jordan scowled for good measure, then broke into laughter. "Oil and water as usual, eh Doctor Cooper?"

"Nah, just old friends who can appreciate their differences."

The ice having been broken, everyone relaxed.

"Speaking of Amanda," Claire added, "she was a teenager the last time I saw her. I remember thinking then that she was going to be a real heartbreaker one day."

"Oh, she is," Shannon answered, proud of her beautiful, smart niece. "Not that she'd ever fess up, but I'll bet there's a whole string of women in California she left pining for her." It was undoubtedly true, but Amanda was the most discreet person about her love life than anyone Shannon knew. You couldn't bribe, cajole, or force personal information out of her.

The boarding call went out, and Shannon looked out at the cold, gray sky one last time. She was a little nostalgic suddenly, but not in an unpleasant way. The next time she returned to Chicago, she would be a married woman. She couldn't wait.

CHAPTER FIVE

Amanda (Las Vegas)

It was like being inside a noisy arcade—the constant dinging and chiming of slot machines rising above the usual airport din. Who ever heard of slot machines in an airport anyway, Amanda Malden thought scornfully. What struck her was that people were playing them mindlessly, like automatons, killing time while waiting for departing planes or arrivals. She supposed bloodthirsty Vegas was trying to suck every last dollar from the tourists before they left. It was sick, and if gambling was the only thing to do in Vegas—besides her Aunt Shannon's wedding of course—she was going to be bored out of her mind. The casinos weren't getting *her* little bit of hard-earned money.

Amanda was tired and had no patience for the pulsing, cacophonous pinball machine she found herself in the middle of. She blew out an exasperated breath and told herself to calm down, she'd be out of it soon enough. Besides, the visit wasn't about her personal pleasure, it was about Shannon and Dani's. She'd not seen much of her aunt over the last eight years, and she was happy to do her part to help make the week memorable and enjoyable for the brides. They were two of her favorite people, and, as Shannon had reminded her just last week over the phone, it would be a much-needed break from school. She could sure use a break. She'd been working her ass off the last few months with school work and her part-time job. While she loved both, the forced vacation would give her mind a rest and hopefully let her reconnect with her aunt.

Scanning the carousel for her bags, Amanda wondered if she'd get much time alone with Shannon. Shannon was her only aunt, but she would have been her favorite anyway. She had been like a second mom and big sister all rolled into one during Amanda's formative years. With her mother—Shannon's sister—dead now, Amanda and Shannon were really the only ones left in the family. For a while they'd been as close as an aunt and niece could be, but not the last few years. Geography was only partly to blame. The rest was Amanda's fault mostly, because she'd chosen to keep a secret from Shannon, and now she didn't exactly know how to dismantle the image that she'd not so much constructed as she'd let her aunt assume was the truth. How could she tell Shannon she was not the person she thought she was? How could she explain her terrible mistake when there was no justification for her lapse in judgment? It sucked now, carrying around this dishonesty, this secret, and she'd have to find a way to come clean with her aunt, particularly now that she would be in her presence all week. It was much easier to keep a secret from a distance.

Amanda claimed her two bags and wheeled them to the automatic doors leading outside. She had just raised her eyes to look for a cab when she heard her name.

"Yes?" She turned in the direction of the voice. A middle-aged woman as tall as herself but stockier smiled politely and held out a hand. Amanda set her bags down and shook it, seeing few signs of recognition in the woman's face. She had short, slightly graying sandy hair and brown eyes that twinkled softly when she smiled. She looked like the kind of stranger you might slip into a coffee shop with to escape a rainstorm, then end up sharing with her your life story. "Please." Amanda laughed self-consciously. "You have to help me out here. You look so familiar, but I'm sorry, I can't place your name."

"That's okay." The woman's voice, low and warm, assured Amanda that she wasn't the least bit offended. "Claire Cooper, your aunt's friend."

"Oh, my God. My aunt's best friend! I'm so sorry, Claire. How could I have not recognized you?"

"Probably for the same reason I barely recognized you. People change a lot in, what, seven or eight years, I guess it's been? But I do remember you being so tall, so that helped me recognize you. And beautiful. That certainly hasn't changed." The last part was said with a simple frankness that wasn't the least bit phony or gratuitous. Amanda was touchy about people commenting on her looks. Compliments were often because someone wanted something, or backhanded because they were jealous. It was almost comical how women clutched their boyfriends—or girlfriends—a little tighter in Amanda's presence. From Claire, however, the comment was a refreshingly innocent observation.

"I'll agree with the tall part, anyway." Amanda didn't place the same value on her looks that others did. Yes, her beauty opened doors, got her noticed, but in truth, it was sometimes more trouble than it was worth. Jennifer had proven this to be true. Jennifer had treated her like she was royalty, as though her looks conferred some sort of rock star status, and then Jennifer had hurt her in the deepest possible way. She had taught Amanda a bitter life lesson—beauty didn't keep a lover, didn't bring you the kind of happiness you could count on. It was just window dressing that, in the end, didn't amount to a hill of beans.

Claire shook her head lightly, still smiling. "Six-foot tall women are a rarity, don't you find? I almost never come across a woman as tall as me, so it's a treat."

"Yes, you're right. It's pretty rare." And yes, it was kind of a treat standing eye-to-eye with Claire now that she thought about it. Jennifer had been a lot shorter; most people in her life were.

Claire picked up one of Amanda's bags and effortlessly slung it over her shoulder. "Must make it a bit of a challenge to find anyone taller than you. Or does height matter in someone you're dating?"

"No, it really doesn't matter to me." Funny how people assumed, probably because of her youth or her looks, that she dated a lot when in truth she was as celibate these days as Mother Teresa.

"Good. Me either. Sorry, I'm rambling a bit. Must be this desert air. It seems to loosen people up or something. Your aunt asked me to pick you up. I rented a car for the week so I could get the hell out of this place if I need to."

Amanda strode alongside Claire, rolling her bag behind her. "That sounds amazing. I swear I'll go nuts if I have to stay on the Strip for the entire week, and I haven't even seen it yet. Just the idea of it is already making me crazy."

"Well, I'm with you kid. Take my car anytime you want."

"Thank you, Claire. It was very nice of you to pick me up."

"I think Shannon just wanted a friendly face here to greet you. Besides, it gave me an excuse to get out of the hotel and make myself useful."

"You can use me as an excuse anytime." Thank God there was a kindred soul in this group, Amanda thought with relief. She didn't want to spend the week in bars or gambling or shopping. The week was supposed to be a bonding experience for the wedding party and the brides, but not if it meant constant crowds and nonstop drinking and foolishness and spending money she didn't have. Amanda felt far older than her years, always had. She was happiest with a book in her hand, or strolling through a museum or art gallery, or chatting with people about her passion—nineteenth- and early twentieth-century architecture. She didn't even know how one went about going a little crazy and

sowing wild oats, or whatever people in their twenties were supposed to do. She was beyond caring what people thought. Well,
almost . . .

"So," Claire said as she opened the trunk of a black Ford
Fusion and deposited Amanda's bags into it. "The last time I saw
you, you were heading off to college. Stanford was it?"

"Yes. God, that was eight years ago. I remember you now.
Shannon threw a big going-away party for me. I absolutely hated
being the center of all that attention. I felt like some kind of
debutante going off to school or something."

Claire walked around and opened the passenger door, the
little chivalrous ritual surprising Amanda. *Wow. Chivalry in
butches still exists.* She smiled to herself. Coming from anyone but
Claire, the gesture would have seemed contrived and silly. But
Claire had such a modest, polite and efficient purpose about her,
it seemed perfectly natural that she should open a door for her.
Amanda had no trouble imagining her as a doctor. Competent
and caring, totally unpretentious.

"I remember you as a very shy teenager. But Shannon says
you've thrived at college and turned into a very confident, strong
woman." She gave Amanda an appraising look that was thorough
but purely academic. "I can see she was right. You're nothing like
the kid I remember."

It was true. She *had* grown into a confident, capable woman,
but she'd had some difficult times where she'd felt anything but.
Jennifer had sucked away some of that fire and confidence. She'd
been making great gains over the past eighteen months in getting
back to herself. Getting strong again. "Sometimes it feels like
I've been in school forever, but I'm in the home stretch now."

Claire started the car and carefully backed out of the parking spot. "You're doing your PhD at the U. of C., right?"

"Yes. I finished my masters at Stanford, took a year off to try
and earn some money. Came back to Chicago last fall to start my
doctorate in art history."

"Art history. Wow. That sounds fascinating!"

"Really?" Amanda chuckled cynically. "When people find

out my major, that's usually when they start snoring."

"Not at all. I think it's wonderful. What's your specialty?"

"Architecture."

Claire gave her a sidelong, appreciative glance, and Amanda's mood instantly brightened. It was rare to receive such genuine interest in a subject she absolutely adored.

"It's the architecture that made me settle in Chicago after medical school."

"You're not from Chicago?"

"Detroit. Well, Bloomfield Hills to be exact, but I went to school at Northwestern and stayed. I love it in Chicago."

"I know what you mean. I sure missed it when I was in California. Once you get the Great Lakes in your blood, it stays with you, you know? It's just such a unique area of our country, all that fresh water and fertile land. And we've had some of the best and brightest urban architects in the entire world call Chicago home. Daniel Burnham, William Holabird, Bruce Graham."

"I wouldn't think of living anywhere else."

Amanda said after a moment, "I don't think I ever will again either. I guess California seems like the place to be when you're young, but it just doesn't have the same bones as Chicago. It doesn't have the same permanence and the deep roots, you know?"

"I do know what you mean." Claire chuckled lightly. "Sorry, it's the way you said California appeals to young people. You're still awfully young. Doesn't it appeal to you?"

It wasn't unusual for people to underestimate Amanda because of her age, or to hold it against her. She was used to it in her line of study, but it still rankled. "The appeal was never really there for me. I like old things, things with character and history and permanence. You don't have to be older to be wise, or to know what you like and don't like. I know what I like."

"You're right. I'm sorry. There are many wines meant to be drunk young."

Amanda smiled. She wasn't upset with Claire. She'd just wanted to make a point. "Okay, being compared to wine is a first, but I like it."

"Good, because I don't mean to insult you. I'm a bit of a connoisseur. In fact, I think wine is one of the world's great inventions."

"I agree totally. But I guess you could say I'm the opposite of a Bordeaux."

Claire licked her lips. "Let's see. You're a Napa Merlot. Or maybe a New Zealand Sauvignon Blanc."

"Crisp and fresh. Bold, young flavors. I'll take it!"

They both laughed like they were old friends. For the briefest instant, Amanda almost wished this older, intelligent, accomplished woman were hitting on her—accepting her as a peer, as worthy of being a potential lover. She didn't want Claire to dismiss her as a lightweight, a youngster.

It might as well have been noon as midnight for the traffic in town. Amanda's eyes nearly popped out of her head as they neared the Strip with all its dazzling bright lights and heavy traffic. Blinking and flashing and dancing in crazy patterns, the lights were blinding. People packed the sidewalks, cars cruised along slowly so the drivers could gawk or be gawked at in their Beemers and Ferraris. It was a veritable human zoo come alive in a video game. "Oh, my God, this place is unbelievable."

"Does give you new appreciation for what we have back home, doesn't it?"

"Everything is so transient here. I can't believe they tear down these hotels every thirty or forty years and build new ones like they're disposable or something. There's no history, just a generation or maybe two. God, I feel like I'm on a Disney movie set or something."

"I know. Incredible, isn't it? Nothing's real." Claire reached over and patted Amanda's arm, and it was a comforting, companionable gesture that sent a tiny, sizzling jolt through Amanda. "I have a feeling we're the odd women out in this group, but tell you what. Let's help each other try to make the best of it, okay?"

"Deal. And if one of us falters, the other has to pick her up and drag her along!"

Claire laughed, shaking her head lightly. "Do we need to develop signals or code words?"

"Yeah. Help! Will that work?"

"Yeah, that'll work just fine."

CHAPTER SIX

Dani

Dani's silence over brunch was deliberate. She was grateful Shannon and Jordan were monopolizing the conversation. She didn't feel much like talking, or much like being in the moment, and so she was present but absent, immersed in feeling sorry for herself. The headhunter working on her behalf to find another job had made no progress so far, which meant she wouldn't be able to keep them above water much longer. The thought of having to confess her failure to Shannon tied her stomach in knots. What the hell was she going to do? She had to find a job, borrow money, do something, because she couldn't fathom losing everything they'd built together so far, everything they'd planned for the future. Would Shannon even stick with a loser like her? Was she finally about to fulfill her parents' prediction that a girl from a working poor family in Nebraska would never amount to anything? She wanted to throw up. She would *not*—could not—let her family be right. She showed them before that she was a success and she'd simply have to find a way to do it again.

"Honey, you're hardly eating," Shannon whispered, full of concern. "Is your stomach bothering you again?"

Shannon had noticed her habit lately of rubbing her stomach. It was her way of trying to calm the churning within. "I'm fine, darling. Really." With concealed effort, Dani began shoveling the omelet into her mouth. Oh yes, she was good at putting on façades, like stuffing her face when she didn't feel like eating, continuing to spend money she didn't have. She could be an actor, and she would do whatever it took to get through this week intact, to keep Shannon's love, to have one more good week at least before the seams of her world split wide open.

It was Sunday, their first full day in Vegas, and talk had turned to how they were all going to spend it.

Across the table, Jordan shot Dani one of those mischievous glances she knew so well—the kind that pleaded for some fun. Fun with Jordan these days was pretty tame. Domestic bliss had clipped Dani's wings, and just as well, too. Jordan was tough to keep up with, carrying on sometimes like she was still twenty-five years old. It didn't bother Dani that Jordan liked women and parties and maybe a drink or two too many. She'd seen Jordan smoke the odd joint too, had even joined her in it a few times before she got involved with Shannon. Jordan sometimes joked about their B.S. days—Before Shannon—and Dani simply retorted that the B.S. really just stood for bullshit. They were bullshit days that she had no desire to return to. Being grown up and sharing her life with Shannon was way better than any drug or booze high, and certainly better than one-night sex with strangers. Dani gave Jordan a secret smile. There was nothing hotter than sex with her Shannon as a matter of fact, and nothing more satisfying than knowing they would spend the rest of their lives together. Jordan could have her life.

In sickness and in health, for richer and for poorer. Dani grew sick inside as the vow she would be saying in a few days repeated in her mind. She'd never given much thought to the words before because they were just words to her. Words to be taken for granted, that had no real meaning. Now the words hammered hard at her. Now they meant something. Now they were a test, because it was easy when life was going your way.

"Well?" Jordan prompted.

"Well, what? What plans are you brewing in that oversexed, alcohol-infused brain of yours?" Dani asked slyly.

Jordan smirked. "Nothing that requires sex or alcohol, believe it or not."

Shannon gave Dani a sidelong warning glance in jest, and Dani squeezed her lover's thigh reassuringly.

"Really? God, are we going to sit around and read a book or something?"

"Very funny, Berringer. I was going to suggest a little black-jack. If you're up to the challenge, that is."

Cards always sent a little surge of adrenaline through Dani. She'd come to Vegas a couple of times with Jordan and they'd spent countless hours gambling. "Oh, I'm up to that little challenge, my friend!" She nudged Shannon. "What about you, honey?"

"I want to spend some time at the pool catching up with my lovely niece." Shannon winked across the table at Amanda. "Even though she just lives on the other side of the city, I hardly ever see her."

Amanda blushed a little before flicking a meaningful glance at Claire. "The pool sounds wonderful, but Claire, please say you'll join us."

Claire shrugged and set her fork down. "If the options are lounging by the pool or playing blackjack, I'll take the pool, thank you."

"It's settled, then," Dani announced. "Us degenerates will hit the tables while you ladies hit the pool. Shall we meet for a drink before dinner?"

Shannon rose and kissed Dani on the lips. "Sounds good, sugar. And don't lose your shirt, unless we're up in the room and I can enjoy the view."

In the casino, Dani grabbed Jordan's arm to halt her from

taking a seat at a fifty-dollar table.

Jordan scrutinized her, puzzlement written all over her face. "We always play at the fifty-dollar tables. What's up?"

Dani hedged. She was too ashamed to tell Jordan the truth about her job. Friends for over a dozen years, back from the days when neither had much money, Jordan had come out clearly ahead in the wealth department. Not that it was a race, but Jordan was undoubtedly working on her second million by now and maybe even her third. They didn't talk about money; that'd be below them. It was expected and accepted that they were both more than comfortable, and anything less would be shocking and shameful. "I'm not feeling especially lucky today," Dani lied. "Let's try the twenty-five dollar tables."

"All right. Whatever." Jordan nabbed two seats at the cheaper table nearby.

Without preamble, Dani said, "You seem to be back to your old self today." She'd noticed Jordan's sullenness at the airport but had been too consumed by her own problems to address it at the time.

Jordan placed two twenty-five dollar chips in the betting circle to Dani's one. "I was a little out of sorts yesterday, but I think I've got my mojo back. I've even decided to stay here with you guys for the week instead of at my condo."

"Great. What made you change your mind?"

Jordan shrugged one shoulder, signaled the dealer with her other hand that she would sit on her seventeen. "I just don't feel like being by myself."

Dani laughed cynically. "Since when are you ever by yourself anyway? You always have some hot little number on your arm when you're not busy with work." She signaled the dealer for a hit on her fourteen and promptly busted with a ten. "Shit."

"True, but hey, I'm trying to ease up a little on that stuff. You know, have some down time once in a while."

"Yeah, I know exactly what kind of down time you're talking about. More like, going *down* on some little Pop Tart, isn't that what you mean?"

Jordan slugged Dani's arm and whispered, "Christ, I'm not that much of a slut!"

"If you say so."

"I'm serious, Dani. Time for me to switch things up a little, that's all I'm saying. After this week, this tiger is losing her stripes."

Dani had never heard her friend talk like this before. And if she wasn't kidding, then something must have prompted this sudden transformation. She couldn't remember a time when Jordan wasn't dating or on the prowl, and always for a younger woman. "What happened? Some cute young thing ask you what it was like before the Internet existed? Or worse, computers?"

Jordan gave her a look that could melt a glacier. "Very funny. I'm serious. I feel like I'm starting to get a little old for certain things these days. I don't know. Like maybe it's time I behaved myself and went out with people my own age."

A cocktail waitress tapped them on the shoulder. She was young, red-haired and doe-eyed. Her skimpy costume thrust her ample breasts in their direction, and both Dani's and Jordan's eyes dropped reflexively. "Would you ladies care for a drink?"

"Sure!" Jordan enthused, her eyes riveted on the young woman's breasts. Fresh color rose to her cheeks, and Dani simply couldn't imagine a chaste version of her friend. It was unfathomable. "I'd love a mimosa."

"Make that two," Dani added before turning her attention back to Jordan. "Christ, maybe she's got a used car she could sell you too."

"Aren't you just full of the one-liners today, Berringer. For your information, there is nothing she could offer me that I would want. Other than a drink."

Dani placed another chip on the table. "Get outta here. You're toying with me."

"Nope. It's true." Jordan placed her bet and watched the cards being dealt. Another winning hand for her, another losing one for Dani.

"Crap," Dani grumbled.

"Since when do you care about losing a couple of hands? Jeez, you've only lost fifty bucks. It's not the end of the world."

Christ, it might as well be. A couple of months ago, fifty bucks was coffee change. But that was when she was a senior manager at one of Chicago's most successful marketing companies, pulling in a couple of hundred grand a year, plus bonuses. Now she was just another jobless sap who'd been chewed up and spit out by the shitty economy.

She deliberately ignored Jordan's comment, not wanting to tip her off that something was wrong. She gamely put another chip in the circle. "Anyway, what's with this new look-but-don't-touch policy of yours? Are you seriously ending your cougar days?"

"Seriously thinking about it, anyway. Or maybe not even dating at all for a while. I don't know yet."

"Wow! I don't know what to say. I'm having trouble imagining it."

Dani had never understood the appeal of Jordan's lifestyle. On the face of it, it seemed exciting—always a hot-looking young woman on her arm, jetting off for weekends somewhere and eating at the most expensive restaurants. Jordan's money, intelligence and her exotic looks insured she had no shortage of lady friends. She knew how to pour on the charm too. But didn't she ever want good conversation? Companionship? A partnership with someone? Didn't she ever want to settle down like everyone else? They'd never talked about it before, but now that Jordan had opened up the subject, Dani was dying to know more.

"Look," Jordan said crustily. "You don't have to make such a big frigging deal out of it. It's not like I just told you I'm going straight or something."

"Okay, now *that* would make me haul you off to the nearest shrink."

The young hottie returned with their drinks, only this time Jordan barely glanced at her. There was a time when Jordan would have provocatively slipped a five-dollar bill into the woman's cleavage, had a little flirtatious fun with her. Not today, and the contrast in her behavior was a little shocking.

"So why the big epiphany?" Dani asked after the cocktail waitress moved on. "It's not because you just turned forty, is it?" Perhaps Jordan's version of a midlife crisis was exactly the opposite of buying a bright red sports car and discovering promiscuity. Maybe it meant finally growing up. "Or because of the ribbing you took from Claire yesterday?"

Jordan shrugged. They were as close as sisters, but true heart-to-hearts were rare for them. Jordan had no one in her life with whom she really opened up. She kept the important things to herself, and Dani suspected something important was going on with her friend. She would talk about it when she wanted to talk about it. Or she wouldn't, but Dani decided she wouldn't force it out of her. Too much true confession time might mean she'd have to open up about her own situation, and she wasn't ready for that.

Jordan sighed. "I don't know. It's hard to explain. I guess I'm just not *feelin'* it anymore. I need a break, I guess."

Dani decided to let it go. Clearly Jordan was a little lost at the moment, but Dani could tell it was as far as she wanted to go with the conversation. Still, a little teasing was too hard to resist. "Wow. I never thought I'd see the day. My little Jordan is finally growing up."

"Look, it's not like I'm getting married or something. I'll leave that part up to you."

"I'm telling you, Jordie, you don't know what you're missing." Dani busted on her hand again and exploded with a curse. "I can't believe how badly I'm losing. Jesus Christ, this sucks big time!"

Jordan looked at her, her forehead wrinkled in concern. "It's okay, Dani. I can spot you a few chips if you need them."

"I don't need them, okay?" Dani snapped. *Shit*. She didn't mean to be so grouchy about it. She took a long sip of her drink to calm down.

"You okay?" Jordan's eyes probed Dani's.

"Fine." She exhaled slowly, settling herself. "Just the stress of the buildup to the wedding probably."

"The wedding's going to be great, and you know you and Shannon are meant for each other. Come on. What's to worry about?"

"I know. You're right." This time Dani took a longer drink. She would be glad when this week was over. She would be glad when she didn't have to pretend anymore.

CHAPTER SEVEN

Claire

Claire sucked in her breath at the sight of Amanda striding onto the pool deck in a sleek one-piece bathing suit the color of emeralds. It matched perfectly the shade of her eyes, and the effect was stunning—so much so that Claire didn't even recognize her own response. Amanda was by far the most graceful woman Claire had ever seen, and not just because of the way she moved. It was her quiet confidence and her natural beauty, which she seemed to wear comfortably yet modestly. So modestly, in fact, that she did not even seem to be aware of her own beauty. Claire recalled her own shock at seeing the tall, dark-haired, stunning young woman stroll through the airport doors. Amanda had been a gawky teenager the last time she'd seen her, and it was really only her eyes—eyes that were exactly like her aunt's—and her height that Claire had recognized. Amanda was certainly no gawky teenager now. She was a lovely young woman full of poise and genuineness, maturity and intelligence. A real head turner.

It had come as a surprise how well they'd gotten on, as though they were old friends. But the real surprise for Claire was her reaction to Amanda, so immediate and powerful. Magnetic, almost. She couldn't seem to stop looking at Amanda, smiling at her, wanting to be around her, like a planet revolving around the sun. *Jesus Mary and Joseph!* What had come over her? Was she having some kind of delayed grieving reaction over Ann? It was ridiculous. *She* was being ridiculous. Claire had no intention of acting on this crazy thing happening to her, least of all with a twenty-six-year-old who was the niece of her best friend. Not a chance in hell. Claire—upstanding, conservative, always one to obey every rule or law, would *never* be interested in someone so much younger. Such a fool thing was far too unorthodox and absolutely out of the question. In fact, she was quite sure she would never date again. Period. Dating was something young people did, or desperate people did. Well, she was neither of those things. She'd had her kick at love, at long-term partnership, and fate had taken it away from her. She wasn't about to try to steal it back.

Claire sucked in a deep, agonizing breath. Where was all this nonsense coming from all of a sudden anyway? It was insane. *Must be the change in altitude, or the dry air, or something.*

Shannon, lying on the chaise beside her, clutched Claire's arm and said proudly, "Did you notice how everyone's eyes are on Amanda right now, men and women?"

Claire pulled her sunglasses back over her eyes. She didn't know or care if everyone at the pool was watching Amanda. It was bad enough that her own eyes had followed her every step. She forced her gaze away, hoping Shannon hadn't noticed she'd been among the gawkers. At least Shannon wouldn't be able to read her mind. "I hadn't really noticed."

"She sure is pretty, isn't she?"

Claire coughed around the lump in her throat. Pretty? *Try breathtakingly beautiful, not to mention sexy as hell and six feet of pure—Oh, God!* This sudden, agonizing attraction to Amanda was like a rogue wave in a calm sea, smashing against her suddenly, knocking her over, turning her upside down, sucking her deeply in. It was totally unexpected. And totally inappropriate in so many ways, she couldn't even begin to list them. She didn't want this.

"Sorry I'm late," Amanda said, towering over them. Her smile was relaxed and friendly, her dimples sending Claire into a new and unwanted stratosphere. "Mind if I take the chair beside you, Claire?"

"Of course not." Oh, Christ, Claire thought, helpless to give any other response. The thought of Amanda lying just inches away from her, the sun kissing her flawless skin and the slight breeze rustling her soft, shiny brown hair, was almost too much to bear. It was smothering her, a weight on her chest she couldn't breathe around. She had to get a grip on herself, and fast, because now she was thinking about her own lips kissing that skin, her fingers touching Amanda's hair. *Goddammit, stop it, you old fool!* What the hell was happening to her? Had Jordan rubbed off on her or something? Was she having some weird menopausal moment? Early senility?

Amanda, thankfully, didn't seem to have the faintest inkling of the crazy thoughts stampeding through Claire's mind. She absently sat back against her chaise lounge, stretched out her long legs, and pulled a book from her bag. *Suite Francaise* by Irene Nemirovsky.

Claire smiled at Amanda. It wasn't like she had a choice; she couldn't look at Amanda and not smile, no matter how hard she tried. "No light vacation reading for you, I see."

Amanda shook her head and flashed those adorable dimples. The effect was like a lightning bolt going straight to Claire's crotch. "I like a book I can really get into. I'm a bit of a nerd when it comes to books."

"Me too. Though at least I look the part. You certainly don't." Claire pointed to the book. "It's good. I read it a couple of years ago."

"You do not look like a nerd," Amanda replied kindly. She

was always so polite. Such a *nice* kid.

"Raised to be kind to your elders, hmm? Did your aunt teach you that?"

"Hell, no," Shannon interjected. "I only taught her to be nice to you, since you're my best friend and maid of honor."

"Hmmm. I'm also the oldest one in our group. Coincidence? I think not!"

Shannon's and Amanda's laughter was virtually identical. They really were two of the nicest women Claire could ever hope to have in her life, and alike in so many ways. Well, she didn't know Amanda very well, but she could tell she was one of the good ones. Smart and funny, just like her aunt. Serious but with a sharp sense of humor too. She must have a veritable parade of hopeful young women in her life, trailing after her. *Lucky them*. She had absolutely no idea what Amanda's love life was like, since Shannon had never mentioned anything beyond the fact that Amanda had come out to her when she was a student at Stanford. It would be surprising if Amanda didn't have a steady girlfriend—another grad student perhaps—and that thought made Claire feel better. Safer, like things were shifting back into their normal place again.

"You know something?" Claire said, emotion suddenly infusing her voice. "You two are so lucky to have each other. I envy that." She missed having that one person in her life she was closer to than anyone else. The kind of person you could be your best with, or your worst, and still be loved and accepted.

"Aw, Claire." Shannon squeezed her wrist. "We're all family—me, Dani, you, Amanda. You know that, right?"

"I know." She missed Ann suddenly, the pain of her death lancing through her, fresh like it was yesterday—an acute reminder of the dark storm clouds that had descended on her in those months after Ann's death, debilitating her, leaving her practically a recluse. She'd emerged from the worst of it, not unscathed, but alive, and yet still sometimes those rain clouds fell upon her again as they did now, pulling her back into darkness. She was afraid sometimes she would be swallowed up, drowned in her grief. Her eyes misted over, and it took effort to pull herself together. She didn't want her friends to see her like this.

Amanda gazed worriedly at her, as though reading her mind, and all Claire could think was how nice it'd be for the four of them to go out for a quiet dinner some time. There was no reason they couldn't; they all lived in the same city. But matching up schedules would be difficult. This week, before the wedding, they could all do lunch or dinner. *Oh, hell!* What was the use? It's not like Amanda would want to spend time with someone twenty-one years her senior and whom she hardly knew. She surely had better ways to spend her time, and in fact, being around her only reminded Claire of how alone she was, of what she was missing, of what it was like to have your whole life still ahead of you. She envied Amanda.

"Oh, I love this song," Shannon declared. It was Lady Gaga and Beyonce, their song "Telephone" bursting from the oversized poolside speakers. "I can't wait for us all to go dancing this week!"

"You always did love to dance, and always to the latest music. You know more of this stuff than I do, Aunt Shannon."

Shannon frowned across Claire at her niece. "How can someone your age not know and love this music?"

Amanda rolled her eyes. "Oh, God, you're not going to start on me, are you?"

"Start what?" Claire asked innocently.

Amanda leaned close. Claire could smell the sun on her skin, and she inhaled deeply. It almost made her dizzy with pleasure. "She thinks I'm a fifty-year-old in a twenty-six-year-old body. In other words, a geek."

"Well, you are, my dear, but you're an adorable one." Shannon chuckled, turning her attention to Claire. "She loves old black-and-white movies and jazz music too. Can you believe it? I think she was born thirty years too late."

"Well, I happen to like that old era of music and movies too," Claire countered, pretending to be insulted.

"Yeah, but you're old. Amanda's not."

Claire huffed noisily. She raised her eyebrows at Amanda. "She's outnumbered. What do you say we throw her in the pool for that?"

Amanda's eyes lit up as brightly as the neon lights of the Strip. "Oh, yeah." Her conspiratorial grin thrilled Claire beyond measure.

"Oh, no, you don't!" Shannon's eyes widened in panic. She was practically shaking. "That's not even funny, Claire Cooper."

Claire laughed unforgivably and leapt from her chair. She was a head taller than Shannon and much stronger. With Amanda's help, Shannon was a sure goner.

Amanda didn't need any more encouragement. Each woman positioned themselves alongside Shannon and clutched her under her arms, heaving her up in one swift move.

"Oh my God, stop it you two!" Shannon's protestations were comical and easily ignored. They carted her off toward the pool, and between the two of them, it took very little effort. "Amanda Jane Malden, put me down right now! And Claire, you're a doctor, for God's sake. You can't—"

On a count of three from Claire, they heaved the still protesting Shannon into the pool. Claire and Amanda laughed so hard they doubled over, clutching their stomachs. It wasn't long before Shannon's head popped up and she joined them in their laughter, spurting water from her mouth at them like a fountain. She splashed them vigorously.

"All right, you two. Get your asses in here."

CHAPTER EIGHT

Jordan

"To Vegas, baby!" Jordan raised her margarita and boister-ously clinked glasses with the others, sloshing some of the sour green liquid onto the table. She'd had a few drinks already, start-ing with mimosas when she and Dani were gambling. She was getting a little sloppy, but to hell with it, she was having a blast. She'd been working a lot of back-breaking hours lately, wrapping up some big land deals with some speculators in Chicago, and soon she'd be tackling a decrepit old motel in Vegas that, with the right buyer, could be transformed into something swanky and profitable. She *so* needed this break from work.

They were all assembled for dinner at the popular Border Grill Mexican restaurant at the Mandalay Bay hotel. Claire was about to offer a toast. She hoisted her glass of wine, her hand steady of course, because the upright, uptight Dr. Claire Cooper never got inebriated. Never made a fool of herself. Probably never even stepped on the cracks in sidewalks.

"To Dani and Shannon. To the start of the best week of your lives. May you always be surrounded by the love of your friends and the excitement and optimism enshrined by this glamorous city."

"Hear, hear!" everyone chanted, clinking glasses heartily.

They tore through their tortilla soup and green corn tamales, the food temporarily sobering Jordan. Next up was a chicken enchilada bursting its seams, and she stuffed herself, not realizing until now how hungry she was.

"Dani, isn't your sister supposed to join us any day?" Jordan asked around a mouthful of enchilada. With five of them, someone was always the odd woman out. It would be nice to have an even number.

"Heather's been sick. She's hoping to be better in a couple more days, and then she'll join us."

"So I'm stuck with you party animals?" Jordan teased, making a face. Heather was straight, newly divorced, and a load of fun. She'd pretty much do or say anything for a laugh, and didn't care a hoot what people thought of her. She might be exactly what was needed to inject a little fun into this altogether too serious group.

"'Fraid so." Shannon winked at her. "Surely by now you must have some wild and crazy friends in this town if we're not lively enough for you."

"Oh, you're lively enough. If I can just get these horses to water, I'm sure you all will take a drink. In fact, I'm counting on it for the bachelor party." If they couldn't get up for *that*, which Jordan had lined up for later in the week, then there was just no damned hope for them.

Claire had to be crapping her drawers about the party, because the mere mention of it had her slinking into her chair like she might become part of the fabric. Amanda was almost as bad. She was lost in her own world, quietly counting the number of tiny lights strung across the ceiling that twinkled like little stars. What was with that kid anyway? She was young, hot and in Vegas. Couldn't she try a little harder to have a good time? As in drinks and dance bars and pool parties? Jordan noticed the way women drooled over her whenever she walked past. Men too, of course. There was a veritable smorgasbord of sex out there if only she would dive in. Yet Amanda took no notice whatsoever, or if she did notice, she could care less. She walked around like she'd rather be anyplace but here. Like maybe a library, perhaps. Or a museum. *Jesus!*

"All right, let's put it to the test," Jordan challenged. "Who wants to come to the Rum Jungle with me tonight?"

"Now?" Dani asked around a yawn. "Hell, I'm still on Chicago time."

"Yes, now. It's almost ten. The city's just coming alive."

"Well, if that's true," Shannon said in a sultry voice, "then I look forward to things coming alive in my room. Honey?" She raised an eyebrow at Dani. "You're not getting sleepy on me, are you?"

"Never, my love. You *know* I can handle anything you want to throw at me."

"Gak," Jordan erupted, not really meaning it. "Can't you two at least wait until the honeymoon before you get all horny on us?"

Dani laughed. "Haven't you always said yourself, why do tomorrow what you can do today?"

"True, I do always say that, don't I?" Jordan turned her attention to Amanda, who seemed to be in need of a little soul rescuing. "You, young lady. You look like you need some fun. Come with me and I'll show you the way to depravity!"

Amanda looked like a doe caught in Jordan's crosshairs, terrified and in need of escape. Jordan let out an evil chuckle. She used to have young girls like Amanda for breakfast.

Claire promptly stood and gallantly threw herself on the sword. "I'll go with you Jordan. But just for a drink. And not at some insane dance bar called Rum whatever."

Man, what a geriatric bunch. "Okay, Dr. Cooper. Let's go. Nighty night, ladies. Sleep tight."

• • •

The Lounge was an upscale bar at the Mandalay Bay, contemporary with glass tables and large chocolate brown, leather wingback chairs—the kind that scooped you up and made you want to stay there forever. A pianist played softly, an old classic by Roberta Flack, and Jordan and Claire claimed opposing seats. It wasn't the Rum Jungle, but it was a place to unwind at least. They each ordered a drink—Jordan a bourbon on ice, Claire a sour apple martini.

"Ooh, a little daring of you, Claire. I like it!"

Jordan had long ago abandoned trying to get Claire to loosen up, but it was still fun teasing her, pushing her a little. She remembered how Claire was with Ann, who was her polar opposite in so many ways. With Ann, Claire had inched out of her shell. They played on a women's recreational hockey team together, headed up a lesfic book club, hosted dinner parties. Now that Ann was gone, Claire did none of these things as far as Jordan knew. A light had gone out in her.

Claire smiled nervously, making small talk until their drinks arrived. Neither blinked at the price—seventeen dollars for the martini and thirteen for the shot of bourbon. It was Vegas, and the only things cheap were the taco stands on the street and the one-dollar margaritas at the one-stars. Jordan watched Claire take bird-like sips of her drink. Nothing ever rattled her, not even, Jordan imagined, a birthing woman bleeding out on the table. Except for tonight. Tonight Claire looked nervous, scared even, like something indeed was bothering her but Jordan knew she'd have to be careful with her. Claire was sensitive, especially since Ann's death, and she didn't like to be pushed too hard or challenged or lectured. They'd all taken turns trying to get her to come out with them, even tried to set her up on a couple of dates. Claire had resisted all the way, had come to resent their efforts. And so Jordan would carefully wait her out, see if there was something she wanted to talk about. Jordan was good at that, letting the other person make their move first, and it was one of her attributes that made her such a successful real estate agent.

It was on their second drink and another round of small talk before Claire approached the heart of the matter. She cleared her throat as though she were about to make an announcement. "You never seem to have an issue with dating younger women. I mean, what's it like?"

Ah, now it was all making sense. Jordan smiled, but not too presumptuously. Now she knew what was up with Claire. "Well, I don't really have a comparison since I've never dated anyone over thirty. But it's . . . different."

"Different how?"

This was no simple girl talk to Claire, not the way she was stiffly leaning forward, her senses keenly on edge. "Well, let's see. They tend to be very energetic, in and out of bed."

Claire colored a little, and Jordan smiled to herself. God, it was tempting to push her buttons and really get into the sex talk, but she resisted. Claire looked far too fragile for that. She was like a teenager trying to confess a crush on someone completely unattainable. Who was Jordan to deflate her by making a joke out of it?

She pointedly steered the conversation away from sex. "They can get bored easily though. Hell, I get bored easily, so I guess that's nothing to do with age. Conversation can be a little superficial sometimes. And things like movies and music are hard to talk about when you're from different eras. One of my recent dates thought Supertramp was the name of a porn star, can you believe that? And forget talking about your career, or things like mortgages or retirement savings or anything like that. They're not there yet."

"It doesn't sound very appealing, the way you describe it."

Jordan granted Claire the point. "No, it doesn't, does it." Her head was a little foggy from the alcohol, but for the life of her she couldn't really think at the moment what appealed to her so much about dating young women. It had to be the sex, right? Or maybe it made her feel somehow more youthful, more lively, more attractive. She shook her head. *How pathetic.*

"You mean the shine is wearing off those brand-new pennies?" Claire's smile was a little smug but not mean.

Jordan shrugged. She didn't want to confess anything to Claire. Didn't want to talk about how she'd unknowingly slept with the daughter of her first lover. It was a bit icky, kind of incestuous really, and she'd never have bedded Krissy if she'd known who she was. She'd come full circle with mother and daughter, and it sobered and scared her. Had her life really come to that? Was she so indiscriminate about who she slept with? And what was she so scared of that kept her continuing this juvenile behavior? Old age? Losing her looks? The answers eluded her, but she somehow wanted to start over, change things up for herself. It was time. "I don't know. I guess everybody's gotta grow up sometime, right?"

Claire studied her drink thoughtfully before raising her eyes. "Maybe not all young women are the way you describe."

"No, probably not. Just the Pop Tarts I happen to choose. Amanda, on the other hand . . ."

Claire jerked to attention, her eyes widening visibly as though someone had just given her a pinch. *Bull's eye!* She started to mumble something incoherent before quickly raising her drink to her lips.

Jordan continued as if she hadn't noticed Claire's discomfort. "Amanda doesn't seem to be anything like the women I've dated. She seems really bright and classy and extremely mature. And good-looking, my God! She's grown into a remarkable beauty, don't you think?"

By the time Claire set her drink down, her composure had returned. "Yes, she does seem like a very fine young woman."

Fine? It was time to call Claire out, push her a little. Come on little lamb, it will be okay, Jordan wanted to say, because it *was* going to be okay. She smiled with what she hoped was understanding. "You're interested in her, aren't you?"

"W-what?" Claire stammered, totally predictable in her denial, but Jordan knew it was only a knee-jerk reaction. She'd noticed how Claire's appreciative eyes followed Amanda, how she seemed so much more relaxed in Amanda's company, how she practically hung on the younger woman's words, smiled

constantly at her. No, drooled, more like. Amanda Malden was
the sun and Claire Cooper the helpless planet orbiting it. *Christ,
I wonder if Shannon knows?* Surely Shannon wouldn't be happy
about this little development. *Oh, well.* It was not Jordan's problem for once, and besides, it was damned good for Claire to show
interest in someone.

"All I can say Claire is hallelujah! It's about time you started
considering someone that way and I couldn't be happier for
you!"

All color drained from Claire's face as she sank down in her
chair. She looked like the guilty family dog that had just stolen
the evening's dinner and downed it in one giant gulp. "Oh, God,
Jordan. I'm not—I mean, I'm just—shit, I think I'm going to be
sick."

"No you're not. Take a deep breath, Claire. You're okay.
You're just being human. You're acting like you just slept with an
underage showgirl."

"For God's sake!" Claire practically wailed. "I haven't
slept with anyone and I'm not going to. She's Shannon's niece.
And she's young enough to be my daughter. Oh my God." She
scrubbed at her temples as though she could rub the salacious
thoughts from her mind. "I think I've lost my fucking mind!"

Jordan couldn't remember a time when Claire had used the
F-bomb. *Jesus, she really is suffering over this.* "So what that she's
younger and she's Shannon's niece. Big freaking deal. Greater
obstacles than that have been overcome in the name of love."

"I'm sure Amanda would be appalled if she knew. *I'm*
appalled!"

"She would be flattered, I'm sure. Don't be so hard on
yourself."

"Oh, God, I can't believe I'm even having this conversation."
Claire finished her drink in one decisive swallow and set the glass
down like a judge slamming down a gavel. "I can't believe any of
this is happening. This is nuts. I'm sure by tomorrow I'll regret
every single thing about this conversation."

"It's okay, Claire, I promise. And I promise this isn't the end of the world. Let me order you another drink so you can decompress a little."

"Thanks, but I think I'll decompress in my room. I've already made enough of a fool of myself."

Jordan reached over and put her hand on Claire's arm. It was about as affectionate as she ever got with Claire. "I'm your friend, Claire. And I'm not going to tell a soul about this. But if you need to talk, I'm here okay? And try to chill out a little."

Claire's smile was fleeting. "Thank you, Jordan. But I'm still embarrassed. I'm not even in a position to, you know . . ."

"No, you're in the perfect position to have a little fun. Just be yourself and let . . . I don't know. Just let yourself *be* for once, you know? Wherever that might take you."

Claire rose and gave the seated Jordan a quick hug. "I'll try, Jordan, but no promises."

After she was gone, Jordan moved to the bar and ordered a beer. She wanted to sit and absorb this new information about Claire. She was thrilled for her friend, but apprehensive too. As much as she teased and goaded Claire about her hermit lifestyle, she worried about her. It was surprising and satisfying to see her testing the waters like this, or at least actually thinking about dating someone, but Jordan seriously doubted Claire had the balls to act on her little crush. It would be a huge leap of faith for her, so out of character, and Jordan couldn't picture anything coming of it.

So absorbed was she in her thoughts, she failed to immediately notice the dark-skinned woman with short black hair slide into the stool next to her.

"Is it something you'd recommend?" asked a deep voice that still managed to sound very feminine.

It took Jordan a moment to surface from the haze of alcohol and the bizarre discussion with Claire. She turned to the stranger. "What, sitting here drinking alone?"

The woman's laughter was another octave richer and deeper, and it washed over Jordan in a luxurious wave. "Actually, I was talking about whatever brand of beer you're drinking." Clear, dark eyes appraised Jordan.

She laughed and shook her head. "The beer, yes. Drinking alone, not particularly."

"Good, then you don't mind if I join you?" The dark eyes softened and posed a silent question.

Yes, Jordan thought, I'm interested. *And why not?* The woman was beautiful and elegant, long limbed and graceful in the way she moved her hands on the bar, smoothing down a napkin and signaling the bartender for a glass of beer. Her only makeup was the bright red lipstick on her full lips, the shade matching perfectly her nail polish. She was probably Jordan's age, maybe even a little older, and she wore her years with grace and without apology. The effect was stunning.

"I would love for you to join me," Jordan answered with a smile. She almost laughed at herself when her eyes remained on the dark stranger instead of feasting on the young woman behind the bar whose blond hair was naturally bleached by the desert sun. No, she hadn't been bullshitting Dani or Claire. She really did want to turn over a new leaf; she just wasn't quite sure where to begin. Maybe this was the place to begin.

"I'm Dez, by the way."

"Jordan." So first names only was how it was going to be—a nameless pickup. Mild disappointment tugged at Jordan. It was clear Dez had no intention of becoming friends, and at one time, instant lovers would have suited Jordan just fine. But now she desired something more than a one-night stand. *Figures.*

"Good to meet you, Jordan." They shook hands softly, then the long fingers closed around the sweating glass of beer. "You were right about the beer; it's good."

Jordan tilted her glass in salute. The beer was good, but she didn't feel like drinking much more. She suddenly wished she wasn't so far on her way to being inebriated. Dez was sober and Jordan wanted to be as well. "Is that a southern accent I detect?"

Dez tilted her long neck and inclined her head closer to Jordan. Her subtle perfume was pleasant. "I'm originally from

Georgia, but I'm surprised you picked up an accent. I figured years of living in New York City and California had decimated it by now." Her laughter was long and low, and it occurred to Jordan that there were centuries of the South in that voice—a cadence to the way Dez talked that reminded her of lazy summers beneath giant century-old oak trees.

"I've never lived on the East Coast, but I've always fantasized about New York City. If you can make it there, you can make it anywhere, as they say."

Dez lightly shrugged a shoulder, the sheer of her pale lemon blouse revealing slender white bra straps beneath. Jordan wondered how the white straps would look against Dez's bare, dark back.

"That's true, but you can kill yourself trying to make it there, and not many succeed. Don't get me wrong, I love New York City, but six years of living there was enough for one lifetime. It's a city that can eat you alive until you don't even recognize yourself anymore. You're pretty small in a place like that, no matter how successful you think you are." There was a note of regret in her voice.

"Then maybe it's better to go there after you've already made it," Jordan suggested.

Dez's smile was wistful. "Maybe it's just better to visit a place like that and not live there."

"Do you miss the South?"

"Hmm. That's like asking a fish if it misses the water." Her accent seemed a little thicker now that they were talking about the south. "You're not from the South are you?"

"The Midwest." Jordan didn't feel like going into any more detail than that. They were playing a little cat-and-mouse game, giving each other enough information about themselves to be friendly, but nothing more. The rules were plain.

"Well, close enough then. So you're visiting Las Vegas?"

"Yes and no. I do a little work here sometimes as well."

"Me too." Dez's smile was an acknowledgment that the line of questioning would go no further. "Are you staying at the

Mandalay?"

"The MGM. You?"

Dez nodded before finishing off her beer, and Jordan hoped she was about to get an invitation for a private nightcap. They seemed to be moving in that direction, Dez giving off subtle signals that she was gay and alone in the city.

"Well, Jordan, if you'll excuse me, I'd better get going. It's getting a little late." She was standing, throwing a bill on the bar.

"Um . . . okay." Jordan felt like a fool, even more now that her voice had suddenly deserted her. Had she read it all wrong?

Dez at least had manners enough to look a little sorry. "It's been nice talking to you. Really. But I don't . . . you know . . ."

Jordan's impulse was to nod and say something equally polite and stumble back to her own hotel, but she didn't want to let Dez off the hook so easily. She wanted her to spell it out. They were not kids, nor was this decades ago where you had to talk in some sort of heterosexually-accepted code. "Actually, I don't know."

Dez's eyes were frank, but not harsh. She really did seem to regret ending the evening. "I don't pick women up in bars. Anymore."

"But if you did, you'd ask me up to your room?"

Dez answered with a smile and walked away.

Well, well, Jordan thought with more amusement than injured pride as she watched her leave. *This is a first.*

CHAPTER NINE

Shannon

Shannon didn't much enjoy shopping, or at least not as much as her closet at home might suggest. The clothes and shoes with their expensive material, handmade craftsmanship and overblown price tags were nice—she couldn't deny they weren't—but they were more about Dani than her. Dani loved her in designer clothes, loved spending money on her, loved her looking like a million bucks. And since it made Dani feel good, it made Shannon feel good to please her. Why shouldn't she do something as simple as dress in nice clothes if it made her partner happy? Dani worked hard, and the extravagance was Dani's reward.

It was this she told herself to alleviate the pang of guilt as she, Claire and Amanda entered the Neiman Marcus store at the north end of the Strip. They had the place practically to themselves, probably because it was Monday morning and the weekenders were on their way home or still hung over and in bed.

"May I help you?" a sales clerk asked, introducing herself as Mary and explaining that she would be their personal shopping assistant. She was eager in the way of someone who wanted to keep busy to make her work day go faster.

"I'm really just looking for shoes," Shannon replied, watching the woman visibly deflate. She didn't want someone shadowing her, so she nodded in the direction of her niece, who was making her way to the lingerie and bra section. Shannon had slipped Amanda a C-note on the way and convinced her to buy herself something nice—something she might not otherwise splurge on. Amanda protested, and Shannon countered that she'd never given her a welcome-back-to-Chicago gift last fall. In reality, she wanted an excuse to treat Amanda, who spent all her money on her classes and books and rarely indulged in anything else.

The assistant went scurrying after Amanda, and Shannon giggled a little.

"That was a bit mean," Claire chuckled.

"I know, but Amanda will forgive me."

"Hmm, I'm not so sure. Would you want someone helping you buy a bra or undies?"

Shannon considered for a moment. "If she was cute, sure."

"God, you sound like Jordan."

"Oh, please. Shoot me if I ever do."

The two laughed guiltily and made their way to the shoe department. Claire wasn't much of a shopper and nodded her approval at everything Shannon pointed out.

"You could at least pretend you're interested in my bridal shoes, you know." Shannon was only kidding, knowing the exercise was akin to going to the dentist for Claire.

Claire laughed gamely. "Just like you tried to pretend you were interested in the book club Ann and I used to organize?"

"Oh, that." Shannon waved her hand, knowing Claire had scored a point. "I can't help it, I like trashy romances. Those big thick Jonathan Franzen and Ken Follett books are just not my thing. Reading that stuff feels like college homework to me."

"I know, I know. You were a good sport to try."

Shannon tried on a pair of Gucci's and decided she didn't like the tight fit, especially when she had to practically pry them off her feet.

"Speaking of unpleasant things," Claire continued. "How did Dani handle your news?"

The question was like a two-by-four across the shoulder blades. Shannon's breath left her in a silent rush. *My news.* She knew exactly what Claire was referring to, and until now she'd somehow managed to file it away in the very recesses of her mind. She swallowed to try to dislodge the unpleasant taste in her throat—the taste of fear and procrastination. "I haven't talked to her yet."

Claire's face fell. "What?"

Shannon distractedly pulled a pair of Jimmy Choos from a box, pulling so hard that she sent a pyramid of boxes toppling. She was angry. Not at Claire, but at the whole goddamned circumstance of it all. She was angry at her body and angry about the timing and angry at Dani for wanting a baby so goddamned bad. It wasn't bloody well fair. "Look, Claire. It's not the right time, okay?" she said shakily.

"When is the right time? On the wedding night? When she starts bugging you again about the fertility clinic?"

"Cut me a break, will you?" Her tone was harsh, too harsh for what Claire deserved, but then, Claire had initiated this little confrontation. "I've only known my test results for six weeks. I need time to process before I tell her. I need some time for myself, okay? Is that so horrible?"

"No, of course not. Come here." Shannon obeyed and sat down beside Claire, who put her arm around her shoulders and pulled her in for a squeeze. "No one wants to hear that they're infertile. It's a tough pill to swallow, especially when you two were going to start trying for a baby. I know it's tough, honey, believe me. And I'm here for you, okay?"

Shannon bit down on her bottom lip. She would not cry, not here and not now. She'd shed enough secret tears. "I know you are, Claire. And I will handle this my own way, okay? I just need a little more time." Like a year would be nice, but that sure as hell wasn't going to happen.

Mary, humming an indecipherable tune, strolled up to them. She was full of helpful enthusiasm. "Have you found anything yet? I can help you if you haven't."

Shannon pulled herself together and stood up, eyeing the black lacy bra and matching underpants Amanda was trying hard to hide behind her back. "Found something sexy, I see. Good for you, Amanda. Someone is going to be very happy with your selections I hope!"

Amanda's face reddened and she tried to slide in behind Mary, but Mary was on the move, pulling more shoes out for Shannon to try.

"She's so adorable when her auntie embarrasses her," she whispered to Claire, but Claire was looking away, almost as red-faced as Amanda. *Jeez!* It was almost like they were cut from the same cloth, a generation apart, so prim and proper and shy.

"Try the Manolo Blahniks or the Pradas," Mary suggested, producing a pair of each like a magician pulling a rabbit from a hat.

Shannon tried to choose quickly, before Claire and Amanda got bored out of their minds. After trying on a couple more pairs, she settled on royal blue Manolo heels that weren't as outrageous as she'd expected—only $220. Mary brightly offered a discount for Claire if she bought a pair too, but Claire gave the poor woman the most withering look Shannon had ever seen on her. She gathered up her purse and the shoes and asked Mary to lead them to the cashier before Claire killed someone.

The sales clerk, who probably made significantly less money than Mary and was incrementally less cheerful, rang up the purchases. Shannon pulled out her American Express, the gold-plated one she and Dani shared.

"I'm sorry," the clerk said after a moment. "But the card's being denied."

She couldn't possibly have heard right. "I'm sorry, what did you say?"

The young woman tried the card again. "I'm sorry, ma'am, but it won't accept the charge."

Shannon's cheeks grew warm with embarrassment. It was obviously some bureaucratic mistake, but she wasn't going to stand here and argue and plead her case like someone desperate. She calmly tried the Visa card she'd kept since she'd graduated from college, relieved when it worked.

"Jesus," she muttered in disgust and relief to Claire, but Claire was too busy trying to avoid looking at the wares Amanda was about to purchase. *It's only lingerie for God's sake. What the hell is wrong with everyone today anyway? Is there a hidden camera somewhere, making our lives into a reality TV show?* She had the absurd idea of flashing her breasts at the ceiling, just in case.

Shannon returned to the hotel quickly, the declined card having spooked her. It might be something fluky, even though it had never happened before. Yet something unspoken and unsettling weighed on her. If there was something wrong, she wanted to know what it was.

She found Dani lying under a palm tree by one of the pools, looking as though she hadn't a care in the world. She was browning nicely already, like bread coming out of the toaster. Her eyes were sleepy and half closed, her arms limp beside her.

"What's up, baby?" Dani asked in a faraway voice.

Shannon sat down heavily at the foot of her cot. "Our American Express card got denied at the department store."

Dani popped one eye fully open. The effect would have been comical if not for the subject matter. "I'm sure it's just a mistake."

"It's not," Shannon responded coolly. She was not angry; she wanted answers. As soon as she'd returned to the hotel, she called the number on the back of the card and learned their credit had been frozen. They refused her an explanation over the phone. "I checked."

Dani's other eye popped open. In those eyes, Shannon saw so clearly the flicker of emotions flare and dim—alarm, concern, maybe even a bit of panic. And then, nothing. The blankness in her lover's eyes threw her, and it was like approaching the edge of a cliff that she didn't want to get too close to. It was frightening, because for the first time in their relationship, there was something hard and impenetrable between them—something besides the baby news. Each woman looked away.

"We'll sort it out later. When we get home," Dani offered casually. "I'm sure it's no big deal." This was not like Dani. She'd always been more than competent at handling their finances. In fact, she was sharp-eyed and precise about it, knowing to the dime what was coming in and going out of the house. Dani should be freaking out about this, not lying there acting like she was being told the bar had just run out of rum and would she settle for vodka instead. No, there was something most definitely false and concerning in her casual attitude.

Shannon's spine involuntarily stiffened. She rose from the cot, her legs a little unsteady. The things that were going on between them—the distance, the secrets—was normal for a cou- ～～～～ as long as they'd been, she told herself. It was noth- ～ t deal with. Later.

CHAPTER TEN

Amanda

The Liberace Museum was on Amanda's list of geeky things to do in Vegas. Same with the atomic testing museum, because anything to do with museums and history made her feel complete. A musty old building or a thick dusty textbook gave her a secret thrill, as if she herself were reaching back through time and becoming a momentary part of that era. She hoped Claire would go with her to the Liberace Museum today, not only because Claire had a car and could drive them, but because it might bring a return to the friendly banter between them. They'd gotten along so fabulously right from the start, and throwing her aunt in the pool was the crowning moment of their budding friendship. Amanda laughed to herself, remembering it. But something had changed in Claire since, because she seemed distant around her now, uncomfortable. Amanda had absolutely no idea what she'd done to cause this change, but whatever it was, she wanted to put things right between them and be friends again. It felt, for reasons she couldn't exactly identify, that Claire was her one true ally here. A kindred spirit.

She listened for Claire with her ear pressed up against her own door—their rooms were conveniently across from one another—and then opened her door just as she heard Claire emerging from her room. "Oh, Claire, hi! Um, listen, I was wondering . . . Would you like to go to the Liberace Museum with me this afternoon?"

Claire looked trapped. "If you want my car, you're welcome to—"

"No. I don't want your car. I want you to come with me."

"Why?"

"Does there have to be a reason? Other than the fact that I thought you might like to." Claire's prickliness caused Amanda's heart to sink a little. Really, did she have to be so defensive about a simple invitation?

Claire softened a little. "I, um, sure. I think that would be fine."

"Look, I'm not asking you to do me a big favor, okay? If you don't want to go, or if you have other plans, you don't have to. It's okay."

Claire seemed to shrink before the starkness of Amanda's words. Her vulnerability was a wild contradiction to the woman Amanda's aunt had always talked about so reverently. She had heard a lot about Claire from the days she and Shannon worked together. Claire was at the top of her field in OB-GYN in Chicago, chief of staff of her department at Prentice Women's Hospital, ran a full practice, even found time to teach at the Feinberg School of Medicine. Shannon described Claire as commanding her kingdom with competence and authority, but was kind and patient too. The kind of person you could go to with your problems, big or small. Shannon worshipped Claire and had grown terribly concerned about her after her partner died. Shannon hadn't said a lot about it, but enough for Amanda to understand that Claire had withdrawn considerably over the last few years. She'd given up her chief status at the hospital and barely taught at the university anymore. She was still damned good at her job—that hadn't changed, according to Shannon, but she was a shadow of her former self. Sad a lot and not much of a joiner these days.

"I-I didn't mean for you to think I was doing you a favor," Claire stammered, fumbling and then dropping her room key card on the floor. She was clearly chastened, and Amanda felt bad for coming on so strongly.

"Please come," Amanda said, reaching for Claire's hand and holding it tight in both of hers. She was surprised at how warm Claire's hand was, and how much it trembled. It was like a fragile bird in her hand, and she held it gently but firmly, surprised by her protective feelings toward Claire. "It'll be fun. Well, not as much fun as it was throwing my aunt in the pool yesterday, but almost!"

Claire's smile expanded slowly. "All right, you sold me on it, kid."

Kid. Shannon and Dani often called her that, but coming from Claire, it was jarring and hurtful, insulting that Claire thought of her as a kid, a teenager, a child—someone not worthy of her respect and attention. Someone unworthy of her friendship. She wanted to scream that she was not a kid and hadn't been for a long time.

"Well, shall we?" Claire said, slowly extracting her hand and picking up her key card to tuck into her back pocket. Amanda's hand cooled quickly at the loss of Claire's. "Let's not keep Mr. Showmanship waiting."

Amanda was quiet on the ride to the museum, but when she saw the building's façade containing a giant music sheet and oversized piano keys, she gasped with pleasure. "Wow, that is so cool, isn't it? I love when architecture is matched perfectly to someone's personality. This is exactly what I would have expected of a museum named for Liberace."

"Must be quite a challenge for architects," Claire commented, "designing a building to match someone's personality."

"Oh, it is. And not only an actual person, but trying to

personify a neighborhood, or an era, or an entire city. There are as many themes for buildings as there are stars in the sky."

"What got you interested in art history from an architecture point of view?"

Claire's interest in her line of study excited her. Surely it was more than perfunctory politeness—or at least Amanda found herself hoping so. Most people tuned out or changed the subject after a moment, but Claire seemed genuinely interested. As they strolled through the museum, Amanda told her more about her studies, about how she loved the lines and dimensions and solidity of buildings over, say, paintings or other less durable forms of art. She explained how the history and beauty of buildings had always fascinated her, starting with her dollhouses and play castles as a toddler. And while she talked, she couldn't help thinking, do you still think I'm a kid, Claire?

They might both be kids in this environment of blue hairs. They had to be the youngest patrons by far, and it made them allies again, the way they'd been allies when they ganged up on Shannon at the pool. Without thinking about it, Amanda clutched Claire's arm in companionship.

"Guess I should know all his albums by heart or something," Claire suggested with a laugh. "I'd better not say this too loudly, but I don't actually own any Liberace CDs."

"Me either," Amanda whispered back. "I barely even remember him when he was still alive. I just thought it'd be cool to come here and look around."

"Hmmm," Claire teased. "Cool if you're seventy maybe."

"All right, maybe cool was the wrong word."

"I do remember seeing Liberace on television when he was in his heyday. The old ladies loved him back then, too. It always seemed to be an age thing, his fans. Or a gay guy thing. But this has to be a new crop of old ladies, since the old girls back then would all be gone now."

Claire looked so serious suddenly that Amanda stopped walking. She hated this talk about age and generational differences. "What is it, Claire?"

"God, I just thought of something. Does this mean when you reach a certain age, like, I don't know, sixty-two or something, that you start to love Liberace? Like maybe it's an age milestone, like menopause."

Amanda laughed and squeezed Claire's arm pointedly. "I don't know, you're the doctor."

"True, but gerontology's not my specialty. Tell you what though, since I'll get to sixty-two, oh, about twenty-one years sooner than you, I'll let you know, okay?"

Amanda sighed grumpily. *There she goes again, making a point of our age difference.* It was like forever being excluded from a certain club, and it rankled her, because she'd never be a part of the forty-something club at the same time as Claire. She'd never be a part of any age group at the same time as Claire. It was an argument she could never win, a race where she could never pull even. She felt defeated before she'd even started.

"Claire?"

They stopped in front of a large glass case of Liberace's elaborate costumes. There were boas and feathers and sequins and jewels, capes, belts and flared pants of all colors.

"Yes?"

"Earlier today," Amanda waded slowly into her question. She didn't want Claire to go quiet on her again, but she wanted to know what lay at the bottom of the distance Claire sometimes put between them, and still did with the age comments. "Sometimes you seem almost resentful of my age or something. Have I done something wrong? Do I offend you? Or should I say, does my age offend you?"

Claire's brown eyes lowered, then raised again slowly, as if her eyelids were heavy and would not permit it. "No, Amanda, you do not offend me and neither does your age."

"Then what? Will you tell me?"

"There's nothing to tell." Claire offered a weak smile. "I was just in a bit of a grump earlier. I'm sorry."

"But it seems sometimes like, I don't know, like you're mad that I'm twenty-six years old. Like my age is a detraction."

"No." Claire shook her head adamantly. "I'm sorry if you thought that."

"I'm sorry I thought that too. I was so worried I'd done something to offend you, or said something stupid, or that I'm a pain in the ass to you."

There was so much sadness in Claire's eyes sometimes, it made Amanda want to say or do something, anything, to make her smile.

"It's just . . ."

"Yes?" she asked eagerly, hoping they were finally getting somewhere.

Claire read a plaque explaining the history of one of the outfits on display. It seemed like a long time before she answered. "I guess there's no easy way to explain."

"You could try."

Claire wouldn't look at her; she pretended to study another plaque as she spoke. "You remind me sometimes . . ."

"Yes?"

"Your youthfulness . . ."

Crap, not that again.

"Your energy, your vitality, your wit, your intelligence. You remind me sometimes that there's a whole world out there, a whole world that's exciting and interesting and worth living. A whole world I'm no longer a part of."

Amanda gasped as tears sprang to her eyes. "Oh, Claire." Emotion thickened her voice.

"It's okay," Claire rasped, equally emotional, looking at her with those sad brown eyes again. "It's not your fault or anything. It's me. I'm sorry."

"Please. Don't apologize." Amanda's voice was stronger this time. She took Claire's hand. Claire's eyebrows rose in surprise, but she didn't resist, and the fragile bird was in the nest of Amanda's hand again. "There *is* a whole world out there, and it *is* worth living. And you can be a part of it any time you want." Please be a part of it again, she wanted to say. She tried to imagine Claire eating dinner alone, waking up alone, sitting alone in front of a TV at night. It made her unfathomably sad.

Claire was shaking her head, her lips pursed. *Case closed. Discussion over.*

They entered a large auditorium containing Liberace's collection of cars—some gold, some silver, a Rolls Royce completely coated in shiny sequins. There was joy in this ostentation. An embracing of life and all its gifts. Amanda suddenly understood what it was about this man that people, especially older people, admired. It was his *joie de vivre*. It was about saying this is who I am and I am living my life to the fullest and having a damned good time doing it.

Amanda looked at Claire, who was clearly not living her life to the fullest. But neither was she, she supposed. She'd given up in some respects, too. And once again, that made them allies.

CHAPTER ELEVEN

Dani

Dani remained a little shaken by how close Shannon had come to stumbling across the fact that they were almost broke. It was news to her that their credit cards had been shut down, but it wasn't surprising. She'd certainly never anticipated that Shannon would be publicly humiliated, and for that she was sorry. It was wrong not to have come clean with her. It was the only thing of such magnitude she'd ever kept from her partner, and the secret was slowly suffocating her like invisible but deadly toxic fumes.

Why, she thought bleakly as she trudged along with the group down The Strip, should she be the one to ruin their wedding with her news? Why did she have to be the Grinch and Scrooge and the Grim Reaper all rolled into one? Hadn't her life been hard enough for the past few weeks, pretending everything was fine, pretending to go off to work as usual when, in fact, she was spending her days at the library or with the employment headhunter looking for work? Hadn't she had enough guilt and responsibility on her shoulders without having to cancel the wedding they'd been planning for a year? Why did it have to fall on her to throw away the life they'd come to expect? It wasn't her fault she'd lost her job. In fact, the day they let her go, they'd told her she did great work. It's just that she was one of the last managers hired, and it was the economy, and blah, blah, blah. Nothing they said had made her feel better or changed the outcome.

Here she was now, deeper and deeper in this morass of lies. Of course it was wrong, but she would *not* disappoint Shannon or ruin the week for everyone. She'd hold it together a little longer, take care of everyone the way she usually did, make everything okay, or at least kill herself trying. She couldn't see doing it any other way.

"Hey, buddy." Jordan slowed and waited for her to catch up. "You look like you got the weight of the world on your shoulders." She grinned. "Not suddenly worried about being tied down for the rest of your life now, are you?"

"Hell, are you kidding me? I'm worried Shannon might finally get some sense and make a run for it." It was meant as a joke but there was more than a kernel of truth to it.

Jordan looked at her worriedly, but only for an instant. "You're right, you better hope she remains blindly in love with you for at least a few more days!"

Dani laughed along with her friend, but it wasn't funny. Her biggest nightmare was that Shannon would wake up one day and realize she was just plain ol' Danielle Berringer from a small town in Nebraska, daughter of a tractor salesman and stay-at-home mother, from a hick family that could have stepped out of a 1950s black-and-white movie. Growing up, she'd been nothing special—just another kid who chose to claw her way out of humble beginnings with no encouragement or expectations from her parents. She'd put herself through college, got lucky with some great jobs, got even luckier with her salary the last few years. But now it had all come tumbling down, and soon Shannon would know the truth. *That* was what scared the shit out of her—that Shannon might deem her unworthy of her love, unworthy of building a future together, and pull the plug on their relationship before she could make things right. For Dani it was a constant battle to keep her world on its axis. She couldn't give up now.

The group paused in front of the Bellagio's massive fountain display, a quiet anticipation rippling through the small clusters of people gathered to wait for the next show. Dani had seen the show on a previous visit, but newbies Claire and Amanda had not. Shannon excitedly explained to them how the show was synchronized to music and lights every half hour, how the hundreds of submerged spigots came to life like underwater creatures. Bored, Dani glanced around. There were a handful of others who looked equally bored, like they'd seen it a million times before, but most looked eager and interested. It *was* pretty spectacular, yet she couldn't get in the mood, not when she was so preoccupied. She wondered how many others around her were just barely hanging on like she was—hanging on to a dream or a hope, or to some shred of normalcy. Things in her life had always worked out for her, she told herself, and they would again. Somehow. They had to.

She watched Shannon's expressive hands move as she talked, her eyes bright with the excitement of describing the show. Innocent, was the thought that came to Dani's mind. Innocent and beautiful—almost exactly as she was when they'd first met seven years ago. So many times Dani had silently and verbally thanked Shannon for choosing her, but now she wanted to scream that she should have picked Claire instead. Claire was a good woman. Claire was a successful doctor. She could provide a future for Shannon—the kind of future Shannon deserved. And yet . . . Shannon hadn't picked Claire. She'd picked her.

"Hey, sexy," Dani whispered into Shannon's ear, bending to kiss the back of her neck.

Shannon smiled and reached for her hand. "I always get emotional at these silly fountain shows."

"I know." Dani squeezed her hand as the first strains of Celine Dion's "My Heart Goes On" played over hidden speakers. Jets of water shot up suddenly from the small cannons poking above the placid surface. Wands of water waved back and forth in time to the music, the spray twinkling and shimmering in the twilight. Even Claire was smiling at the water pulsing in time to the music. It really was a romantic sight.

Shannon leaned against her and spoke quietly. "It's so beautiful. I never get tired of this. And it makes me remember how much I love you." She turned to Dani, her eyes moist with unshed tears. "That's how I feel about us, you know, that song, the words, and how the water and music are so perfectly in tune with each other. I don't ever want anything to happen to us, Dani. Ever."

"Oh, baby, nothing's going to happen to us." She pulled Shannon into her chest and hugged her.

"How can you say that? You don't know. Nobody knows what's going to happen. For all we know, our lives could change in an instant. Nothing goes on forever."

"That's true, but I know my love for you is never going to change. And that's the one constant I can count on."

Shannon responded by kissing her softly. "You're right, and that's all that really matters. Sometimes I get so scared, that's all."

"Of what, my love?"

"That things can't stay this good, this wonderful, forever."

"Well then, if that's true, we'll just have to get through the bad stuff together. As a team." And they would find a way to get through this financial nightmare together. *Just not right now!*

"You're right. Of course we will."

Dani sucked in her breath to steel herself for the next lie. She hated this, but the need to keep a few more days of peace won out. "I'm sorry about that credit card mixup. I'll check with the bank tomorrow and make sure they fix whatever they've screwed up. I don't want you to worry about it, okay? Everything's fine."

"I'm not worried, honest. Besides, there's nothing else I need to buy this week anyway. I do want to check on all the flower arrangements tomorrow. In fact, I want to double check everything now, make sure we're not being followed around by some little black cloud of screw-ups all of the sudden."

Claire drew closer. "Did you say something about tomorrow?

Aren't we all driving out to the desert after breakfast?"

"Oh crap, Claire. I forgot to tell you, Dani's sister Heather is supposed to fly in tomorrow afternoon and we should be here to meet her. And I want to check on some of the wedding arrangements. How about Wednesday? Or Thursday?"

"Oh, no," Jordan interjected. "Thursday night is the big bachelor party and I don't want anyone late for it or stranded out in the desert." There was a wicked gleam in her eye. "Besides, I can promise you it's not something you all want to miss anyway."

"Wednesday's my big wedding assignment," Amanda added, "so that won't work."

Shannon stepped between Claire and Amanda and placed her arms around their shoulders. "You two go tomorrow. It'll be fun, and besides, Dani and I have been out to Red Rock Canyon before. It's beautiful, but I don't mind skipping it if we need to."

There was no mistaking the look of panic on Claire's face, and Dani did a double take. Claire was always so calm and in control.

"What about you, Jordan?" Claire asked with a note of desperation.

Jordan winked slyly like an evil big sister. "Maybe I will, if you don't mind me tagging along. Or maybe I won't, if you'd rather I didn't."

"Of course you should come," Amanda answered casually. "Why would you consider yourself to be tagging along?"

"Oh, no reason," Jordan said innocently. She was being such a brat that it made Dani smile.

As they watched the rest of the fountain show in silence, Dani kept glancing at Jordan as though she might be able to find in Jordan's face the reason behind that little exchange. She finally decided it would take more mental energy than she had right now. There was plenty on her plate without trying to decipher secret codes or unravel some kind of childish drama. There was always something going on with Jordan; Dani rarely concerned herself with whatever it was.

The Bellagio seemed like a good place for an evening drink

and the five of them sauntered in, discussing at great length the right way to make an authentic Cuban mojito. Jordan was adamant that the lime juice had to be freshly squeezed. Amanda debated the merits of simple syrup versus powdered sugar. They all ordered one after carefully quizzing the waiter about how the bartender was going to make it. Shannon added that it wasn't authentic without real Cuban rum.

"Where the hell did you ever taste real Cuban rum before?" Dani asked her.

Shannon shrugged and looked guilty of a misdemeanor, but not sorry. She playfully stuck out her tongue.

Dani rolled her eyes. "Oh, I forgot. That Canadian woman you dated a long time ago. The Cuban rum up there was part of your foreign experience, I suppose?"

Jordan waggled her eyebrows. "French kissing too, Shannon? And petting beavers?"

"All right, all right," Dani growled, more for show than anything real. "It's probably bad luck to talk about exes right before a wedding. Though you, my dear Jordie, could certainly write an entire book about exes."

Jordan laughed with self-deprecation. "Unfortunately, every chapter would read the same."

Their drinks arrived and they toasted to no more talk of exes.

"So what do you two think of Vegas so far?" Shannon said to Claire and Amanda.

Amanda hesitated as though she didn't want to say anything negative. She was a sweet kid, always thoughtful before she spoke. "Now that I'm here, I think it's someplace everyone should experience at least once. It's . . . different, that's for sure."

"The hotels are spectacular," Claire said. "Now I know what a couple of billion dollars looks like in 3-D. But what I'm really looking forward to is the drive out to the canyon tomorrow, seeing all those desert colors I saw from the air."

"You should try a show one night this week," Jordan suggested. "There's every kind you can imagine. Concerts of every genre, all the Cirque de Soleil shows, dinner theater." She hopped up and plucked a magazine from a nearby table. It contained a listing of all the shows for the week. She flipped through the pages quickly. "Kenny Chesney's here, Taylor Swift . . . ugh, Barry Manilow!" They all roared with laughter as Jordan began singing "Copacabana." She went back to the magazine. "Bette Midler, Lady Gaga, John Mayer—"

Dani seemed to be the only one who noticed Jordan's face turn stone white. The others began chirping about Lady Gaga, but Jordan seemed frozen on the same page, unable to go further.

Dani leaned in and whispered to her, "What's up?"

"N-nothing. I think Barry Manilow nearly made me toss my cookies."

Dani peeked at the page she clutched tightly. There was a black-and-white photo of an African American woman with short hair, impossibly luscious lips and prominent cheekbones. She looked like an African princess sitting at a piano, long legs crossed. Deziree Adams, opening every night at the Monte Carlo for Smokey Robinson, it said in a breezy, italic script.

"That looks interesting. I love R&B," Dani said, still unsure why Jordan was acting so weird. "Let me guess. You've already seen her perform and didn't want to let us in on this hidden treasure?"

Before Jordan could answer, Shannon interrupted. "Ooh, did someone say R&B? I would love to go see some R&B acts! How about it, you guys?"

Amanda clutched her hand to her chest. "Oh my God, yes! Especially if it's old R&B stuff. I *love* old soul music. The Spinners, Motown, Barry White, Gladys Knight!"

Claire gave Amanda a peculiar look and smiled widely. "I'll go get tickets. Jordan, you in?"

Jordan sprinted from her seat like it was a race. Obviously she had recovered from her temporary paralysis. "Are you kidding? You couldn't keep from it. C'mon Claire, I'll go with you to get tickets."

CHAPTER TWELVE

Jordan

For the entire thirty-minute set, Jordan couldn't take her eyes off Dez up on the stage, roaming it and commanding it like a big prowling cat. She sang with confidence in deep resonant tones, songs such as "Best of My Love," "Ain't No Mountain High Enough," "Tell Me Something Good." On a stool at center stage she later sat, her long legs crossed elegantly, her hands caressing the sleek microphone like a lover's thigh for "Midnight Train to Georgia" and "You'll Never Find Another Love Like Mine." The audience lapped it up, mesmerized by her voice and her graceful beauty. Her sensuality too, which had an almost paralyzing effect on the audience, riveting and dazing them. Jordan's attention was trance-like, and there were brief moments she could have sworn Dez was looking straight at her, singing the lines just for her. It was an illusion, of course. Dez wasn't singing to her and probably wasn't even looking at her, but rather on a fixed point on the wall behind her. But Jordan wanted to believe otherwise, no matter how silly the idea was. She wanted Dez to remember her, to mean something to her.

"She's really something," Dani whispered.

Jordan could only nod, not willing to remove her attention from Dez. She didn't want to miss anything—not a note or a single movement. She wondered, though, why Dez hadn't mentioned to her that she was a singer. But then again, they hadn't gotten as far as careers in their discussion.

The half-hour set ended far too quickly, though the audience was rewarded with a duet between Dez and Smokey Robinson—a slick, sensual rendition of "Ooh, Baby Baby." Jordan's body always told the truth in its responses, and it was telling her plenty of things now. She wanted to be the microphone, stroked by Dez's long fingers. She wanted to be held and coaxed to life as Dez had done with each song. Most of all, she wanted to be the inspiration behind Dez's voice and the words she so expertly and emotionally sang. What would it be like, she wondered, to be the kind of lover, to have the kind of love that someone wrote or sang about? She had never experienced such a thing and wondered if it were even possible.

This is crazy, she chastised herself. She was attracted to Dez, wanted to sleep with her, spend a little more time chatting and listening to that lush southern voice. But that was it. There was no reason to think Dez was any different from her multitude of superficial conquests over the years, except for the one fact that she was at least Jordan's age this time. Any deeper considerations than that were just some strange pull of the music along with the commanding and mesmerizing aura of Dez's stage persona. Jordan was simply mixing up feelings of admiration for something more, she told herself.

At the ten-minute intermission, as they all stood and stretched their legs, Dani said she vaguely remembered reading an article about Dez some years ago in a magazine.

"She was supposed to be the next Anita Baker," Amanda supplied, saying she'd read about Dez too. "About twelve or fifteen years ago, she had a couple of number one hits and she was the talk of the R&B scene."

Shannon patted her niece's arm. "You're so cute, knowing all this obscure music stuff from an era when you were just a kid."

Jordan noticed the sympathetic look Claire gave Amanda, who was probably annoyed but calmly said to her aunt, "I happen to love R&B from any era, Aunt Shannon. The way someone can appreciate art, whether it was made yesterday or a hundred years ago." She turned to the others, and Jordan thought, *good for you.* "Anyway, Dez Adams disappeared off the charts and off the radar shortly after those hits. I don't really know what happened, except she quit performing and cutting records for a long time."

Jordan wondered why. Maybe Dez preferred smaller audiences, like this. Or maybe something had happened to derail her skyrocketing career. She would love the chance to ask her.

The show resumed without Dez. It was Smokey's show now and it was clear Dez's part was over. Jordan whispered to the others that she was turning in early and made a hasty departure before Dani or the others could bug her about it. She didn't want them guessing the depth of the impact Dez's concert had had on her. She wanted to find Dez. Wanted to have a drink with her again and talk more, perhaps even try to seduce her and figure out if it was sexual attraction behind this need to be with Dez, or something much more mysterious and baffling. Dez had made it clear that she didn't pick up women in bars anymore, but they kind of knew each other now, didn't they? It would be okay on a second meeting if they ended up in bed together, wouldn't it? Jesus, she'd never worried about this kind of thing before. *Crap. Next thing you know, I'll be trying to figure out what kind of flowers to buy her!*

Jordan hopped the tram to the Mandalay and slipped into the same bar and into the same seat where she'd first met Dez last night. She ordered the same imported beer and tried not to look like she was on a mission. God, what an adolescent idiot you're being, she told herself. *Waiting around here like some groupie hoping she'll show. Could you be more pathetic?* She couldn't help herself though, and she wondered suddenly if it'd felt this way for any of the women who'd chased her—hoping Jordan would notice them, hoping she'd choose *them*, like trying to stand out on a shelf full of identical soup cans.

She finished her beer and ordered a second one. She'd drink it up, then leave. If Dez didn't show, oh well. There would be absolutely no failure in going back to her room alone at the MGM, watching a little TV or reading. She'd already determined she was done with the one-night stands, fast sex and flimsy relationships. Done, done and done, she reminded herself. *Yeah, right. Then why are you waiting around here hoping to get lucky with Dez Adams?*

She began to argue with herself. *Dez is not the same as the others. She's interesting and mature and beautiful and incredibly talented. I'm only interested in her because she's special. She's not like the others. This is not like the other times!*

As the beer in her glass diminished, so did the hope that she was succeeding in outwitting herself. So what if Dez was older and more mature than the Pop Tarts she'd dated. The end result she was hoping for was still the same as always—a satisfying fuck or two, maybe dinner, end of story. Same box, different label. Well, that crap wasn't who she was anymore, no matter how alluring Dez was. Matter of fact, Dez could walk in here half naked with a blatant proposition and she would simply turn her down flat. Yeah, that's what she'd do, by God, she'd say no. That's—

"This seat taken?"

Oh, God! That unmistakable voice. "Help yourself." Jordan turned and smiled, let her eyes drink Dez in. She'd changed out of her stage outfit into jeans and a loose white cotton blouse that showed enough cleavage for Jordan to have to cross her legs and will away the sudden wetness.

"So," Dez answered softly, claiming the seat and signaling for a beer. "You've discovered my little secret about what I do for a living. I saw you in the audience tonight."

"I guess you didn't think to mention earlier that you're a famous singer?"

"Well, if I was so famous, how come you didn't recognize me?"

Jordan laughed and mentally scored a point for Dez. "At least I can't be accused of being a groupie."

Dez's dark eyes glinted. "And I can't be accused of taking advantage of an exuberantly willing fan."

"Sounds like the perfect combination."

Dez's eyes were frank in their appraisal. "No. What would be perfect is getting out of here and going up to my room."

Jordan didn't quite believe she'd heard right. She also didn't quite believe her luck. "Are you asking?"

Dez blinked, the only evidence of hesitation. "Yes."

In the elevator, Dez's eyes again swept over her body like a bold caress. No hesitation there, and no hesitation in the greedy smile that hinted at devouring Jordan in one bite. Oh, she could stand being devoured by Dez, plundered by those long fingers and strong hands, subjugated by those soft but demanding lips, immortalized by that mouth. Yes, Jordan thought with a little gasp of astonishment and a sly smile. *I want to be your bitch tonight.*

Inside the penthouse suite, Jordan barely gave a glance in the direction of the floor-to-ceiling windows overlooking The Strip. Its lights of bright pink and green and blue illuminated the otherwise dark room in a hazy glow, and Dez's dark skin shone beautifully in the soft, dancing light.

"Care for a drink?" she asked.

"No." Jordan walked up to Dez and boldly clasped her arms around her waist. "I only want you."

Her lips claimed Dez's. Dez closed her eyes and both women abandoned themselves to the kiss. Kissing wasn't usually essential to Jordan, but was this woman good at it! Her lips were soft and assertive, playful yet bold in the way they responded. The kissing was a little like playing with fire, and yet the flame, so hot and hypnotic, beckoned in a way she could not resist. Maybe it was because she didn't have to be in charge for once. She could let this very capable, very skilled and very sexy woman take the reins. Let her take what she wanted. And oh, she wanted to give to Dez. Dez's tongue was now dancing inside her mouth, and then roughly she thrust Jordan up against the wall and began grinding—so slowly and sweetly—against her, that she wanted to melt on the spot.

Jordan moaned loudly, not caring that she was so weak and so desperately in need of a good fucking. Let Dez think she was in charge because, by God, she was. Her fingers were wending their way inside Jordan's pants. They roamed there, bringing Jordan to a whole new level of wanting. She was so wet and so hard, and those fingers were massaging and tickling and exploring her, driving her insane, making her harder and wetter. It was almost too much.

"Oh, God," Jordan uttered, breathless and shaking. She wouldn't beg. Never had and never would, but dammit, if Dez didn't give it all to her soon, she didn't know what she would do. Her legs quivered, her pelvis rolled and pushed hard against Dez's hand. Dez's mouth was at her neck, kissing, sucking, nibbling, biting, whispering incomprehensible things. Oh, how she just wanted it hard and fast and now! *Oh yes, hard hard hard!* She might have even whispered it out loud, because Dez's two fingers suddenly thrust deeply into her, filling her instantly. She jerked in response, then gushed new wetness and opened wider for Dez, wanting her deeper and faster. Her hips enthusiastically met each thrust, increasing the friction and depth. With a greed and hunger that knew no bounds, she wanted—*needed*—Dez's mouth against her and her tongue inside her too, and the vision of this pushed her over the edge. She came with a ferocity that frightened her for a moment, having climbed to a great height and then fallen long and fast and hard. It frightened her that she might never be able to reach such heights again with anyone else. She was ruined now. Ruined and collapsed in this marvelously wet and quivering heap in Dez's arms.

Moments later they were lying in the massive bed, naked and facing one another, caressing each other's bodies as though they had all the time in the world. It was the antithesis of fast and hard, but oh, it was so sweet. It was going to be a very long and very satisfying night.

CHAPTER THIRTEEN

Claire

Standing outside her car, hand impatiently on her hip, she punched in Jordan's cell phone number one last time, caught between exasperation and annoyance. Jordan hadn't appeared at the appointed time in the lobby for their trip to the desert. *Typical Jordan. She probably hooked up with some tramp last night and can't get her ass out of bed this morning.* The phone rang half a dozen times before Jordan finally picked up.

"Where the hell are you?"

"And a good morning to you too, Claire."

"I thought you were coming with us today?"

Jordan laughed devilishly, making Claire instantly regret that she'd confided in Jordan her feelings about Amanda. Jordan would never let her forget this. She'd lord it over her, make fun of her for, oh, about the rest of her damned life. She shouldn't have said anything, but she so desperately needed to talk to *someone*, and Dani and Shannon were definitely not the ones she could talk to. Jordan, however, was enjoying this far too much. Claire could practically hear her saying, *Have fun you little lovebirds!* Or perhaps, *Don't do anything I wouldn't do*—some childish refrain like that. "Sorry, I can't," was all Jordan said.

"What? What do you mean?"

"I can't, that's what I mean. I'm busy today. Sorry, bud." Another woman giggled in the background and Jordan whispered something unintelligible to her.

Shit. She should have figured Jordan would stand them up like this. It was unforgivable! "All right, fine."

She disconnected angrily, then tried to scramble for an excuse to cancel the trip. She couldn't possibly be alone with Amanda all day. Could she? They'd talk, and Amanda would ask all kinds of personal questions and they'd find even more things they had in common, and Amanda's eyes and dimples and that gorgeous smile would melt her again and again, suck her in so deep that she'd forget about Ann, and she'd forget she was forty-seven years old, and she'd forget how crazy and inappropriate all this was. She'd be unable to resist acting like she had every right in the world to flirt and spend time with this adorable and wonderful young woman.

Christ, Claire, get a grip. It's not like that. It's not like that at all. It's just your imagination going a little crazy after being alone so long. You can do this. You can have a nice day with a nice woman who's practically family. And what's the worst thing that could happen? It's not like this new car is going to break down and your phone's going to quit working and you're going to have to shack up for the night with her in some little hick town motel with one room available and one bed that sags conveniently in the middle. Though it would be kind of fun, she had to admit.

"Something wrong?" Amanda asked as Claire climbed into the driver's seat.

"Jordan can't make it."

"Oh. Is she all right?"

"Yup. Found something better to do I guess." *And someone better to do it with.* She started the car, cranked up the air conditioning, and carefully pulled out of the parking lot.

After another moment of silence, Amanda asked, "Is everything okay?"

"Of course. Why wouldn't it be?"

"I mean, with us taking off for the day like this."

"Sure. What makes you think it wouldn't be?" *Ah, the old saying, the best defense is a good offense!*

"Okay. You seem a little upset about Jordan not coming, that's all."

Jordan wasn't the issue, but she wasn't going to tell Amanda that. The only issue was with herself, and she was going to get over it, dammit. She took a quiet, calming breath and forced a smile. "It's fine, honestly. We're going to have a great day and I'm looking forward to it."

"Good, because I'm kind of glad it's just you and me."

Claire swallowed nervously. "You are?"

The look Amanda gave her was hard to decipher, and maybe that was a good thing. Oh, God, she thought, what the hell am I doing? But her panic subsided when Amanda reached for the satellite radio dial and found the classic soul station. "Ain't No Sunshine When She's Gone" was playing and Amanda began singing the words. Too shy to sing, Claire hummed along and soon the city disappeared behind them in a haze of dust, the voice of Bill Withers filling the car. They found other songs to enjoy, and the respite from conversation was having a calming effect on Claire. It was refreshing, invigorating, to just *be* for a change.

Rust-colored mountains dotted the horizon, looming closer with every mile, and it occurred to Claire how hilly and mountainous the desert really was and not as flat as she might have believed. The colors were amazing—every hue of brown and orange and red imaginable, rich textures that ranged from smooth to jaggedly rough. The highway unfurled before them like a roll of tape along a seam, and with it came a liberating sense of irresponsibility and freedom. She was free. They both were.

"Wouldn't it be amazing," Amanda said, "to do this drive in

a convertible?"

"Yes, it sure would." She could picture it in her mind perfectly, blasting their old tunes out into the dry, endless air. "And to have absolutely no agenda would be wonderful." No one to answer to, no patients to worry about, nothing to rush back to.

"Oh my God, yes. To not even know where you're going to end up or how long you're going to be gone. Wouldn't it be amazing to take off like that?"

Claire couldn't help laughing out loud at the absurdity of the idea. She had patients and a crap load of obligations. Enough to keep her busy for years. She shook her head, a little mournful that her time for such whimsy was long past her. "Yes, it would be amazing, but totally unrealistic."

"Yes, I know exactly what you mean," Amanda said on a long sigh.

"See, the thing about getting older is that stuff like that is just a fantasy. Something you think would be cool, but you know is never going to happen. You end up with so many obligations, you can't just jump off the merry-go-round and drop out. Work, bills. You, on the other hand. Whatever you want to do, Amanda, do it now before you get locked into jobs and relationships and mortgage payments."

"That's just the thing. I've got obligations and bills to pay too. I already took a year off from my education, and now it's full steam ahead."

"Did you do anything fun on your year off?"

"Worked two jobs, and no, I wouldn't call it fun. People think that just because you're young, you've got it made. Like you have all kinds of freedom and nothing to worry about. And you know what? It pisses me off. It's not fun not knowing how you're going to pay your tuition and your living expenses, how taking a part-time job might totally fuck your school work, how you're going to graduate with good enough grades so you can get shortlisted for the best employers. And as for a mortgage, I probably won't even be in a position to have one for at least ten years." Amanda whipped off her sunglasses. Her expression was hard, implacable.

"I'm sorry. You're right." Claire reached over and touched her arm. "People like me sometimes forget life is no picnic when you're young. We see it nostalgically as a time of freedom and lack of responsibilities, and not for what it really is."

Amanda was not appeased. "That's another thing that upsets me. You act sometimes like you're so much older than me. Like we're a different species because of it."

Shocked, Claire could only look at her as she continued. "I'm not a kid, okay? Why do people do that anyway? Why do they assign us into categories based on our age? Make us feel incapable and inferior because of something as arbitrary as age? It's insulting. Saying I'm too young to understand something, or that you're too old to try something new, is every bit as horrible as saying black people can't do something because of their color, or a girl can't do something because of her gender. It's stupid and I hate it."

Jesus, Claire thought, chastened. *There's a lot of fire in there when she's pissed off.* The image of Amanda angry, flushed, so fired up and feisty, made her smile. And appreciate her even more. "You're totally right. It is stupid. I don't mean to act like your age is some kind of impediment to anything, okay? I'm really very sorry."

Near tears, Amanda said, "I get that kind of crap from Aunt Shannon all the time and I just . . . I don't want it from you, okay? I don't want to be a kid to you."

"You're not, Amanda." Her ass suitably kicked, Claire swallowed her pride. Amanda was right. It was time to treat her like the intelligent, mature, capable woman she was. It happened to be easier to think of her as a kid only because it was safe that way. Claire could never fall for a kid, could never be tempted by a kid. But by a woman, she could. She felt her voice quaver with emotion as she said, "You're a beautiful, bright, wonderful woman. I respect you and I like you very much, and I don't ever mean to hurt you or demean you in any way. Okay?"

Amanda's smile was in direct contrast to the tears pooling

in her big green eyes. They looked like shimmering emeralds, Claire thought, and she gasped a little at their beauty.

"Thank you," Amanda said. "And I'm sorry I lost it."

"No," Claire said. "I'm glad you set me straight. I needed it."

When Amanda's hand crept into hers on the console, it felt good, damned good—like they'd held hands many times before, and neither was in a hurry to pull away. A week ago, she never would have guessed she'd be driving through the Nevada desert with a beautiful young woman, holding hands. Even if it was just platonic. And kind of surreal. *God, Maria would pee her pants if she could see me right now!*

"Hungry yet?" Claire asked.

"I'm always hungry!"

"Me too. Unfortunately I don't have the body you do, so it takes a considerable amount of self-restraint to keep from blowing up like a whale."

"Oh, Claire, you are so funny sometimes. I think you look absolutely perfect."

Claire did a double take after seeing something in Amanda's eyes she hadn't expected—something that hinted at much more than just an innocent compliment. It sent her heart into a momentary arrhythmia until she convinced herself she was imagining things—imagining that Amanda was attracted to her. Surely to God *that* was a fantasy.

"I thought we'd have a little snack at a picnic area before we hit one of the trails," Claire said.

"Wow, we're here already. That was fast!"

"Only thirty miles from Vegas, but it's a world of difference, isn't it?"

"Oh yeah. *This* is what I came to Vegas for!"

Claire paid the five-dollar toll and drove past the welcome center to a parking area near a picnic shelter. Behind them the red jagged mountains, beautiful against the blue sky, beckoned. "You up to a little hiking?"

"Anything you want to do sounds great to me."

Anything? Claire thought roguishly. For a moment she allowed herself thoughts of lying on the beach next to Amanda, pulling Amanda's short-sleeved blouse aside enough to kiss the base of her neck, those lovely eyes looking at her with lust or perhaps even love. *Oh, stop it! And stop thinking everything she says has a double meaning*! To distract herself, she retrieved a picnic basket and two nylon roll-up chairs from the trunk, then led Amanda to the picnic shelter. Three-foot-high cacti and an even taller Joshua tree gave them privacy from passing cars.

"Wow, you've thought of everything, Claire. I'm impressed."

Claire laughed, but she was flattered. "If this impresses you, I'm glad I didn't go to the bother of getting one of the big restaurants to cater this."

"Well, I *am* a poor student don't forget, so I don't need fancy things to impress me."

"I'll remember that." She didn't know why she'd just said that, but she would remember Amanda's words. And yet she also wanted to spoil Amanda if the opportunity ever arose.

They ate cheese and crackers and drank nonalcoholic strawberry coolers and talked about one of Claire's favorite topics—books. They discovered they'd both read Wally Lamb's latest, as well as Jonathan Franzen's. They both loved Sue Miller, Anne Tyler, Alice Munro—character-driven novels. Claire went on at length about her latest visit to a bookstore and her discovery of a new author. "Actually, she's been around for a long time, since the 1970s, but she's only written a few books—Hilma Wolitzer. I loved *In the Palomar Arms*."

"Can I borrow it?"

"Of course. I'll dig it out for you when we get back to Chicago. It's funny how your aunt hates those kinds of books."

"I know. I swear the only books she reads are lesbian romances."

Claire smiled, thinking of the bookcase in her own bedroom that was full of them. "Actually, there's nothing wrong with lesbian romances. Some of them are really quite good."

"I know that."

"You do?"

Amanda's face colored at her confession. For a moment Claire was tempted to press, but chose not to. She was dying to ask which of the lesbian novels were her favorites, but didn't. She was dying to know too if Amanda had a girlfriend, or if she'd ever been in love with a woman. She was too shy and didn't want to make Amanda uncomfortable.

"Ready for a little hiking among the rocks?"

"Oh yeah!"

CHAPTER FOURTEEN

Dani

So much for lounging in bed and a little premarital sex. Shannon had torn out of the room at the ungodly hour of nine o'clock to meet with the florist, then the caterers. To Dani, tending to such wedding details was like a trip to the dentist. Oh, she wanted the gorgeous, perfect wedding, all right. Was more than happy to pay for it. Well, *had been* more than happy to pay for it when she thought the bottomless well that was her job was going to keep bringing up those golden buckets. But Shannon loved the details and loved being busy. Planning the wedding was pretty much her domain, and Dani was glad for it.

In their room, she was on her second cup of coffee and the third section of the *Las Vegas Review* when Shannon returned.

"Hi, love!" She blew Dani a kiss.

"Hi yourself. How'd it go?"

She kicked her sandals off and joined Dani at the little bistro table by the window. "Any more of this coffee left?"

Dani nudged the carafe toward her. "Help yourself."

Shannon poured herself a cup. "Can you believe it? No hitches so far! The flowers are going to be awesome. The orchids are absolutely beautiful, you should see them!"

"And the food?"

"Oh my God, I've been sampling things all morning. You should see these little canapés shaped like hearts, they're so cute."

"Hearts?" Dani snickered.

"And the champagne fountain is like nothing I've ever seen before! It's eight feet high, can you believe that? It's like something out of a Food Network show."

Dani winced. *Christ, this shit is going to cost a bloody fortune.* But now was not the time to dwell on the negatives. It was too late to scale back anyway; they'd have to suck it up. "Back to the food," she said, deliberately lightening her tone. "See anything pink and succulent and that belongs in my mouth? You know, kinda rosebud shaped?"

Shannon studied her hard, straining to figure out what she was talking about before Dani's lewd intent dawned on her. "Dani Berringer, you're a pig!"

Dani stuck her tongue out and waggled it acrobatically. "You know you want it."

Shannon's face predictably grew heated as her gaze settled on Dani's tongue. Oh yeah, Shannon knew what that tongue could do to her. *Let's see her resist it!* Shannon was squirming in her chair a little, getting hungrier, her defenses clearly weakening. It wouldn't be long.

"Dammit, Dani. We have to go to the airport and pick up your sister in a few minutes."

Dani stood and reached for her lover's hand as though she were asking for a dance. She led her to the king bed. "We've got at least ten minutes before we need to grab a cab. C'mon baby, let me do you. You know you want me to."

A gentle nudge sent Shannon toppling backward onto the bed, giggling and protesting mildly while simultaneously Dani stripped off her shorts and underwear. Shannon never could resist an oral display of Dani's love for her, and Dani, for her part, *loved* going down on Shannon. Many times at work she had sat at her desk with the vision of getting down on her knees, pulling Shannon to the edge of the bed and burying her face in the sweet, willing wetness that felt and tasted like home to her. It made the afternoons at work crawl by when she longed to slip home for a little afternoon delight. Now she dropped to her knees and ardently performed, her tongue, lips and mouth giving endless pleasure to her lover.

"OhGodohGodohGod," Shannon muttered in breathless ecstasy over and over again. "I love when you suck me off. Oh Dani, suck me!"

Dani loved the verbal urgings, loved how Shannon's hips pushed in sync against her mouth, loved the hands that tangled in her hair and roughly pulled her in, mashing her face against the slick velvetiness. Even as Shannon, dripping wet and bucking wildly, came in her mouth, she didn't want to stop. She kept it up until Shannon pulled away and turned over, still writhing and spent.

"God, I love doing that to you," Dani whispered excitedly, softly stroking Shannon's back. "I could do that all day."

"Honey, if you did that all day there'd be nothing left of me. And nothing left of your tongue."

Dani laughed. "Well, we could always try it and see if your theory is correct."

"Oh, God, you're trying to kill me with kindness."

"Is there a better way to go?"

"Please tell me the sex isn't going to dry up after we get married."

Dani gently turned her over and kissed her deeply. "Never, my love. Even when we're dead tired and the baby's crying in the next room, we are *not* going to stop having sex."

"Shit, look at the time. We need to get going."

Dani sighed loudly. "I know, I know. God only knows what kind of trouble Heather might get into if we leave her alone in

Vegas." She was kidding, but not entirely.

Heather, three years older, had been the first to rebel. Not long out of high school and working as a bank teller in their hometown, she successfully seduced the older, married branch manager. The scandal erupted when, at twenty-one, she became pregnant, and much to everyone's surprise, her thirty-six-year-old lover actually left his wife for her. The problem was compounded by the fact that the wronged wife was the local Baptist minister's daughter, and so Bob and Heather were pretty much run out of town on a rail. They ended up in Portland, Oregon, and married on their son's second birthday. With an older sister bringing such scandal and unforgivable shame upon the family so early on, Dani's taking off to college and supporting herself, and then her avowed lesbianism, didn't spark quite the same fireworks. Not that her parents approved of her by any stretch of the imagination, but it would have been worse without Heather having blazed a trail. She owed a debt to Heather for being her own person, for raising her middle finger to the world and making her own choices, because her actions had given Dani the confidence to do the same.

Thirty minutes later, in her short shorts and tight, neon pink tank top, Heather hugged them both. "How are my two favorite girls?"

Dani smirked and couldn't resist teasing. "I thought your two favorite girls were compliments of that talented boob doctor in L.A."

Three years ago, newly divorced from Bob and dating a guy fourteen years her junior, Heather had gotten an expensive breast augmentation with her alimony settlement. The boyfriend was gone now, but the boobs remained. Heather rolled her eyes. "Dani Berringer, I know you're a boob woman, so don't even pretend to disparage these babies."

Dani shook her head. Her sister always knew how to put her in her place.

"How's your cold?" Shannon asked.

"Much better, thank you. Good drugs help, and the lure of

coming to Vegas! It's so nice and warm here, I love it. By the way, how are the blushing brides doing? You guys okay?"

"Nerves of steel," Dani answered. "Thanks for coming. Seriously."

"Aw, sweetie, I wouldn't have missed it for the world. Just because the rest of our family are a bunch of jackasses, it's their loss not to be here."

Dani had never been able to write off her family as effortlessly as Heather. As much as it pissed her off, a small part of her still craved her parents' approval. She knew it was a waste of time and a waste of her emotional energy, but just once she wanted them to say "good job," or "well done," or "we're proud of you." Her sensible side knew it was never going to happen, but she couldn't stop trying to figure out why the sun continued to shine out of her younger brother Jim's ass and never hers. He was a high school dropout, twice divorced and a hard-core alcoholic, and yet he could do no wrong in their parents' eyes. Same with the youngest in the family, Mary. She was the good girl, and so she probably actually deserved her parents' admiration, except that she knew it and ate it right up. She dutifully and happily conformed to the script her parents would have written for all of them. She'd gotten a job as a secretary out of high school, then quit in her mid-twenties to marry a solid, nerdy guy from the same church. Mary also lived up to her name, for she was very religious, perhaps even more so than their parents. Seven years younger than Dani, they weren't close, but that hadn't stopped Mary from condemning Dani's "sick and perverted lifestyle" several years ago. Yes, she'd used those very words in a letter Dani had committed to memory before burning it. They hadn't spoken since.

"Yeah, well," Dani quipped, "there's probably a big Cornhuskers basketball game on this weekend. You know, something *important*."

"Yeah, or a sale on Budweiser at that gas station down the street."

The three of them laughed, knowing the comments probably

weren't far off the mark. Their parents had been sent an all-expenses-paid invitation to the wedding, but the returned RSVP simply said they couldn't make it, without explanation. Well, that was fine, Dani told herself. Maybe she wouldn't be able to make it to their funerals one day, either.

Later over a glass of wine, just the two of them, Dani asked her sister how she was really doing. She looked older, a little more worn down since the last time they'd seen each other nearly a year ago. Her latest boyfriend, this time younger by only single digits, was taking a little time out from the whole committed relationship thing at the moment, Heather explained with rolled eyes. But her job at an investment company was good and her son Jack, a college sophomore now, was doing great. He was the one bright spark in her life, a good boy who treated his mother right and was excelling in his pre-med courses, she said. "But don't worry, Mom and Dad wouldn't be impressed even if Jack discovered the cure for cancer."

"Yeah, well, fuck them."

"If you really meant that, then why'd you invite them to your wedding?"

"How about if I blame Shannon and say it was her idea."

"Nice try."

"All right." Dani sighed loudly, having no legitimate explanation. "I don't know, okay? I guess I try to keep rewriting the story, hoping the ending will magically change. You ever read a book or watch a movie, and you don't like the ending, so you kind of make up a whole new one in your mind and then believe that's really the way it went down? Like Romeo and Juliet used body doubles or something and ran off together. Or Hitler actually got offed in one of those assassination attempts."

Heather looked at her quizzically. "Dani, I wouldn't know a happy ending if it bit me in the ass, okay? Anyway, you're better off just forgetting about them, like I do."

Dani shrugged and sipped her wine. Heather was right, of course, but it was hard to give up something she'd secretly yearned for most of her life. Wanting that parental connection and approval seemed especially important now that *she* was getting closer to becoming a parent. So she battled with the pragmatic and cynical part of herself that was like Heather and knew it was useless; the other part wanted to try one more time. "It'd be nice if just once—"

"Don't even go there, sis. Listen to yourself."

"I know, I know. Pathetic, isn't it?"

"What's pathetic is there's no good-looking young guys in this place." She scanned the lounge until she spotted the only man under thirty-five—a cowboy type with the makings of a beer belly. "Anyway, baby, life goes on, you know? You got the world by the balls. A gorgeous fiancée, a job that pays you more money than you know what to do with, and pretty soon a baby too."

Something heavy, like a lead ball, lodged deep in her belly. It was a sense of foreboding because for the first time today, Heather was not right about something. Dani couldn't bring herself to contradict her and tell her about her job.

CHAPTER FIFTEEN

Amanda

They heard the commotion before they came upon the cause of it. Someone was yelping in pain. Terrible pain. Claire was off and running like a shot, quickly disappearing on the trail ahead.

By the time Amanda caught up, Claire was bent over a gray-haired man lying on the ground, her attention on his leg. She looked solemn, concentrated, totally in doctor mode. The man's face was pale, constricted in pain, and upon closer inspection, Amanda saw that his ankle was badly broken. She had never seen a broken ankle before, but the fact that his foot was facing the wrong direction was a pretty good indication of how badly it was broken. Someone was on their cell phone calling 911 and Claire was asking the man questions to keep him conscious, checking his pulse at the same time. She directed Amanda to collect jackets or extra clothing from people to help keep him from going into shock.

"Is there anything else we can do?" Amanda asked after she'd completed her task, her stress spiking at the whimpers of pain from the man. What she really wished for was that Claire could fix him, stop his pain, but of course that was impossible.

"His pulse is fairly strong, his breathing is a little ragged. His BP is probably on the low side. I'd like to keep him from passing out and going into shock. Other than that, we need to wait for the paramedics." Her expression was grim as she whispered to Amanda, "He'll need surgery right away."

Amanda couldn't keep looking at the crooked foot without wanting to throw up. She engaged in conversation with a couple of the others who'd stuck around to see if they could help. She was fully confident and relieved that Claire was on the job. If she were injured or sick in any way, she would want Claire by her side, offering comfort and reassurance, just as she was doing now.

It was a good thirty minutes before the paramedics appeared, though it felt much longer. Probably to the poor guy too, who seemed to be holding his own thanks to Claire's attentiveness.

"Jeez, I felt so useless back there," Claire confessed quietly on the hike back.

"Are you kidding me? You were totally professional and a huge comfort to that guy. I'm sure he would have been in a lot worse shape if you hadn't been there to help. The rest of us would have been in a lot rougher shape too I suspect. We'd have been whining like helpless babies."

"I highly doubt that."

"No, you were amazing. You knew exactly what to do."

"Just basic first aid was all it was. If he'd been having a baby instead, I would have felt much more at home."

Amanda laughed. "Now *that* I would like to see!" She was too shy to show how totally impressed she was. In a crisis, Claire acted just as she'd expected she would—calm, in command, compassionate, competent. Her respect for Claire took another leap forward, and she tried hard not to seem like she had the biggest crush in the world on the very capable Dr. Cooper. "Anyway, you did great."

"I think I've worked up an appetite. And I could use a drink after all that. Do you mind if we head back and look for a restaurant on the edge of town somewhere?"

"I'd love to."

The sun was beginning to set by the time they pulled into the parking lot of an Italian bistro. The colors of the desert and the mountains seemed to ignite under the setting sun, seared with golds and pinks and burnt oranges.

"What do you think of the desert and all the open space?" Claire asked after they were seated at a small table beside a large window. A votive candle shimmered from a bowl of rose-colored water in the center of the table, lending a decidedly romantic air to the environment.

"It does feel a little strange here after being surrounded by skyscrapers everywhere back in Chicago. But as an architecture nut, I can understand why you would ask me that, and I like the change. It feels like you can actually breathe here with all the open space. Nature and architecture don't necessarily have to be at odds with one another."

"Have you ever thought of becoming an architect?"

Amanda smiled at the question. "You mean instead of just studying the art and history of it? Yes, and I still might one day. But I've always wanted to be a student of architecture before ever becoming an architect myself. I want to be an expert in the history and appreciation of it before ever trying to build something myself. I don't think you can build anything new without understanding what came before it."

The bottle of Chianti Claire had ordered arrived, and they waited for the waitress to fill their glasses and take their dinner order—chicken parmesan for Claire, gnocchi for Amanda—before Claire said, "That makes sense, actually. Kind of like learning about the history of wine and how it's made in different cultures before trying to make it yourself."

"Yes, exactly. Mmm, this wine is good." Amanda rarely drank but tonight she felt like knocking back a couple of glasses and relaxing. "You understand what I'm trying to do, but not many people do. I think my aunt, for instance, thinks I'm a perpetual student who keeps going to school just for the love of going to school."

"You're right, this wine *is* excellent." Claire closed her eyes for a moment as she savored the taste. It was a classico riserva from Tuscany, with a seventy-dollar price tag, but Claire had insisted.

"That was stressful today, with that man breaking his ankle like that," Amanda remarked. "I imagine you're pretty used to stress in your line of work."

"It does have its moments, but I actually kind of like the stress. A tense situation seems to sharpen every sense in your body, makes you prioritize and concentrate on the immediate situation. It's almost like being in a tunnel, where everything else drops away and you focus on the job at hand. But afterward you kind of crash from the adrenaline rush, like now."

"I can always drive back if you're too tired."

"I might take you up on that."

Their food arrived, smelling delicious, and both women tucked into it ravenously.

"It seems," Claire said around a mouthful of chicken and noodles, "from some of the things you say, that your aunt doesn't understand you very well."

Amanda shrugged. "It's not her fault. We haven't been very close the last few years, which is mostly my fault, actually."

"Mind if I ask why? From what she's said, I know you two were extremely close until you went off to school."

Amanda considered how much to tell Claire. She didn't want to come between such good friends, nor was it fair to put Claire in the middle. She had absolutely nothing negative to say about her aunt—she loved Shannon like a mother or a big sister, and she knew Shannon's love for her was equally unconditional. The problem between them came down to her own shame about herself, her own fears. She was afraid to let her aunt see her as someone who could make a mistake—a huge mistake. There was something about Claire, however, that made her feel safe to be herself. Yes, that was it. Claire was *safe*. Claire wouldn't judge her for making mistakes.

"We were very close, it's true. Don't get me wrong, I love my aunt more than anyone in this world."

"But?"

"But nothing." Amanda took a bolstering sip of wine before looking Claire straight in the eye. She was quickly caving in, wanting to confide in Claire. She needed to. "There were certain things in my life I've kept from her, and it's created some distance between us."

Claire looked pensive. "I've seen secrets destroy relationships. If you and Shannon love and support each other like you say, why the need to keep things from her?"

A simple question that deserved a simple answer, except that it wasn't simple. It was complicated because Amanda had made it complicated. Tears sprang to her eyes suddenly and for the moment she couldn't speak.

Claire's hand closed the distance between them and slipped into Amanda's on the tabletop. The tender gesture sent Amanda's tears slithering down her cheeks.

"Oh, Amanda. I'm sorry. Can you tell me why you're so upset?"

"I'm ashamed," she whispered after a moment, looking into Claire's soft brown eyes and finding solace there. "You see . . ." She had to take a deep breath before speaking the words she was so ashamed to say. *Say it, say it. Claire will understand.* "I'm married."

Surprise registered in Claire's eyes. She started to say something, stopped. Her hand, slightly tremulous now, continued to hold Amanda's. "Okay. I didn't see that coming. I thought you were gay?"

Amanda smiled through her tears. "I am. I married a woman."

"Oh. Okay."

The release of the admission made Amanda feel a little nauseous, yet it felt good being honest with Claire. It dawned on her that she'd had the urge to be completely up front with Claire since meeting her at the airport. Maybe she was just tired of carrying around the shame of her actions, or maybe telling Claire was a dress rehearsal for coming clean with her aunt. In any case, she *wanted* to share this part of herself with Claire. Desperately needed to be *herself* with Claire.

Claire looked more confused by the minute. "It's kind of an important announcement, isn't it? Getting married is not something you sort of forget to tell someone you're close to, like telling her you changed your hair color or that you've grown fond of Russian poetry or something." Claire looked peeved, perhaps a protective posture for Shannon's sake.

"I know, and you're right."

Claire shook her head in mystification and removed her hand from Amanda's very slowly. "I'm sorry but I don't understand. Why would you keep something like this from Shannon?"

"I meant to tell her before but lost the courage. The problem was with *who* I married. And the fact that it turned out to be a big mistake."

"It did? Will you tell me about it? I've got all night, you know."

Claire's smile was infectious and Amanda smiled too. "Thank you, and yes, I would really like to tell you. I was in my last year of undergraduate studies at Stanford when I met a second-year law school student, Jennifer, at a party. We started hanging out, and I knew right away we'd be lovers. I hadn't had many lovers before, but I knew Jennifer was special. The intensity of my feelings for her scared the shit out of me at first, but I was in love. I went with it. I was so happy then, I wanted to share it with the world. And I did. Shannon flew out to meet her, and that's when the problem started."

"What happened?"

"Aunt Shannon took a disliking to Jennifer."

Claire topped up their glasses with wine and leaned a little closer, captivated. "That doesn't sound like Shannon."

"She caught Jennifer flirting with some guy one night when

we all went out to dinner and a dance club. She told me about it the next morning, said she didn't trust Jennifer's intentions. I blew it off because I was blinded by love, I guess. I don't know." Amanda was still disgusted with her stubborn disbelief in her aunt, and disgusted at her own inability to see through Jennifer. Jennifer had told her she was bisexual, but she'd never guessed that meant Jennifer thought she could act on her attractions even within the confines of their relationship. "I refused to believe there was a problem. Refused to believe I couldn't trust Jennifer, even though I knew she was bisexual. I didn't question her hard enough, didn't pick up on the signs. I was stupid."

"Not stupid. Trusting. You shouldn't be sorry for trusting someone."

The next part was hardest for Amanda, because she did not admit to failure easily. "That wasn't the worst of it. After five months together, Jennifer and I got married. In California."

Claire's eyebrows shot up. "Legally?"

"Yup." There were times when Amanda felt old. Old and battle scarred. Now was one of those times.

Claire kept her thoughts close, her voice neutral. "Wow."

"I know. Shocking, isn't it?" Amanda shook her head severely, her self-loathing evident in her voice. "Not only did the smart, ambitious, cool-headed Amanda Malden do something as impulsive as run off and get married on practically the fourth date, but she went and married the wrong girl."

"Oh no. I'm sorry. What happened?"

"Three months into the marriage, we both knew it was a mistake. We weren't compatible. Suddenly, everything we thought was endearing about one another grated on our nerves. And I suspected Jennifer wasn't monogamous with me. We kept it going for another month or so. I guess I kept hoping it would work out, you know? I wanted to try some more, get some counseling, but Jennifer announced that she was going back to men and that she didn't love me."

This time Claire let her emotions show. "Oh, Amanda. I'm so sorry that happened to you. It must have been such a tough time for you, and to go through it without family support. Are you okay now?"

"Yes and no. It was the worst time of my life then, so yes, things are better now." It was the one spontaneous thing she'd ever done in her life and it had ended in failure. Amanda looked at the ceiling for strength because tears were threatening again. "It's just . . . I couldn't believe I'd screwed up my life so badly. To be married and then not married before I was twenty-five. And to have Jennifer go back to men, it seemed like a double whammy. A double mistake. It was devastating." She remembered the sting and the irrevocableness of Jennifer's words. *I don't love you anymore, Amanda. And I don't want to be with a woman anymore.*

Claire's face looked pained. "So you couldn't tell Shannon because you were embarrassed?"

"Yes. She's always thought so highly of me, always so proud of me. I didn't want to destroy the image of me she'd built up in her mind. I didn't want to disappoint her and I didn't want to admit to myself that she'd been right about Jennifer."

"Shannon would never be disappointed in you. She loves you. And she would never throw something like that in your face."

"I know that." She let a tear fall freely down her cheek before swiping it away. "I've been so afraid. Afraid to tell her, afraid to make it real by admitting it, afraid to fall for anyone again."

Claire nodded. "I know. I understand. But they say the truth sets you free, so to speak."

Amanda shrugged. "I'm moving on from it now. Our divorce is tied up in the courts, and it could be a while with all the politicking going on in California over gay marriage. But I want it to be over, and you're right. I can't do that until I deal with the truth."

"You're a brave woman, Amanda. Braver than you think, and your heart's in the right place." Claire reached for her hand again and held it loosely. She seemed to know exactly when Amanda needed a comforting touch. "We all make mistakes. I know that as well as anyone because I've made my share. Shannon has too."

"It's going to shock the crap out of her."

"Yes. But she'll be okay, and so will you."

"I trust in what you're saying, Claire. Thank you for believing in me. But now can we please change the subject and talk about something fun? Like the wedding cake I'm supposed to design for them?"

Claire laughed. Flagging down the waitress, she ordered coffee. They'd successfully killed the bottle of wine. "What's that all about?"

"Didn't you get a little wedding party assignment? Mine's the cake, Jordan's is the bachelor party."

"Ah, yes. I'm supposed to compile a photo album of all the candid shots from this week. Guess I better get working on taking some photos or I'm going to get fired!"

"Tell you what. I'll help you take photos if you help me design the wedding cake."

"I'm not much of an artist. Not like you, Miss Architectural History Doctorate. But nice try on attempting to make a deal with me."

"Oh, come on, you know you want to help me and you know you could use another person taking photos this week."

Claire blushed a little, and it was an adorable contrast to her serious side. "All right, busted. When are you supposed to come up with this design?"

"Tomorrow afternoon. I'm supposed to meet with the pastry chef and go over it."

"Tomorrow afternoon? Wow. Are you a last-minute crammer or something?"

"Sometimes." Amanda laughed. "Especially if it's something I'm putting off. We could have lunch together tomorrow and come up with something?" *Yes, lunch together would be perfect.* There was something exciting about making plans ahead of time with Claire, especially plans that didn't involve anyone but the two of them. It produced a little tickle in her stomach.

"All right. I can see I've been roped into this. Lunch tomorrow, but let's see if we can at least come up with some rough ideas on the drive back tonight."

"Deal."

Amanda took the wheel for the drive back to Las Vegas. They joked about the cake, jockeying to come up with the silliest idea. Amanda thought the cake should look like a ball and chain, Claire two breasts in profile touching one another.

"Ooh, Claire, I didn't know you had it in you to be such a dirty girl!"

Claire's laughter, so genuine and deep from her belly, made Amanda laugh too. "Don't you dare tell anyone, especially not your aunt! I'd never hear the end of it."

"Don't worry, your secret's safe with me." Amanda parked the car in the hotel's underground garage and cut the engine. Neither woman made a move to get out. "Thank you for listening to me tonight. And for not judging. It means so much to me."

Claire pulled her in for a hug, the spontaneity of it catching her off guard a little, but she let herself be held tightly and took refuge in the broad shoulders and heavy breastedness of the older woman. It was comforting, nourishing, and perhaps something more, but she didn't want to go there. Not yet.

Still holding her tight, Claire said encouragingly, "I'm here for you. And your aunt will be too if you give her the chance."

"I know. I will. I guess I just needed to know it was going to be okay."

She didn't want to pull away and could have stayed in Claire's arms all night, but she felt her stir and begin to release her. When she looked into Claire's eyes, shadowed by the dimly lit garage, she had the faint impulse to kiss her. Their mouths were not far apart, and Claire was looking at her tenderly, perhaps a little expectantly.

No, Amanda thought. *Impulsiveness has only gotten me into trouble, and I won't do it again.* She could get herself and Claire into so much trouble right now, but she resisted because it was really her only choice. It was hard, dammit. She needed the comfort of another woman so badly right now, but she would settle for the talk and the hug, and not the kisses and the full body contact she craved.

CHAPTER SIXTEEN

Jordan

Exhausted and sore from the hours and multitudinous positions of lovemaking, Jordan couldn't be happier. She was energized beyond all reason, as if she'd been chewing on caffeine pills or amphetamines nonstop. She'd never known this kind of thrilling energy. It was empowering, invigorating, stimulating. It made her want to leap across tall buildings in a single bound, scale walls like a comic book superhero. It was the most intense high she'd ever known; nothing else compared.

They hadn't left Dez's room since after last night's concert, and now, some twenty hours later, the remnants of the room service dinner shoved back out in the hall, Jordan ached for a quickie before Dez needed to get ready for her show.

"I'm sorry, Dez, but I can't get enough of you," she purred.

"I don't think you're sorry at all."

"Okay, you're right. I'm not sorry."

Dez laughed and tugged Jordan along. They didn't make

it to the bed. The sofa was more than adequate for the job. Dez wore only a bathrobe, which was perfectly convenient for what Jordan had planned. She climbed into Dez's lap and began kissing her neck and her luscious throat—that throat from which such beautiful music was given life. Her talent was a gift from the gods, and Jordan was privileged to lay her hands and mouth on such a gifted woman. Her fingers separated the silk robe as her mouth inched its way down, until finally she fell to her knees on the floor. *Beautiful.* Tenderly she took Dez into her mouth, lovingly ministering the needs of her erect clit and moist lips. Patiently and expertly her tongue swirled and her mouth sucked until Dez's moans filled the air. *Oh yes, sing to me baby.* It was the most beautiful song she'd ever heard Dez sing. It was a song of desire and supplication, of joy and then fulfillment. It made Jordan's own desire soar and overwhelm her.

Afterward they lay tangled on the sofa, touching, kissing, unquenched in their thirst to touch and be touched. Jordan marveled at their physical inseparableness. She'd never spent this many consecutive hours with a lover before. Had never wanted to be *inside* another person the way she wanted to be inside Dez. It was confusing and it was uncharted territory, wanting and needing this. Maybe it was because of the wedding bells in the air, she reasoned, because surely it couldn't be love. In any case, Dez didn't seem to be minding the intensity. In fact, Dez seemed as much into her as she was into Dez, and the reciprocity was something to marvel at too. Typically Jordan's conquests were far more into her than she was into them. Like a thousand percent more. Clingy and sentimental and sickly sweet. This was completely different, and while she didn't particularly feel like analyzing the reasons why she felt as she did with Dez as she lay in her arms, she at least allowed herself to enjoy this immersion in the comfort and peacefulness that was Dez.

Moments later, as Dez showered and changed for the show, Jordan fleetingly wondered how Claire and Amanda's day in the desert had gone, or was still going. Maybe they'd grabbed some crappy little motel room for the night so they could have at each other without the rest of the wedding party knowing their business. That's what she would have done if she were in Claire's shoes. She'd have just boldly pulled into a motel and blatantly seduced—and then screwed—the daylights out of Amanda. She tried to imagine Claire doing exactly that and the vision caused her to chuckle. Claire wouldn't have the guts to make the first move. She was too hung up on their age difference and the myth that Amanda was unattainable. Well, Jordan could care less about the age difference, and as for Amanda being unattainable, ha, that was a joke. Amanda looked at Claire with the same affection and lust as Claire looked at her. *God, life would be so much simpler if they'd just jump each other's bones instead of making googly eyes at each other and acting so childish.*

"Hey, baby." Dez leaned over and gave her a heart-stopping kiss. "I'll leave a ticket for you at the door, okay?"

"I have to share you with two thousand other people tonight?"

"Afraid so. Those two thousand people are going to help me pay my bills."

I could pay your bills, Jordan thought, shocking herself. She'd never *kept* any of her previous girlfriends, if you didn't count paying for dinners and shows and the occasional trinket. She didn't want to buy Dez dinner or a trinket. She wanted to buy her a house with beautiful flowers in the front garden and a heart-shaped swimming pool in the backyard and a front porch for them to sit on in the evenings. *Oh my God, Jordan, what the hell has gotten into you? You have the best sex of your life and now you want to play house with this woman? Plan a future with her? C'mon, give your head a shake.*

"You okay?" Dez asked, eyeing her suspiciously.

"Fine, darling." Jordan laughed quietly. A momentary loss of her sanity, that was all. A little post-sex exuberance that was turning her into a silly heart. She'd get her head about her again, and the sooner the better.

• • •

On stage Dez was sexier than ever, if that were possible. Maybe it was the glow of all those orgasms, Jordan thought with a self-satisfied smile as she watched Dez in a tight-fitting, slit-to-the-waist burgundy cocktail dress stalk the stage singing "Sweet Thing." During another Chaka Khan hit, "Ain't Nobody," Jordan's attraction to Dez rocketed higher. She loved the way she moved gracefully, athletically, seductively around the stage. The way she raised an eyebrow at the audience, the way she stroked the microphone, the subtle sway of her hips, the way her expressive hands conveyed the emotion of the song. Jordan easily flashed to an image of Dez covering her with her naked body in bed, the two of them rising and falling together, mouths, fingers, hands, breasts, Dez's dark creamy curves joining hers. Her mind was not her own anymore, nor her feelings, which were alien now. She was obsessed. Possessed. Totally immersed and engrossed in this—*what? Affair?*

She wanted to know everything about Dez and yet she hardly knew anything at all. They'd talked a little about their childhood and teen years—Dez about what it was like to grow up in a poor family of six kids and doting grandparents who lived next door, Jordan about growing up in a nuclear family of two career-obsessed professionals. They hadn't talked yet about their careers, about future plans, politics, religious beliefs, current affairs, past loves. There were weeks of conversations they'd yet to have and Jordan couldn't wait to get started.

The thirty-minute set flew by, and while Jordan was sorry to see it end, she was also thrilled she would soon have Dez to herself again.

They shared a bottle of champagne in Dez's room and talked about the concert and music in general. Jordan asked her if she would come to Dani and Shannon's wedding with her Saturday and sing a song for the brides. Dez's answer came in the form of silence and an unmistakable frown.

"Just one song. Their wedding song. You know The Pretenders' 'I'll Stand By You?' It would mean so much to them, Dez. And to me." She knew she was pleading but couldn't help it. "It would be the defining moment of the wedding if you sang it."

The silence stretched out before Dez quietly said, "I don't know."

"We could work it around your performance schedule. I'd pay you too, if that's—"

"No, that's not what I meant. I don't want your money," Dez said irritably.

"Then what's wrong?"

"The wedding is days away."

Jordan began growing impatient, worried. "Yes, I know that. It's four days away. Are you leaving town or something?"

"No, no. It's . . . Look, we've had a great twenty-four hours together, okay? It's been wonderful. But now you're talking about . . ." Dez tightened the belt of her robe. She looked decidedly uncomfortable, nervous perhaps, or else it was a good act. "Look, you're asking me to make a commitment to being your date at a wedding that's days away, and, well . . ."

Realization was slow to dawn on Jordan, but when it did, she was horrified, then embarrassed, then incredibly hurt. Dez was dumping her. They'd had their fun as far as Dez was concerned and now it was over. Jordan searched Dez's eyes for the joy and desire that had been so plainly evident moments before. She looked for evidence of the companionship and caring that had emanated from Dez's every expression, every action, such a short time ago. But there was nothing now. A curtain had come down. The show was over.

Jordan rose unsteadily, half drunk from the alcohol, in shock and with a growing despair that was sure to produce a monsoon of tears any minute. She couldn't identify these feelings at first, so foreign were they. "I thought . . ." She couldn't finish.

She gave Dez one last beseeching look that she hoped conveyed the depth of her feelings, of her hurt. But Dez was looking away. Dez had cut the cord and Jordan had no choice but to leave.

She stumbled to her room at the MGM Grand and sat in

the dark, numb and devastated. So this was what it felt like to be dumped by somebody you really, *really* liked. It was a detached observation, clinical, like she was looking over a business proposition. Was this what some of the women she'd dumped over the years had felt like? Was this what she'd put Brooke through six years ago? Sweet, dear Brooke, who'd come the closest to being considered a bona fide girlfriend. They'd dated exclusively for a couple of months, had grown quite close. Brooke clearly loved her, was clearly prepared to make Jordan her main priority in life. They were marching toward being a real couple—perhaps U-Haul territory even—when Jordan pulled the plug. It was the merciful thing to do. With Brooke, her feet felt like cement, unable to move. The same cement that encased her heart. No matter how much she had liked Brooke and cared for her, she could not bring herself to break old patterns, to remake herself, to cultivate feelings that would simply take too much work to nourish and maintain and would probably just die anyway. She could not bring herself to allow Brooke to crack that casing around her heart, and so she had ended the relationship before, she hoped, it would devastate Brooke.

Dez was an entirely different situation. Dez had broken through without even trying. Without even intending to, she had cracked that cement and it was like a bolt of lightning out of nowhere on a clear, sunny day—totally unexpected and deadly accurate. Jordan didn't even know or understand how she had come to feel this way, just that she had. And now Dez was trashing it all. Dez didn't want her. Dez was the mirror image of Jordan, an exact replica, it seemed—callous and cavalier in the dating department. *Use them and send them away.*

Had she missed a signal from Dez? Had she misread her in her blind attraction to the singer? Had she let her own growing feelings color reality? What had she done wrong that had made Dez turn away from her? Or was it predestined to end this way? Dez had told her she didn't do this kind of thing anymore, these quick pickups. And yet she was a pro at it, had done it so effortlessly with Jordan. Why had Dez gone and done this? Why was she treating her like yesterday's newspaper, used and discarded?

Slowly, the tears began to fall. She was alone and unwanted by the person she wanted most, and it was absolutely the worst feeling in the world—the most helpless and frustrating and lonely feeling in the world. *It sucks the big one, Dez Adams, when all I wanted to do was love you.*

CHAPTER SEVENTEEN

Shannon

It was amusing to watch Heather and Dani poke gingerly at breakfast in their hungover state. They'd stayed up late in the sitting room part of Shannon and Dani's suite, drinking white wine and talking about old times, and now they were paying for their alcohol-fueled trip down memory lane. Each nibbled tentatively on her omelet between huge gulps of coffee.

"Aren't you looking smug," Dani commented with a tired wink.

"Not smug, just happily virtuous, sweetheart."

Heather narrowed reproachful eyes at Shannon. "There's always a goody two-shoes in every family."

Shannon laughed, taking no offense at the teasing. She enjoyed seeing Dani and Heather together, both so different and yet so close, the way sisters should be. It was the way Shannon would want it if her sister were still alive. The rest of Dani's family was a source of frustration for her, even anger. They treated

Dani so grievously—worse than they probably treated strangers. Their cold absence from her life was cruel, so apparent by their failure to send a few kind words her way now and then. A letter, a card, an e-mail seemed like some kind of overwhelming and worthless task to them. Well, Christmas usually produced some awful ultrareligious card from them—one that implied judgment and condemnation. Rejection and criticism were all the Berringers seemed capable of showing Dani. Shannon was glad they weren't coming to the wedding, because while Dani thought it might mean something if they did, she knew it would only make things tense and unhappy, their unforgiving and intolerant ways heartbreaking all over again.

Amanda strolled into the casino restaurant, spotted them quickly and took a seat at their table. "Am I interrupting anything ladies?"

"Only if you're another goody two-shoes!" Heather pointed her fork accusingly, then laughed heartily. "I don't think we've met, though I've heard a lot about you. All nice things, of course. I'm Dani's sister, Heather."

Amanda reached over the table to shake hands. "Nice to meet you, Heather. I suppose my reputation as a goody two-shoes precedes me?"

"Well," Heather chuckled, "if the shoes fit!"

Amanda winced a little as the women laughed, and Shannon thought it prudent to change the subject. Her niece had always been a little on the sensitive side when it came to being teased, especially if had to do with her quiet, reserved ways. "Where's Claire?"

Now her niece's pained look morphed into something totally different, like a flower blossoming suddenly. Amanda's smile was ethereal, almost otherworldly, and Shannon sat stunned for a moment. In the twenty-six years she'd known her, she couldn't ever remember seeing her smile so beatifically before.

"We were pretty late getting back last night. She's probably still sleeping."

"How was your day in the desert?" Dani asked.

Shannon tuned out a little as Amanda accepted a cup of coffee from the waiter and began describing her day at Red Rock Canyon with Claire. She talked about hiking on rocky trails, a broken ankle, Claire helping someone, Italian food. And Shannon couldn't help thinking all the while how *happy* Amanda looked. It suddenly occurred to her that it was the first time her niece had seemed happy all week. Come to think of it, she didn't really know where Amanda was at in her life these days, whether she was happy or not. Happy in her own life, Shannon hadn't thought to question Amanda's happiness. It only occurred to her when someone was extremely unhappy, the way Claire had been in her years of grieving for Ann. It was hard to miss extreme unhappiness, but simple contentment or even ambivalence was always much harder to detect. She wished she could put her fork down, halt the polite conversation and straight out ask her, *Are you happy, Amanda?* The answer seemed important suddenly. But unfortunately it would have to wait.

"Amanda," she said pointedly when the conversation died down. "What do you say about a little together time tomorrow, just the two of us? I read about this great spa where we can get a manicure, pedicure, a massage and a steam bath. What do you say?"

"Sure," Amanda answered quickly. "As long as we don't miss the big bachelor extravaganza Jordan's got lined up for us all tomorrow night. She'd kill us if we did."

"Oh, God," Shannon groaned. "I'm scared to even think what she's going to do."

"Not me," Heather chimed in. "In fact, I can't wait!"

Dani chuckled knowingly from behind her coffee cup.

"Okay," Shannon challenged, sharpening her gaze at Dani. "Spill it. What do you know?"

"Nothing, I swear!"

"Hmm, why don't I believe you?"

Dani held her hands up in innocence. "Would I lie to you, my love?"

No, Shannon thought, I don't think you would. *But I would.*

Maybe not lie so much as not tell you the truth. She could play with the semantics all she wanted, but an omission of the truth was as bad as a lie, wasn't it? Not telling Dani, who so desperately wanted them to have a baby together, that they couldn't have one was far more serious than the time she'd not told her mother about a bad report card. Worse than when she failed to tell her first girlfriend that she wasn't really in love with her. Those things she could excuse, but this was much harder to justify. She had to tell Dani, of course she did, and she would. But there was always a reason to put if off—too many people around, wedding plans to make, events to attend like the bachelor party tomorrow night, the wedding itself on Saturday. There were always good reasons.

"Well," Shannon finally said, "if Jordan were here we could probably beat it out of her."

"Yeah, where is she?" Amanda asked. "She pooped out of going to the desert with Claire and me yesterday."

"She texted me yesterday," Dani said with a gleam in her eye. "Seems she's been holed up in that singer's love nest since Monday night."

"Dez Adams?" Amanda asked in awe.

"The one and only."

"Oh, my God!"

Dani shrugged, unconcerned. "I'm afraid we'll just have to guess what she has in store for us all. Anybody want to wager on whether there's a stripper involved?" She raised her eyebrows hopefully, and Shannon reached across the table to give her a playful smack on the shoulder.

"Oh, no," Heather said. "I'm not betting against that. In fact, I rather hope there *is* a stripper involved. That would be such a blast!"

Amanda made a face. "Not my cup of tea."

Shannon patted her niece's arm sympathetically. "I don't blame you. I think it's a bit silly myself, but totally something I could see Jordan springing on us."

Amanda visibly flinched at the comment, but her reaction

was lost in Heather's outburst. Heather exclaimed, "Well honey, I don't think it's silly at all! I would love to have a gorgeous woman dance naked in front of me. I *totally* get why men are so enamored with the whole scene. It's so, I dunno, *sexy!*"

Dani nudged her sister playfully. "Maybe you could ask Jordan if *you* could be the stripper."

Heather laughed until she nearly fell out of her chair. When she could speak, she said, "Are you kidding me? I would *love* to dance to a roomful of hot and horny lesbians! Oh, my God, please pick me! I would pay money to do that."

Shannon easily imagined the gregarious Heather dancing on a stage. She loved attention, loved to have fun and make a spectacle, and she had the looks and sensuality to pull it off. The sisters were both athletic and graceful, and Heather, with the same dark hair, blue eyes but with killer cheekbones, was a more feminine version of her younger sister.

Dani shook her head as though regretting having introduced the subject. If nothing else, this bachelor party was going to be an adventure, her look seemed to say, and they were all going to be helpless participants.

"How's the cake design coming along?" Shannon asked Amanda.

"Great. Claire's helping me with it."

"Really?" Shannon answered in surprise. Claire was hardly the artistic type. It was a huge stretch to expect her to take photos of the week and compile them. But helping design the cake? It was a shocker that Claire would volunteer to help with it, but somehow, it seemed Amanda had managed to talk her into it. "Well, I guess I can trust you two to come up with something tasteful." She cocked an eyebrow toward Dani and Heather. "You two on the other hand . . ."

In unison, they both dropped their mouths in pretend shock.

CHAPTER EIGHTEEN

Claire

It surprised Claire how much she was looking forward to lunch alone with Amanda. The hot excitement in the very pit of her stomach surprised her too. There were all the hallmarks of a very special first date—the sweaty palms, dry throat, nervousness that kept her from eating breakfast, the indecision over what to wear. You're a fool, she kept telling herself, except she didn't really believe it was the awful thing her conscience wanted her to believe it was. There was something insanely liberating about feeling like a fool. Claire smiled, as she always did when she thought of Amanda. So beautiful, so smart, so much fun to be around. Amanda's youthfulness was like a beacon, beckoning her to let herself feel young again. Not young in the sense of immature, but young in an optimistic, weightless way. It was like suddenly coming out of a long expanse of dreamless dark nights.

They'd reserved a table at Canaletto at The Venetian, their

love for Italian food making it an easy choice. They hopped the monorail together for the ride to the north end of The Strip, sitting side by side, not looking much at one another as they made small talk. It was a little strange talking about the wedding, the weather, current events, after the deep and very personal conversations of last night. Amanda's confession had shocked Claire, because she didn't seem the type to run off and marry someone she barely knew, or to ignore warning signals and then to end up with a failed marriage. But everyone made mistakes, Amanda included, and she'd undoubtedly learned valuable lessons from the experience. It certainly cleared up the mystery about whether Amanda was single or not, and Claire wondered nervously if her feelings for Amanda, her connection to her, would intensify. She hoped not, in the way one hoped not to be enticed by a fattening but oh-so-tempting dessert. The deliciousness and forbidden nature of this attraction to her best friend's niece was, in reality, not a dream but a nightmare. It could bring nothing but trouble for both of them. And yet she couldn't help but step closer, couldn't help opening her heart just a little more each time she was with her.

Canaletto was beautiful, with its sixteen-foot-high ceilings trimmed with thick dark wood, its polished hardwood floors and romantic leather-covered booths. They chose the indoor patio however—safer and less secretive, Claire figured—where they could look at the shops and the indoor canal in St. Mark's Square, the massively high mural ceiling of blue sky and faint clouds making it feel as if they were outdoors.

Both women had unknowingly chosen nearly identical clothing—dress shorts and a well-tailored short-sleeved shirt. Claire wore leather loafers, Amanda heeled sandals.

They debated the soups and salads on the menu before they both boldly declared they were going for the good stuff—pasta. It would be her meal for the day, Claire said, and Amanda happily concurred with the little pact. They had a couple of hours before they were scheduled to meet with the cake designers. They could take their time, order a bottle of wine. God, it really was almost like a date. But then, last night in the desert had seemed a little like a date too. It was really just her imagination running away with her or loneliness, Claire told herself, because it had been so long since she'd been on any kind of date.

They placed their order—Claire the *vermicellial pomodoro*, Amanda the *casonzei con stracchino e pere*—and agreed to share samples. Amanda protested but only mildly when Claire ordered an Amarone—a rich red wine that cost a small fortune.

"Have you ever been to Venice?" Claire asked, because she could picture Amanda there, exploring, checking out the remarkable architecture. Closer to the truth, she could picture the two of them there, having a romantic dinner in a restaurant much like this, taking a ride in a gondola with a gondolier singing romantic songs in Italian.

Amanda shook her head sadly. "I'd love to one day. What about you?"

"I haven't and would love to as well. Mostly Ann and I traveled within North America. And since then, I—" She stumbled a little. She hadn't planned on mentioning Ann, and yet she'd said the name so effortlessly, as though every part of her life were an open book for Amanda. "I, ah, haven't really been anywhere since, except for medical conferences."

Their bottle of wine arrived, the waiter pouring them each a glass with a flourish.

"Oh," Amanda gushed after a taste. "This is wonderful. I've never tried an Amarone before. God, I don't think I could ever afford to, but I've always wanted to. Thank you."

"You're welcome. Until last night, I think it'd been a couple of years since I ordered a bottle of wine at a restaurant. It was nice." The delis and roadhouse restaurants she typically frequented when she didn't feel like cooking either didn't serve liquor, or didn't serve any worth drinking. She'd missed this. And missed eating with someone. "I need to be thanking you. This is lovely. I'd forgotten how special it is to eat out at a nice restaurant and to enjoy a nice wine with a meal." She raised her glass to Amanda. "The company makes all the difference."

"Thank you and I agree. Great food without great company is just food and not an experience to remember."

"You're so right."

Amanda settled an appraising gaze on her. Her eyes exhibited curiosity but mostly sympathy. Claire expected her to make a comment about Ann's death, but instead she said, quietly, "What was she like?"

Have you got all afternoon? Claire wanted to ask. She began to smile as she started speaking about Ann. "She was kind of the opposite of me. Real outgoing. Made friends easily. Liked to try new things. Got us to do things like cycle around the island of Cape Breton in Canada, hike up Mount St. Helens, go on a wine tour in the Napa Valley. And oh my, she loved to dance. She even signed us up for ballroom dance lessons once." Claire remembered the women's dances Ann would regularly drag her to. An adept dancer, Ann wouldn't sit down all night, and soon Claire would find herself having a good time too, trying to keep up. Ann was the one who'd brought such joy to Claire's life for more than a dozen years. She'd been her light, the true north in her compass.

"She sounds like a marvelous woman. Did she work with people?"

"How'd you guess?" Claire's smile broadened. "She was an elementary school teacher, and in the summers she'd volunteer to do activities at a home for seniors. She always said she didn't want to restrict herself to working only with kids. She liked people of all ages."

"Were you together a long time?"

"Ten years when she got her diagnosis. Two more after that." It would be fifteen years now if Ann were still alive.

"I'm so sorry."

Claire shrugged and looked away. "I had twelve wonderful years. I guess that has to be enough." For her it was. She'd had her one true love. Twelve years with a soul mate were more years than most people ever got.

The food arrived. Claire's dish was angel hair pasta with

chopped tomatoes, marinara sauce and fresh basil and gar-
lic. Amanda's was ravioli filled with roasted pear, parmigiano-
reggiano and tossed with asparagus and stracchino cheese. It
smelled divine, almost too good to eat, but it wasn't long before
they were shoveling forks into it and trying each other's. The
wine suited the meal perfectly, and Claire yearned for the lunch
to last all afternoon. And evening, for that matter.

"I know I'm out of line saying this," Amanda said after a
while. "But you seem, I don't know, incomplete being alone."

"Unhappy you mean?"

"Partly, yes."

In her soul, she was lonely, and that must be what Amanda
perceived. Amanda was alone too, and yet it didn't seem like a
source of sadness or emptiness for her. Claire's aloneness was
sharp and more painful, like a piece of her was missing. "I think,"
Claire answered slowly, "that when you've been with someone for
a long time, someone you're close to and in love with, a part of
you is gone when they're gone. I feel like half of me is missing."

"That makes sense. I didn't have that with Jennifer, but I can
see that it's true for you. But you can remake the part of yourself
that you still have, don't you think?"

Claire took a long, deliberate bite of food before she spoke.
"I guess so." But you have to want to, she felt like saying. *And
then you have to figure out how to do it.* "It's not easy," was all she
could manage. It was especially not easy doing it alone. Regaining
herself was a mountain to scale, and most days she simply didn't
feel up to it.

"You're right. Starting over is never easy, no matter what the
circumstances."

Claire was reminded that Amanda, while perhaps adapt-
ing much easier to being alone, had had to rebuild her life too.
Divorce was never easy, she supposed, even in a short marriage.
"It's been hard for you too, hasn't it?"

"Nothing like what you went through. I haven't been grieving, like you. I've just been feeling stupid for being so—"

"Human?"

"Yeah. For being a stupid human."

"You're awfully hard on yourself, do you know that?"

"Yes, I guess I do know that. I guess I'm a bit of a perfection-ist; I hate failure. But you're pretty hard on yourself too, in my opinion."

Claire studied her glass and its ruby red contents. "All right, how about this. How about we make a deal that we'll stop being hard on ourselves for at least the rest of this week?"

Amanda's quiet laughter made Claire want to agree to anything. "Deal," Amanda said, raising a questioning eyebrow. "How shall we seal it?"

Claire stared at Amanda's mouth with what she imagined was obvious hunger; she couldn't help remembering last night in the car, when they'd nearly kissed. Unless it was all a figment of her overactive imagination. *She* had wanted the kiss to happen, she knew that much, and the urge had so shocked and disgusted her that she'd had to take half a sleeping pill when she got back to her room. Surely Amanda wasn't about to suggest kissing on their deal. No, that was just fantasy talking. And foolishness. Kissing Amanda had the abstract quality of something distant that she was never going to reach, and so now she allowed herself the luxury of wondering how it might really feel. Would a kiss simply make her want more? Would it send her into a kind of paralysis? Scare the crap out of her? Make her feel like she was betraying Ann?

Claire tipped her wineglass at Amanda and hoped like hell she hadn't read her thoughts. "Let's drink to it."

"You got it."

After they drank a toast, Claire remembered the wedding cake. "Oh, crap, aren't we supposed to be talking about cake designs?"

"Did you do your homework?"

"No," she answered guiltily. "I tried to think about it as I fell asleep, but I don't have an artistic bone in my body."

Amanda reached for her purse and pulled out pieces of paper. "Luckily I do." She spread the pieces on the table. "I like this one the best." She pointed to a careful sketch she'd done of a four-layer cake, each layer meticulously decorated to look like an elaborately wrapped present. Each succeeding layer was smaller than the one below and positioned at an off angle. On the top was a fancy bow that would be made of frosting.

"Wow Amanda, that's incredible!"

"You like it?"

"Yes, I think you did a great job, and I know Shannon will love it. How'd you come up with that?"

"I don't know. I was thinking how life is full of surprises, you know? And gifts. And that it'd be great to have a theme of gifts."

"Well, I think it's absolutely perfect."

"Thanks. I'm so glad you like it. You kind of inspired me, actually."

"I did?"

Amanda looked shy as an adoring blush worked its way up her neck. "I feel like getting to know you this week has been a gift. And a lovely surprise. Thank you, Claire."

Claire felt a hitch of emotions in her throat. No, she wanted to say, *you're* the lovely surprise.

Amanda cleared her throat nervously and nearly dropped her fork. "I'm going to tell my aunt tomorrow, by the way."

It took a moment or two for Claire to figure out what Amanda was talking about. For an instant, she thought she meant she was going to tell her aunt how they'd become special friends. "Wow, that's really great. I'm proud of you for doing that, Amanda. And I know it will be fine."

"Well, I hope I don't chicken out."

"You won't."

"How can you be so sure?"

Early on Claire had pegged Amanda as the kind of woman who always held up her end of a deal. She was responsible, good to the core. She'd do the right thing. "Because you know it's the right thing to do, that's why you'll do it." In fact, maybe Amanda's bravery would rub off on Shannon and she would tell Dani her own bit of heartbreaking news, if she hadn't already. Secrets ate away at relationships, and Amanda's secret had eroded the close relationship between aunt and niece. Perhaps after tomorrow the two of them would be able to bridge that gap again. She and Ann had never kept secrets from one another, and she had trouble imagining what it would have been like if they had.

"Yes. You've convinced me it's the right thing to do. Thank you for that, Claire. Thank you for giving me the courage."

Claire's heart opened further toward this young woman who had so quickly become a friend. "You already had it in you, believe me. Is there anything I can do to help?"

"Maybe just be there for my aunt if she needs to talk about it."

"Of course. And I'm here anytime you need to talk too, okay?" Day or night, she wanted to add, but she was afraid the comment might sound like some kind of cheesy come-on.

Amanda's eyes misted over. "How did I get so lucky finding you?"

No, Claire thought. *I'm the lucky one.*

CHAPTER NINETEEN

Dani

She knew something was wrong from the tone of Jordan's text. It was simple enough: *Need to get together tonight, just us.* She had enough history with Jordan to know it was a rare—in fact, almost unheard of—plea for help. Jordan needed her. She immediately withdrew from the group's plan to see a Cirque de Soleil show, earning a few words of irritation from Shannon, and texted Jordan back to meet her at the Monte Carlo casino at eight o'clock.

Dani liked the Monte Carlo because it was upscale but quiet and less ostentatious than some of the others. One look at Jordan—dour, unsmiling, uncommunicative—and Dani led her to a ten-dollar, single deck blackjack table. They wouldn't have to talk right away, and there was the added bonus of a young, sexily clad woman dancing on a small stage not more than fifteen feet away. Cards and eye candy. A perfect distraction that was sure to boost Jordan's spirits.

"You must really be worried about me if you're putting me at a ten-dollar table," Jordan quipped but there was no humor in her voice.

"I don't want you to lose your life savings if you're in some kind of funk." It also wouldn't hurt Dani's pocketbook as much.

They played blackjack silently for a while. Jordan's luck was awful and she was down seventy dollars within minutes. Dani's was much better, for a welcome change. As Jordan lost, Dani won, and soon her chips were stacked in neat little columns a few inches away from Jordan's shrinking and chaotic pile. The losing, understandably, seemed to darken her friend's mood. Dourly, Jordan ordered a vodka straight up with a slice of lemon.

"Aren't you drinking anything?" she asked in astonishment after Dani ordered a Diet Coke and lime.

"Nope. I tied one on pretty good with my sister last night. I need to behave tonight—let my liver breathe a little before tomorrow night's big bachelor party. Speaking of which, I think the group's a little scared of what you might have planned."

"They should be. Wimps."

"So. What *do* you have planned?"

"Oh no. You're not getting anything out of me, no matter how many drinks you ply me with."

They chatted for a while about nothing of consequence, played a few more rounds. Jordan knocked back a second vodka and began to get a little loose around the edges. She started paying more attention to the dancer than to the cards, and her losing streak continued.

"Hey," Dani urged. "Alcohol and cards don't mix. Remember our little golden rule?"

"Screw that. I don't care if I lose anyway."

That was a new one. Jordan took her card playing very seriously. Usually. And she *loved* to win.

"Why don't we color up and go sit in the sports lounge for a while?"

She had to somehow get Jordan talking about what was

wrong, because watching her lose at cards and get drunk wasn't very appealing. Or helpful. Theirs wasn't a friendship of many heart-to-heart talks—each reacted awkwardly to touchy-feely conversations and typically tried to avoid them—but clearly Jordan was in some kind of free fall. Dani was the only one who could help her right now, if indeed she could be helped, and it might take a small miracle.

They claimed a couple of big leather La-Z-Boys in the sports betting lounge. The wall of television screens broadcasting hockey games, basketball games and horse races would give them all the privacy they needed. Two women in deep discussion was no competition with what mattered to the die hard sports fans scattered around the lounge, loudly urging on their teams or their horses.

"Okay my friend. What's going on?"

Jordan stared at her benignly, sipping her third vodka and lemon. She wasn't going to give it up easily.

"Please tell me there was a good reason you got me in shit with my soon-to-be-wife tonight. Somehow I don't think she would be convinced that sitting here with you watching six hockey games trumps a Cirque de Soleil show."

Jordan shrugged, but Dani could see the slow gathering of courage in her eyes. Her face crumpled a little but she struggled to remain stoic. It wasn't in Jordan's DNA to cry or fall apart. She said simply, "I guess I needed to talk."

"Okay." It was not the time to make a joke and certainly not the time to tease her best friend about this sudden and unusual need for verbal intimacy. Jordan was upset and Dani wanted to help. "Will you tell me what's wrong?"

Whatever was tearing Jordan up inside was slow to come to the surface. With effort, she shook her head sternly—the kind of bitter head-shaking that meant she was angry at herself. "You know, if you'd told me I was going to take one of those trips into space you can pay a billion dollars for, I'd have believed you before I would have believed . . . *this*."

"What?"

"This . . . This falling in love bullshit. Or whatever the hell you want to call it. *If* that's what it is."

"What?" *Falling in love*? What the hell was she talking about? "Can you please slow down and speak English? Because whatever language you were just speaking, it kind of sounded like something to do with falling in love. And we all know Jordan Scott doesn't fall in love. Ever."

Jordan made a face. "All right, all right. Tease me about it. I deserve it. Yes, I said falling in love. And yes, as fucked up and hard as it is to believe, it might actually apply to me."

It might just as well have been a two-by-four that had slammed Dani across the back, she was that shocked. This confession was going to take some time to digest. She'd never known Jordan to be in love before. Briefly infatuated, yes. In lust, for sure. But in love? Never. In fact, it seemed to go against Jordan's basic principles. And yet, Jordan looked absolutely miserable, and only people in love could look this miserable. "You're serious, aren't you?"

Jordan drew a long breath before she spoke, and then the words cascaded out of her like a bottle of vodka suddenly turned upside down. "Christ, Dani, it's insane. Absolutely insane. It was supposed to be just a night of fun, or maybe two, I don't know. She was gorgeous and sexy, and we wanted each other and it was so perfect, you know? No strings, no complications, just a good time. Except I suddenly started thinking about more than a couple of nights. I started thinking about bringing her to your wedding as my date. About spending time with her after that. About . . . Christ, I don't know. I was getting the sweaty palms and the pounding heart and the dry mouth when I was around her. I mean, *Christ*!"

"Wow. It does sound a little like falling in love."

She gave Dani a momentary look of horror. "I know I want to be with her more than anything else. I want to fall asleep in her arms. I want to wake up with her. I want to make her coffee and breakfast and start my day with her. I want to phone her and text ten times a day. I want to kiss her, hold her, *be* with her.

I know it sounds nuts, but she's not like anyone I've ever met, Dani. She's not like any other woman I've ever been with. She's smart and fun, and so good at what she does. She's got this great sense of humor, and she's so wise, you know?"

"Okay, wait. We *are* talking about Dez Adams, right?"

"Of course we are! Jesus, who did you think I was talking about, the fucking chambermaid?"

"All right, all right! No need to get so pissed at me."

"Sorry, you're right. I'm just so . . . so, fucking uptight and pissed off and . . . and goddamned hurt."

"Why, what happened?"

Jordan finished her drink in silence, as though considering how much to tell Dani, or maybe it took her that long to find the courage. Finally, she said with astonishment, "She fucking dumped me. Twenty-four hours of pure bliss, and then she suddenly showed me the door."

"Wow. Okay. That was pretty harsh."

"Oh, come on. It's no worse than what I've been doing for almost twenty-five years. I've been a fucking dickhead, Dani, and I wish you'd told me what a dickhead I've been all these years."

She wanted to laugh at Jordan's language, but it was the language of someone distraught, frustrated and half drunk. Jordan was being completely serious and looking at Dani challengingly.

"Okay, look," Dani said placatingly, "it's not my place to—"

"You're my fucking best friend! Of course it's your place to tell me anything and everything. Or at least the truth."

A few people turned from the television screens to stare at them in annoyance; they didn't want to be distracted from their games. Dani lowered her voice. "Jordie, you and I don't have heart-to-hearts. It's not what we do, okay? And if I'd told you that you treated women badly, you would have jumped all over me and denied it. Or told me to go to hell."

Jordan signaled the cocktail waitress for another drink, earning from Dani first a frown, and then a sigh of understanding. Jordan was well on her way to getting shit-faced. Pain could do that to you. It had taken all of Dani's strength not to hit the bottle when she lost her job. Escaping, dulling the pain with alcohol would have been the easy thing to do, but she'd successfully resisted. She had too much to look forward to—a future with Shannon, a baby perhaps—and those things had kept her on the rails.

"All right, I might have done those things if you'd called me on it," Jordan admitted, her words beginning to slur. "I'm a fucking asshole, okay?"

Dani reached across the small table between their recliners and clutched Jordan's hand. They held hands for several quiet minutes before Dani spoke. "Jordie, you're not an asshole. You're a wonderful friend. And an intelligent, caring woman. I've known you for a hell of a long time, and I picked you to be my best woman because I love you."

"Oh, Dani." Jordan squeezed her hand affectionately. Her voice quavered. "You don't have to say those things, you know."

"Yes, I do. We don't say it to each other enough. In fact, pretty much never. But I appreciate you and I need you in my life. You mean the world to me."

They relied on each other regularly, but not usually in mammoth or profound ways. They often lifted each other's spirits, distracted one another, had fun together, lived the little moments that added up to a deep friendship, gave each other unspoken support when it was needed. It was rewarding to know that they could lean on one another in bad times, and Dani regretted now that she hadn't shared her job loss with Jordan. She'd been too embarrassed to tell her, and yet she knew deep down that Jordan would not have judged her or criticized her or pitied her. She would have been there for Dani if she'd given her the chance. She would confess now, except Jordan was too preoccupied with her own troubles, not to mention inebriated.

"I love you too," Jordan said, smiling sloppily and clutching a fresh drink. "Thank you for believing in me and sticking with me, even if I am a dick sometimes."

"I'll always believe in you, dick or no dick."

"Yeah, well, we both prefer no dicks." At least she was

smiling a little now. "You know something Dani, I never knew before now what it was like."

"What do you mean?"

"Getting dumped by somebody you like. Or love. It really, really sucks."

"Yes," Dani laughed shortly. "It does." She remembered getting dumped by Julie, Shannon's predecessor and the only other woman she'd ever truly loved. Or thought she'd truly loved. At least it seemed so at the time, but now she wasn't so sure, because it was nothing compared to how she felt about Shannon. Fresh out of college, she and Julie were a bit too much oil and water and both far too career obsessed to give their relationship the energy it needed. Julie simply put them out of their misery by breaking it off, though Dani hadn't been so enlightened to see it that way at first. She was devastated for a good year afterward.

"God, I can't believe I put so many women through this same kind of bullshit." Jordan was staring into her drink, shaking her head bitterly.

"Well, don't flatter yourself too much, my friend. I'm sure some of them weren't overly surprised, or maybe not even all that heartbroken. It's not like you promised them a ring or something."

"I know that. But a few of them were pretty upset." She stared for a long time at nothing. "I didn't know any other way then. I was scared. Too scared to commit. It's how relationships worked in my world. Hell, when I was a teenager and in my early twenties, I always dated older women who weren't looking for anything serious. Then I started dating younger women, hoping *they* weren't looking for anything serious. It was really *me* who didn't want anything serious."

"What is it that you're afraid of?" The question might be too serious for Jordan in her current state, but what the hell. They were on a roll.

Jordan turned tortured eyes on her. "Christ, what are you, my shrink?"

"Yes, except I'm a hell of a lot cheaper."

Jordan laughed until there were tears in her eyes, and Dani wasn't sure if they were laughter tears or sadness tears. "Oh, God, I don't know. Afraid of being rejected once they really get to know me, I suppose."

Dani knew about that. It still scared her that Shannon might suddenly discover she wasn't such a good person after all, that she simply had too many faults.

Jordan continued. "Afraid of me needing someone too much, or someone needing me too much, and then disappointing them. Afraid of failure, afraid of being too happy, afraid of compromising too much, afraid of lesbian bed death. Christ, it's quite the list, isn't it?"

Dani raised her eyebrows in amusement. "I can assure you that not all long-term relationships end in LBD. Trust me on that one."

"Well, I'm glad for you, but Shannon's one in a million. I never expected to find my one in a million. Told myself that even if there was someone out there, I never wanted such a thing anyway, so it didn't matter."

"Ah, but you found Dez, even when you weren't looking. You can't give up now."

Jordan laughed morosely. "Yeah, right. She's given up on *me*."

"So why should that stop you?"

"What, are you suggesting I become a stalker or something?"

"Oh, hell no. Look, you don't give up on those million-dollar real estate deals you're always talking about when they get tough. You're a pit bull at work. Why can't you be a bit like that now, huh? Are you going to let yourself drown in your own medicine? C'mon! You've got more balls than that."

Jordan polished off her drink and thought for a long time. Then she stood, swaying a little, and Dani jumped up to clutch her arm.

"Let me get you back to your room."

Jordan complied, letting Dani guide her back to their hotel and up to her room. At her door, slurring, she turned to Dani and said, "So what the hell do I do to get her back?"

Dani smiled, fully confident in Jordan's abilities. "You'll think of something."

CHAPTER TWENTY

Amanda

Reclining in the warm thrashing water of the hot tub, Amanda barely listened to Shannon's endless questions and attempts at conversation. Instead, she tried to imagine the words she would use to admit she'd married—and was now divorcing—Jennifer. It was difficult to concentrate with such an event looming over her. Shannon was asking her about school, about her plans for the summer, about her part-time job as a downtown tour guide of architecture in the city—a walking tour she conducted every weekend morning—and numerous other subjects. She tried to answer as best as she could but knew she was too distracted to be convincing.

It shouldn't be this hard to admit the truth. Shannon loved her and would forgive her—Claire was surely right about that. Shannon would probably be hurt that such an important secret had been kept from her; Amanda could understand that. Still, she worried that her aunt—her only close family member—might think less of her now. How could she not? Amanda had always been careful in her decisions, always thought things through intelligently and objectively. Letting her emotions rule when it came to Jennifer had been disastrous—something Shannon had tried to warn her about. She hadn't heeded the warnings; she'd screwed up. But she was finally accepting that her emotions hadn't been the enemy; blinding herself to everything else had been. She was finally beginning to accept that she could move on from her mistake, and maybe Shannon's forgiveness and acceptance of her past would be the beginning of her own forgiveness and acceptance. It was time to put an end to the secret and it was time to regain the closeness with her aunt.

Amanda luxuriated in the massage that followed the hot tub; it relaxed her further. Thankfully there was no more conversation, giving her time to gather her courage and plan her words. Funny how confessing to Claire had taken no such planning and courage gathering—it had spilled out of her effortlessly and was an example of how talking intimately with Claire came incredibly natural. Unusually so. She'd shared things with Claire in their short time together that she'd not shared with anyone since Jen. She and Claire simply clicked. The intensity of their connection surprised her, but not to the extent that she feared or doubted it. As a matter of fact, she embraced it and enjoyed it. Yes, I enjoy Claire so much, she thought with satisfaction. She appreciated Claire's angle on things, her intelligence, her warmth, her humor, the easy way she had about her. And yes, the way Claire sometimes looked at her, like there were things she wanted to say and do. There was an undeniable attraction between them, and the realization slammed into Amanda, making her involuntarily suck in her breath.

Her thoughts wound their way back to how they'd nearly kissed in the car the other night. Amanda couldn't deny she had wanted a kiss to happen. She had delighted in the tender hug from Claire and the warmth and softness of her body, but the thought of Claire's mouth on hers had undeniably made her tingle with heat and anticipation. At lunch yesterday she'd managed to put aside thoughts of kissing Claire, even as waves of heat kept pulsing through her like a small, rumbling volcano in search of release.

The attraction still mystified her a little, but in a good way. It was not something she had been looking for and certainly not something she had expected. Claire was at least twenty years older, well established in her profession, a mother figure in some respect, perhaps. But Amanda didn't need or want a mother figure; she was fiercely independent. So it wasn't that. It wasn't that she was lonely either. She'd not even been remotely attracted to anyone in the fourteen months since her separation from Jen. And yet here she was out of the clear blue sky attracted to Claire physically, emotionally, intellectually. Claire couldn't be more opposite to Jennifer, yet it felt exactly right to be attracted to her. She was handsome in a distinguished way with graceful lines and a strong body. Her eyes were warm, her smile genuine. She was kind, intelligent, accomplished, and she was the kind of woman who knew how to love deeply and how to appreciate another woman. She was well experienced in how to be a good partner, a loyal lover for life, and the knowledge of that gave Amanda a rush of warmth.

The masseuse stopped suddenly. "Am I hurting you? You've really tensed up."

"No, it's okay." She glanced quickly at her aunt, who seemed to have taken no notice of the emotions hurtling through her.

"Well, we're pretty much done here anyway. Are you ladies ready for the wet sauna next?"

Shannon groaned happily. "Could we be any more spoiled?"

Yes, Amanda thought happily, Claire would know precisely how to spoil a woman. She was sure of it. She smiled dazedly at her aunt, then sobered abruptly. The time was approaching, and she vowed to get it over with in the steam room if they were alone. No more procrastinating.

They were very much alone in the sauna. Amanda didn't know whether to be thankful or frightened, and like a taut string on a violin, she tightened inside. Wrapped only in a towel with classical music playing in the background, she breathed in the eucalyptus-scented humid air that spewed out in warm, thick clouds. It was now or never. She took the plunge.

"Aunt Shannon?"

Shannon reclined lazily against the wood-paneled wall, her eyes closed. "Yes, sweetie?"

Amanda swallowed hard. "There's something I've wanted to tell you for a while. I was scared to before, but now—"

Shannon's eyes flew open. "What's wrong? You're not sick are you?"

"No, no, nothing like that." Shit, this wasn't easy, and all the rehearsing in her mind suddenly spun away from her, useless. "The thing is . . . What I needed to tell you . . . You remember Jennifer Morgan, the woman at Stanford I was dating?"

"Of course I remember her. Don't tell me you've started seeing her again?"

"No, I haven't."

"Well, that's a relief. To be honest, I'm glad you broke up with her before things got too serious. I never quite trusted her."

"I know you didn't. And I'm sorry I didn't put enough stock into your feelings about her."

"Well, it's all in the past sweetie. It doesn't matter now. You said she went back to men?"

"Yes, she did." Amanda had told her aunt after the marriage ended that she wasn't with Jennifer anymore, but she'd spared the most important details. "See, the thing is, we got married. In California."

For a long moment Shannon didn't say anything, and the heavy steam made it impossible to read her expression. Amanda repeated herself. "We got *legally* married."

"What?" Her voice was like the crack of a gun.

"Shortly after you visited me and met her, we went down to city hall and had a civil ceremony."

"Amanda Jane Malden! Are you serious?"

Crap, Shannon was really pissed off. "It's okay. We're not together anymore. It didn't work out. We separated a few months after we got married. I'm trying to get divorced but it's taking forever."

Shannon's voice shook. "Why didn't you tell me any of this?"

Because I'm an idiot and a coward, Amanda wanted to say. She swallowed her guilt and pride instead. "I knew you didn't like her, and I was embarrassed that I could make such a stupid mistake. I was afraid to admit any of it to you."

Disapproval and disappointment were not things Amanda had ever experienced from her aunt before, but now they felt like a real possibility. Shannon was only marrying Dani after being with her for seven years, and in contrast, Amanda's poor judgment and impetuousness surely would not be up to Shannon's careful standards. *You're twenty-six years old, for God's sake. Quit worrying about what other people think and trust Aunt Shannon to deal with this.*

"I don't know what to say. I'm shocked."

Amanda willed herself to be patient; she understood it was shocking news. She inhaled the eucalyptus deeply until it singed her nasal passages, then let her breath out slowly, evenly. "I'm sorry, Aunt Shannon. I made a huge mistake, and then I made it worse by not telling you."

For a long time, neither woman spoke. Tears pooled in Amanda's eyes. She was so sorry she hadn't included Shannon—the only family she really had—in what was the biggest event of her life, followed by one of the worst times in her life. She should have included her aunt, she understood that now, but all she could do was vow to never shut her out again. "I'm so sorry. I wish I'd done things differently."

"I wish you'd done things differently too, kiddo." Shannon sighed, and with her expelled breath went her anger. "But that's over now. So what's going on? Are you okay? It must have been an awful time for you. Did you have anyone to help you through it?"

Tears erupted from Amanda suddenly, catching her by surprise as much as they did Shannon.

"Oh, sweetie." Shannon pulled her in for an embrace and stroked her damp hair.

Amanda let herself cry for a few moments, let herself be loved and forgiven. It was about loving and forgiving herself too. She wouldn't pretend that she was over the sting of a failed marriage yet. She wouldn't pretend she'd fully forgiven herself, and Jennifer too, but with Shannon's love and support now, maybe true forgiveness was more a possibility than she thought.

"I'm so sorry, Amanda."

"Me too. Sorrier than you could ever imagine. And yes it was an awful time, but I'm okay now. I'll be even better if I know you don't hate me for this."

"Oh honey, of course I don't hate you and I'm not mad at you. You need to know that I would *never* think less of you because of this. You know me better than that. You know you can always come to me. With anything. And that I will always love and respect you."

Amanda supposed confessing a crush on Shannon's best friend might be the one exception. She smiled at the secret thought. "Thank you for understanding. But I'm still ashamed."

"Look, you were happy and you took the step of wanting to be with this woman for the rest of your life. It didn't work out. You made a mistake. All you can do is move on and learn from that, right?"

"I know and I have, believe me."

"I'm still shocked that you got married before I did. Please don't ever elope on me again young lady!"

Amanda laughed, relieved to be free of this burden, relieved her aunt still loved her. "I promise that next time you will be walking me down the aisle to give me away."

"Damn right I will!"

"You're my hero, do you know that? I do want to walk down the aisle for real one day, like you're doing. And who knows, maybe even have babies the way you and Dani are planning."

Shannon released her from her loose embrace, sadness in her slumped shoulders. "Well, I'm not so sure about that."

Amanda, still distracted by her relief in the emotional reconnection with Shannon, said, "Not so sure about what?"

"I'm not going to have babies," Shannon said quietly. "In fact, I'm not even going to have one."

"What?"

Shannon turned sad but tearless eyes on her. "I can't have children. My ovaries are dysfunctional and can't produce eggs anymore."

"Oh my God, I'm so sorry. How long have you known?"

"Not long. A few weeks."

"Shit, that's terrible. Isn't there something they can do? What does Claire have to say about it?"

She shook her head. "There isn't anything they can do and Claire can't help me. I've been checked and triple checked. Consultations, second opinions. There's no hope."

This confession was far worse than her own, and Amanda felt foolish and selfish. "I wish I could help, or at least do something. I'm so sorry."

"Well, short of having a baby for us, I'm afraid there's nothing you can do."

"Dani must be crushed by this."

"Dani doesn't know yet."

"What do you mean she doesn't know yet?" Amanda was astonished.

"Once I knew there was a potential problem, I didn't tell her about all the tests. And then I didn't tell her about the results either."

"Oh, crap."

"You said it." Shannon sighed miserably. "You and Claire are the only ones who know right now. But I'm going to tell Dani soon. I know I have to. I just hate how badly this is going to hurt her, and I really didn't want to have to tell her before the wedding."

Another bond between her and Claire, being privy to

Shannon's secret. "I understand, but you need to help each other through this, don't you think?"

"Yes, I know. Claire's quite pissed at me for not telling Dani sooner. In fact, for not having Dani in on all this from the beginning. It's just that she's so damned excited about having a baby. She has her hopes up so high. I absolutely dread disappointing her."

"Disappointing people is sometimes a sad fact of life, whether we want to or not."

"Yes, I know. I keep hoping I'll wake up in the morning and the news will be different."

"You can always adopt or get a surrogate or something, can't you?"

"Yes. There are options. Right now I just want to forget about all of it and maybe go back to work, take some time to get used to it all and figure out the next step."

The scale of her aunt's disclosure was only beginning to sink in. These were huge changes for Shannon and Dani's relationship, a huge shift in their future, and she hoped with all her being that they would find a way to weather it. "Are you going to tell her before the wedding?"

Shannon was noncommittal. "I don't know yet, but trust me, this is not something that's going to put our wedding or our relationship in jeopardy. Dani and I love each other, and we'll get through this test. I promise."

Amanda simply nodded, not really comprehending. She'd not had enough relationships to know what they could withstand. She and Jennifer sure as hell hadn't been able to stand any real tests, but then, their love had not been the real thing like Shannon and Dani. She gave Shannon's hand a squeeze to show she believed in her.

CHAPTER TWENTY-ONE

Jordan

Jordan tried hard to get into the spirit of the bachelor party; after all, it was her baby and she'd planned it for weeks. Partying, however, wasn't exactly what she felt like doing, not when Dez still permeated her every thought. If she closed her eyes, she could still smell Dez on her fingers, on her skin. Could still hear her rich, soulful voice singing, repeating her name in ecstasy. Could still feel Dez's velvety touch on her face, on her neck, on every part of her body. She could not get Dez out of her heart, and most tormenting of all, didn't want to. She was not ready to let her go, and the driving need to hold on to her scared her a little. She did not want to be a desperate, obsessed, crazed ex-lover. She'd had women do that to her—leave love notes on her car for weeks afterward, make hang-up phone calls, give her unwanted gifts. She hated that kind of obsessive behavior, and yet this morning she'd ordered a bouquet of flowers sent to Dez's room with a note pleading to see her again. Dez had not responded, and while her silence didn't surprise Jordan, it hurt. At least the bachelor party tonight would keep her from sneaking into the concert venue to watch Dez sing.

The party started in the lounge of their hotel's biggest bar. Jordan had instructed the five other guests to wear comfortable clothes and to bring swimsuits. They'd start with a few drinks before a casual dinner at the Wolfgang Puck Bar & Grill. Tonight was for fun, not for a classy time out. The wedding would be first rate in the class department, but the bachelor party was an opportunity to raunch things up a little. She was careful not to go overboard, though it was not easy restraining herself. Slyly, she thought of Claire dying a thousand deaths having a stripper force a lap dance on her. She chuckled to herself. Might almost be worth the deep shit she'd be in for arranging a little one-on-one show for Claire. *That'd teach her to be such a prude.*

"Ah, my little lambs," she said to their eager faces. "Beer or wine or something stronger to start with?"

Shannon eyed her suspiciously. "I have a funny feeling there's going to be a ton of alcohol tonight, so maybe we should ease into it with wine and beer."

The others quickly agreed and Jordan complied with a pitcher of beer and a bottle of merlot. To start the proceedings, she ordered each of the bridal party members to take a turn offering a toast to the brides, with the toast based on a physical attribute. The answers were entertaining. Claire prudently chose to remark on their eyes, and they all drank to Shannon's and Dani's lovely eyes. Amanda, giving it some thought, suggested Shannon's graceful hands and Dani's strong shoulders were worth toasting. "Now we're getting somewhere," Jordan smirked as she drank to the brides. Heather offered a toast to Dani's charming smile and Shannon's beautiful blond hair. Jordan grinned devilishly and suggested Shannon's breasts and Dani's ass, drawing good-natured protests from the brides and agreeable but shy chuckles from the others. The next round was reserved for the brides' non-physical attributes, and this took more time. The beer and wine helped take the edge off.

Jordan led the group to Wolfgang Puck's Bar & Grill on the far side of the casino and to a reserved table that would keep them well away from the other patrons. They ordered three wood oven pizzas and another round of beer and wine. Jordan tacked on half a dozen strawberry vodka shots to the order.

"New rule tonight," Jordan announced. "Anyone who says the words *Dani* or *Shannon*, *bride*, *wedding* or *married* for the rest of the evening has to drink a shot. And that includes the guests of honor."

"Oh, God," Shannon groaned. "What am I supposed to call her?"

They all had suggestions for Shannon: lover, wife, fianceé, darling, sweetheart, honey, love machine, stud. The list went on until Shannon surrendered, palms up. "All right, I have no excuses then, and lots of lovely substitutes."

Over pizza the women tried to lure each other into stepping on the verbal land mine. Amanda nudged Claire and whispered, "I need the pepper way down there, would you be so kind?"

"Dani, can you please pass—"

The others guffawed and pointed accusing fingers at Claire. A shot was placed before her. "Oh, for God's sake." She gamely downed it, making a sour face before turning to Amanda. "Better watch your back after that one, young lady. I have a long memory."

"It's okay, you don't scare me."

It wasn't long before Claire got her revenge. She got Amanda to talk about the time Shannon took her to see the movie *The Wedding Singer* when she was a teenager. "Fine," Amanda said after drinking her punishment and reproachfully sticking her tongue out at Claire. "We're even."

Their playfulness reminded Jordan of what she was missing with Dez. She glanced at her watch. Dez would be getting ready for the show. The flowers had been a wasted effort. Time to up the pressure a little—show Dez that she was not yet ready to give up, that she wasn't about to take it lying down. Well, actually, lying down and taking it from her would be perfect about now, but that wasn't going to happen. She wondered what she could do to prove how much Dez meant to her and how serious she was about her.

She thought about the word *serious* and how it could possibly apply to her, after all the women she'd dated over the years. But it did apply to her. She was serious about Dez. She was in love with Dez, as strange as the words felt tumbling around in her mind. She had not seen it coming, had not expected it or even dreamed it was possible for her. And yet it had happened, just the same as if she'd been walking down her street minding her business and a bolt of lightning hit her. It was almost as though she were observing all of this happening to someone else, and yet the tickle in her stomach, the constant clenching in her chest, assured her that it really was happening to *her*.

Once dinner was leisurely consumed, Jordan told the group that their limo was waiting and that they should all bring their swimsuits. "Oh, and one more thing before we go to Old Town." From a large paper bag she withdrew a pair of handcuffs lined in fuzzy pink fleece.

"Oh, no," Dani protested, backing away. "Get away with those things!"

Claire quipped, "Did you pull those out of your collection, Jordan?"

"Yes, and you can borrow them after tonight if you'd like."

Claire reddened and promptly clammed up. It was so easy to embarrass her. In fact, there was little challenge in it for Jordan, but that was okay. There were plenty of other targets to pick on. Briskly she grabbed Dani's left wrist and locked a cuff around it, then secured it to Shannon's right hand.

Shannon looked at Dani helplessly and shrugged. "Guess this means you're stuck with me."

CHAPTER TWENTY-TWO

Shannon

They piled into the limo and lost no time in opening a bottle of champagne. They toasted the sacrifice of the grapes, then toasted Vegas, toasted the chauffeur, toasted one another, until there was nothing left to toast and the bottle lay empty and rolling around on the carpeted floor. They were getting giggly, and what the hell, Shannon thought, *why not?* Why not act like a silly ass tonight? They could all pretend they were college freshmen let loose on the town. In fact, it might be rather liberating. And if nothing else it would go a long way toward making her forget the weight of childlessness, forget that she needed to tell Dani they wouldn't be having any children. For just tonight maybe she could forget the one thing that had dominated her thoughts for weeks.

Oh God, she thought. Her stomach churned endlessly. *We're too late. We're too late to have kids now. Maybe . . . maybe if we'd tried three or four years ago it would have been okay. It was still early in our relationship then but we should have done it, dammit, because now it's too late. It's too late, too late.*

Her thoughts often went in the same lamenting circles since she'd been told her ovaries were no longer producing eggs and could not be coaxed into doing so, regardless of medical advances. The news had come about from routine testing before attempting artificial insemination, and it had come as a shock. She spent days afterward in disbelief, quite sure her doctor had made a mistake. She confided in Claire, asked her to go over the results with her, had her take a second blood test and a second ultrasound to confirm things. The news, unfortunately, didn't improve. She was infertile, and the truth was, she wasn't so much heartbroken for herself as she was for Dani. It had never been her overwhelming dream to have children. If it happened, she was good with that, knew she would be a good mom and would love whatever little being came into her life. But for Dani, having a child meant everything. Dani saw herself as a mom, saw it as one of the great roles she was meant for. There was no doubt her childhood was a major motivator. Shannon knew Dani's childhood had not been idyllic, that she'd not been blessed with involved, supportive parents and very early on had been cast as the outsider, the failure. Dani was a survivor, a fixer, and she wanted to atone for her parents' mistakes, perhaps even reset her childhood button. If she'd not needed a hysterectomy from severe endometriosis by the time she was thirty-three, Dani would have most likely given birth by now, perhaps even years ago.

What shitty luck that neither of us can give birth. Sure there were other options, like adoption and a surrogate mom, but she couldn't think of those right now. Her own failure was all-consuming, as was the thought of giving the devastating news to Dani. How do you tell someone their dream is over? How do you tell your loved one that she can't share the miracle of childbirth, that you can't give her the one thing she wants most in this world?

After the limo deposited them on the doorstep of Old Town, Jordan cheerily handed out cigars. They were little ones, thankfully, about as big around as a pencil. Jordan systematically went around with a lighter, lighting them all, encouraging them to smoke the celebratory cigars. "Yes, even you," she said to Claire, who was frowning like it was pot she was being asked to smoke.

Shannon sucked at her cigar before exhaling smoothly. The tobacco was rich, giving off a pleasing scent. A few mild stares were directed their way as they walked and talked boisterously and smoked their expensive cigars, the pink fur-lined handcuffs announcing that it was a special night. Their behavior was not at all unusual for Vegas. The thousands upon thousands of neon lights blinked and raced overhead in signs and displays. Noise spilled from the open doors of the casinos—people having fun, slot machines dinging and clanging. A girl danced suggestively in a large plate glass window, her eyes set on nothing, her body moving for everyone and no one. Vendors of trinkets called out from kiosks in the street that was closed to vehicular traffic. Street performers dressed like Marilyn Monroe, Elvis, Ozzy Osborne and Cher tried to engage the tourists.

Claire sidled up to Shannon and whispered in her ear, "You doing okay? You look a little down."

Dani, attached to her wrist, was busy gabbing with Heather. Shannon stared straight ahead and said, "I'm okay Claire. I'm going to have fun tonight."

"Promise?"

"Yes, I promise."

"It's going to be okay, you know."

She wanted to believe her. "Yes, it is." There was no conviction in the statement, and yet it had to be okay, one way or another. Life would go on.

She looked at Claire. Claire's life had gone on after Ann's death. Perhaps not in the happiest of ways and certainly not in the most fulfilling, but Claire had somehow found a way to soldier on. Amanda too, who was happily puffing on a cigar and looking surprisingly pleased with herself, had moved forward. She had survived the untimely death of her mother—Shannon's only sister—from a rare form of leukemia, a life-altering event for

Amanda that had happened right before she went off to college.

And then there was news of the marriage she'd shockingly divulged. Marriage and divorce! Part of her wished she'd been able to save Amanda from all of that. Wished Amanda had listened to her misgivings about Jennifer. But she couldn't protect Amanda and certainly couldn't govern her life. Amanda was her own woman, it was just that she'd had no idea she was capable of going off and legally marrying her girlfriend so impulsively. But as she thought more about it, she realized that if gay marriage had been an option when she was young, who knows, she might have gone off and married her first serious girlfriend too. Marriage was about hope and optimism, and being hopeful and optimistic was a hallmark of the young. Marriage certainly wasn't reserved for the wise and aged, and she realized that binding herself in matrimony to Dani was the most hopeful and optimistic thing she had done in her life to this point.

She hoped Dani felt the same way. She'd told Amanda that Dani would still love her, that they would work things out over the baby issue. It seemed to be the thing to say, but was it really true? Maybe Dani wouldn't want a future with her if it meant no baby. Maybe a vessel for delivering a baby was more important to her than the love they shared. How was she to know until it was put to the test? How much did Dani truly love her for who she was?

A drag queen dressed as a Vegas showgirl stopped them on the street and fluttered his hands wildly in the direction of their handcuffs. "Oh, sister girls, what's up with those lovely handcuffs? Don't tell me you've been having a little fun with those?"

"They're getting married this weekend," Jordan answered. "Tonight's a test. If they can stand being handcuffed together all evening, then they were meant to be together."

He batted long, fake eyelashes. "Honey, take it from me, it all comes down to good sex. If you can be married and still have good sex, you'll be just fine." He leaned closer and whispered loudly, "But those little handcuffs will help spice things up, if you know what I mean."

Dani puffed her chest out adorably, possessively. "I don't think we need any help from these things."

"Accessories never hurt, darlings. Take it from me. In fact, if you don't need those handcuffs after tonight, I'd be glad to take them off your hands."

Claire pointed at Jordan. "You'll have to fight her for them if you want them."

Jordan shot Claire a menacing look, and Shannon thought, oh no, poor Claire. *You'll never get the last laugh with Jordan.*

"I have plenty more where those came from, Claire, so I am more than happy to let you have them. In fact, they haven't even been broken in yet. Perhaps you'd like to give them a go tonight? I'm sure you can find *someone* willing to help you out. In fact, I'm more than sure."

Sparks were now flying, the claws out, and Claire began huffing and stammering. Well, you did walk into that one, Shannon thought with amusement.

She turned her face up to Dani and kissed her long and hard on the mouth, drawing a few oohs and ahs and a loud *woohoo* from the drag queen. She didn't often go for public displays of affection—it wasn't really her nature—but she wanted to give Dani a possessive, melting kiss at that moment, and undeniably it was partly to reassure herself that Dani was still hers.

"What's that for?" Dani asked in a sultry voice that indicated the kiss had turned her on.

"Just because I love you."

"I love you too, but I think I need more of those kisses. Like how about every ten minutes?"

Shannon laughed. "I'll see what I can do, darling."

"Good. I'm going to hold you to it."

CHAPTER TWENTY-THREE

Claire

The casino at the Golden Nugget was every bit as disagreeable as any other casino to Claire. Noisy, smoky, full of weak souls with nothing better to do. It wasn't that she had a moral aversion to gambling; she considered it a mindless waste of time that was potentially dangerous if it got out of hand. Looking around, she supposed Ann would have liked it here with its collection of interesting people, and the thought caused her to lighten her censorious grip a little. Ann had loved to people-watch, and being the competitive sort, she'd probably have tried her hand at a little inexpensive gambling. Claire, however, would much rather sit and read a book or do just about anything than mindlessly pull the lever of a slot machine. As for the rest—blackjack, roulette, craps—she hadn't the foggiest idea of how to play them.

Jordan guided them to a roulette table and ordered them to plunk down twenty bucks apiece for twenty one-dollar chips. They obeyed—Claire the most reluctant of them all—and bet their chips on Dani and Shannon's wedding date, which was the number three for the month of March and the number twelve for the day, as well as both women's birthdays.

Amanda turned to Claire and in an urgent whisper asked, "What's your birth date?"

"Oh, no. I'm not going to contribute any further to this delinquency."

"Like hell," Jordan interrupted before promptly ratting her out and telling Amanda that her birthday was April 2.

"Good, thank you." Amanda smiled triumphantly and placed a chip on the numbers four and two.

Petulantly, Claire made a face at Jordan. Could she not get away with anything since she'd fessed up about her crush on Amanda? Well, crush wasn't exactly the right word. It was more like a fondness and a mild attraction, or maybe a friendly attraction. A passionate friendship? Whatever the phrase, it was harmless and under control, innocent and certainly nothing for Jordan or anyone else to make a big deal about. And yet a tiny part of her felt guilty, like she held a provocative secret or had been caught doing something illicit, like the time she and her best friend had played house underneath her bed on her seventh birthday, kissing clumsily in their own rendition of being husband and wife. A guilty pleasure, that's what this was.

Amanda brushed against her in the excitement of the roulette wheel nearing the end of its spin. Oh, God, Claire thought with a pulse of her own excitement that started in her crotch and shot straight to her throat. *Okay, so maybe it's a little more than a mild attraction, but it's nothing I can't handle.* Jordan would tell her she simply needed to get laid, that her hormones were flaring up because she'd not had regular sex in such a long time. Well, that might be true, but she was not about to do the one-night stand thing again, nor was she interested in dating anyone—especially not a young woman who was her best friend's niece. So for now, she was stuck with this sudden and unwanted awakening of her libido. And if it would not go back to sleep, well then perhaps she'd better get busy with herself, and soon.

Claire's heart continued to pound and she dared not speak because her voice would surely come out tight and high-pitched like a little girl's, giving away the fact that she was putty in Amanda's hands. When the little ball and the wheel finally came to a stop, Amanda let out a squeal and squeezed Claire's arm until it hurt. The winning number was two—Claire's birthday.

"I knew it!" Amanda yelled, hopping around in a little victory dance. "I knew you would be my lucky charm!"

She'd bet two dollars on Claire's birthday and now the dealer slid a pile of chips worth seventy dollars her way.

"How about sharing a little of that luck," Heather suggested hopefully. "In fact, screw Dani and Shannon's lucky numbers. What are your other lucky numbers, Claire?"

"No way," Claire protested. "I'm not going to be responsible for your winning or losing, thank you very much!"

Shannon joined in by announcing that Claire's jersey number from her hockey playing days had been seventeen. Claire tried for a withering look, but Shannon looked so damned excited and happy in those silly pink handcuffs, so she shrugged her resignation instead.

"Seventeen it is," Heather announced, and they all towered a bunch of one-dollar chips on the number, except for Claire, who accepted a glass of wine from the young waitress making the rounds. She was drinking a lot this week. More than she'd probably drunk in quite a while, but what the hell. What was Vegas without a little alcohol after all? And a little gambling, much as she hated to admit it. The business of winning had some merit to it. Who knew it could almost be *fun*.

Her eyes nearly popped out of her head when seventeen hit for the win. The group shrieked and carried on like they'd just won millions.

"Oh my God, Claire, you're a natural!" Jordan enthused. "Who would have thought you were the reckless type?"

"It's always the quiet ones you have to watch out for," Dani interjected. "You should know that by now, Jordan."

"You're right," Jordan said, slipping a wink to Claire. "It's always the innocent looking ones who are full of trouble. Right Claire?"

She caught Amanda looking at her like she wanted Claire to mix up a little one-on-one trouble with her. *Oh Jesus, Amanda, you have to stop looking at me like that or your aunt's going to catch on.* She swallowed the desire in her throat. "You're not going to become a gambler now to finance your way through college, are you?" Claire wasn't entirely kidding. Amanda was smart, sensible, had a good head on her shoulders, but if she was going to be seduced by gambling after this little experiment, Claire was going to bloody well kill Jordan.

"No." Amanda laughed reassuringly, touching her arm again in that pleasing, affectionate way she had. "But I am enjoying this little windfall. In fact, I'm enjoying a lot of things about this week. It's been full of surprises." She turned soft, shining eyes on Claire. "Wonderful surprises, as it turns out."

Claire felt naked in a room full of clothed people, sure that everyone could see the sparks between them. She especially didn't want Shannon to notice anything. *God, what would Shannon think of this . . . this thing between us?* It was taboo, both the age difference and the fact that Amanda was Shannon's niece. And while forbidden relationships could be thrilling and seductive, it wasn't that way for Claire. She wasn't trying to be a rebel. She connected with Amanda, loved spending time with her, because spending time with her was so effortless and so natural. Joyful too. They had a great time whenever they were together. In fact, Claire couldn't remember the last time she'd felt this light, this free of the burden of grief she'd been carrying around for so long, as if she might have permanent imprints from it. There was nothing inappropriate about this bond, and yet, she couldn't help but feel naughty whenever she positioned herself for Amanda to touch her, as she did now, or when she'd welcomed the hug in the car and her body had responded with a mind of its own. It was absolutely prohibited that her hormones should do a happy dance whenever she and Amanda touched, and yet, she couldn't *not* touch Amanda or be touched by her, and she couldn't *not* respond. She was the moth to Amanda's flame, the blossom reaching out to her sunshine. She was young and alive and full of spirit whenever she was around Amanda. She sighed in frustration, unsure and unwilling to stop all this, but unwilling to fully accept it all too.

An hour or so later, she was caught totally off guard in the hot tub when Shannon, slipping into the water beside her, leaned close and whispered, "Claire, do you think Amanda is happy?"

Claire blinked stupidly. "What?" Amanda was still in the change room and Dani, handcuffed to Shannon, chatted loudly and obliviously to Heather on the other side of her.

"She told me today that she married her girlfriend in California, but it didn't work out and now they're trying to get divorced."

Good, Claire thought, instantly proud of Amanda for having gone through with it, but she played dumb for Shannon's benefit. "Wow. That's pretty surprising news. How do you feel about that?"

"You mean after I got over the shock? I was hurt she hadn't told me sooner, but it's her life. She's a big girl who can make her own decisions, and she's mature enough to handle it when those decisions don't work out. I just want her to be happy. You've spent a lot of time with her this week—a lot more than I have. Do you think she's happy?"

How does anybody really know whether someone else is happy? It was a loaded question, but Amanda certainly seemed happy in her company this week. She'd been through a lot the last couple of years, and before that with her mother's death, and so it was understandable that Shannon was concerned about her. "Yes," she answered simply. "I think she's reasonably happy."

"I hope so. She deserves to be, you know?"

Yes, Claire thought, I do know.

"And so do you," was Shannon's stern admonition.

"I'll take that under advisement." God damn, was that some kind of permission she'd just been given? Was she trying to say it was okay for the two of them to be happy *together*? Or was it just a coincidental juxtaposition?

"I'll tell you something," Shannon said, a menacing edge to her voice. "The next woman who hurts her, I'll kick her ass."

Claire wanted to laugh, relieved because she knew it would never be herself hurting Amanda. She would never hurt Amanda.

The wine was making her introspective, but when Amanda emerged and walked gracefully—*sexily*—to the hot tub, all introspection went down the drain. The sight before her rendered Claire completely speechless and paralyzed. For all she knew her mouth was hanging open and drool was spilling down her chin and into the hot rushing water. Amanda wore an emerald green two-piece bathing suit Claire had never seen before, and it was especially revealing and singularly sexy. The fabric was shiny and smooth over her luscious breasts, which swelled in firm twin mounds Claire itched to put her hands on. Her stomach was tight and slender—*ah, youth!*—and the bikini bottom dipped low and provocatively over her hips and into her nether regions. Claire sucked in her breath when Amanda chose the spot on the other side of her to sit down, and she wondered crazily if Amanda had worn this bathing suit just for her. Well, if she had, she'd surely gotten Claire's attention and she'd surely noticed Claire's eyes following her so closely.

"Goddamn," Heather whined loudly. "If I had your body Amanda, I sure as hell wouldn't be sitting in a hot tub right now with a bunch of old hags!"

"Hey!" Jordan protested. "Speak for yourself! Not all old hags are created equal, you know."

"All right, all right," Shannon chided before turning to Claire. "Claire, I think you might need to be Amanda's bodyguard tonight, or at least for as long as she's wearing that . . . that . . . God, does it even qualify as a bathing suit, Amanda?"

"Yes, Aunt Shannon, it does, I promise."

Jordan was shooting Claire all kinds of shit-eating grins and her eyebrows were dancing on her forehead like they were in the middle of a disco competition. *Great.* Jordan could be such an ass sometimes—crude, exasperating, ill behaved. But no matter what her antics, she'd forever endeared herself to Claire after Ann's death, when she'd offered to take the boxes of Ann's clothes and give them to charity when Claire didn't have the strength to deal with them. Other things she'd done for Claire too—helped her write notes to people after the funeral, made sure her cupboards were full of groceries. And so she wasn't truly peeved at Jordan now, she just hoped she'd keep her mouth shut.

Claire closed her eyes, let the warm churning water soothe her skin, and luxuriated in the warmth of Amanda's bare shoulder and thigh that were warm and soft against hers. Soon her skin was on fire. She let her mind wander. It was the wine and champagne—she was half drunk—so it wasn't really her fault that she wanted Amanda's hand on her leg. Wanted that hand to possessively, lovingly, run up and down her thigh and then, feather light, come to rest between her legs. *Oh, God!* One touch like that, she imagined, and she would probably come right there against Amanda's hand. Her every nerve ending was on fire, and only Amanda's touch could put out the flames. It was never going to happen of course, not in a million years, but for now, her head lolled back against the hot tub and her eyes firmly closed, she imagined a different truth—one where she and Amanda could indulge in what their bodies hinted at and ached for. No consequences, nothing forbidden, just love and lust all rolled into the sweetest, deepest orgasm ever.

CHAPTER TWENTY-FOUR

Jordan

Jordan was having way more fun than she'd expected. Being a lovesick idiot should have left her miserable, but the alcohol and the antics of the bachelor party had done their magic and lifted her spirits. She'd made herculean efforts to shove thoughts of Dez to the very outer limits of her mind and simply enjoy the evening and the company of her friends. She felt almost normal again. Almost.

She'd purposely kept the party fairly tame. Until now that is, she thought wickedly. The final *coup de grace* for the evening would be a visit to a gay and lesbian dance club. Well, that part wasn't going to be the pinnacle—the exotic dancer hired to do a lap dance for the brides was going to be the crowning glory. *Wait til they get a load of that, they're going to die!*

Jordan made sure Dani and Shannon were seated comfortably at a small table. They were completely unaware, like lambs before the slaughter, and she smirked to herself as she waited for the song "Naughty Girl" to start, which was the cue for Jessie, the bra-bursting, spectacular-looking blonde she'd hired for the job. Oh yeah, it was going to be so much fun unleashing Jessie on the unsuspecting wedding party, and Jessie, she was sure, would be more than worth the two hundred bucks she'd paid her for the little show.

Beyonce and L'il Kim's duet began blasting from the speakers when Jessie strode purposefully up to Dani and Shannon, trailing her little whip behind her. She was dressed in black fishnet stockings and a little leather bra and matching thong. She wore a red leather cape that matched her scarlet lips, and she stood tall and menacingly before the group, black stilettos spread apart in a challenge.

Oh yeah, this is going to be good!

She saw the amusement flash across Dani's face—Dani knew a good time when she saw it—and a look of subtle surprise settle on Shannon. Dani and Shannon were cool and would take it in stride. Heather, party girl that she was, predictably whooped and cheered on the dancer. She would undoubtedly whip herself into a frenzy pretty soon. Claire—*poor Claire!*—was trying her best to shrink into invisibility, horror widening her eyes. Well, Claire could act horrified and disgusted all she wanted, but she was as much a sexual being as the rest of them. She needed to loosen up a little, let herself experience the world around her a little more, take people for what they were and worry less about the consequences and the judgment people were quick to cruelly dole out. Jordan's glance flicked to Amanda, who calmly and somewhat drunkenly smiled and sat back to appraise the little show. Amanda was the cautious type who thought carefully before she spoke or acted. Or so it seemed. But there was a tendril of wildness in the young woman that indicated she knew how to live, knew how to take the occasional chance in life. She'd probably be a good influence on Claire, if Claire would let her.

The dancer shook her cape loose and twirled it to the floor. Her hips gyrated in time to the music, the thin leather whip cascaded seductively around her legs, and a full pout swelled her scarlet lips. She blew kisses at the wedding party, then, one by one, snaked her whip around each of the women's shoulders. Dani and Shannon played along, good sports that they were, and laughed loudly at all the appropriate moments. Heather bounced in her seat like she was raring to join Jessie in the dance. Claire was taking a different tact now, trying hard to look nonchalant, as though she were used to this sort of thing—that this was nothing. Amanda's eyes flicked curiously between Claire and the dancer; she was sizing up the situation, seeing how much Claire could handle, Jordan guessed. A good-natured crowd began forming around them, laughing, clapping, encouraging. Jordan had cleared the little dance job with the bar's management, since it was a regular nightclub and not a strip joint. She'd even greased the manager's palm with a couple of hundred dollars to seal the deal. It was just one song and one dance and she wasn't going to get completely naked. What harm could it cause?

Jessie moved closer, gyrating her hips above Dani's and Shannon's laps. She draped her arms around them, ran her fingers seductively through their hair, pressed her scantily clad breasts toward their faces. Shannon, feeling no pain, boldly and uncharacteristically pushed her face into Jessie's cleavage for a moment, earning a loud whoop from the crowd. As the song finished, Jessie wound the whip tightly around the guests of honor's shoulders, joining them much closer than the handcuffs. Only when they kissed did Jessie release them. She saluted them a final time, kissed each of them on the cheek, then sassily sashayed away.

"Oh, my God!" Heather protested. "Come back here, missy! You can't leave yet! You're just getting started! How much are they paying you?"

Dani laughed and loudly accused her raucous sister of going gay.

"Whatever. It sure as hell seems like more fun than I've been having lately!"

Dani tugged Shannon from her seat. "C'mon you naughty thing, you. Good thing Jordan thought to handcuff you to me, or who knows what trouble you'd get into around here!"

"I only want to get into trouble with you, my love."

"Perfect. Let's see what trouble we can get into on the dance floor."

Soon Heather was dancing as well, and with a very tall tranny. Amanda slowly guided Claire onto the floor, Claire somehow managing to look both eager and shy. The song was called "Dirty Talk," the singer singing about pantyhose, legs up, in the back of a car, doing dirty things tonight. Jordan's pulse began to match the beat of the music. She thought of Dez's long legs, wished she could grind up against her on the dance floor, the heat and sweat from their bodies mingling as they sizzled together, their desire for one another in full throttle. She'd not had a chance to dance with Dez, and she regretted it, especially as she watched Amanda and Claire move in time, their hips rhythmically coming together, their hands touching in this dance of innocent foreplay. There was a certain sexual grace on the dance floor between two people hot for each other, whether the attraction had been consummated or not, and Jordan missed the excitement of new desire. She missed Dez and she was getting turned on in the worst way.

"Care to dance?"

Jordan turned toward the voice and the honey-skinned woman who could have been Dez's younger sister. "Okay."

They were not at all awkward with each other, as two strangers often were. Jordan, well lubricated from the evening's alcohol and the flood of hormones helplessly cascading through her body, relaxed into the dance. "I'm Jordan. What's your name, beautiful?"

"Savannah."

Jordan winced at the reminder of Georgia, Dez's home state.

"I haven't been able to keep my eyes off you since you came in," the woman continued, her gaze bold. "I have to tell you, I think you're sexy as hell."

That got Jordan's attention. Dez wasn't here. Dez had

banished her for good. Screw Dez. Savannah was ready, willing and present—the three criteria that mattered. Savannah made no secret of wanting her, and so she began turning on the famous Jordan Scott charm, began dancing closer, touching Savannah, making her desire known, muttering the right words, moving seductively. The game was in full operation.

Three songs were all it took. Savannah looked at Jordan, raised her eyebrows with the unstated question, and Jordan followed her out. She caught Dani near the door, told her she'd make her own way back to the hotel later, and tossed her the key to the handcuffs.

Dani laughed and shook her head. "You're not in a hurry to have these things back, are you?"

"Hell no. You go, girl!"

She followed Savannah to the parking lot and hopped into her Mustang convertible—definitely a babe mobile. Savannah, it seemed, was well practiced in the art of picking up women, but what the hell, so was Jordan. It made things simple.

At Savannah's apartment, tall drinks were poured and the small talk on the sofa was superficial. It wasn't long before Savannah moved onto Jordan's lap and began kissing her deeply. She nibbled on Jordan's lips, kissed her deeply again, moved her tongue deep inside while Jordan cupped her round ass, pulling her closer. Savannah began moaning as she placed Jordan's hands on her full breasts, her nipples already pebble hard. Jordan squeezed lightly, brushing her thumbs against Savannah's nipples. She moved her mouth roughly to Savannah's neck and shoulder. She sucked and bit the flesh, kissing it softly too. Punishment and reward. God, how she wanted to fuck and be fucked. Hard. She wanted to squeeze those tits hard, shove her hand forcefully against Savannah's crotch, rip and tear at her clothes, plunge two, maybe three fingers inside. No mercy. And then she wanted this woman to suck her breasts and then suck her clit, hard and fast as she could. Oh yeah, she wanted it all hard and fast tonight.

Savannah removed her blouse, pushed a breast into Jordan's eager mouth. Oh yeah, Savannah knew how to give it too. *Perfect.*

Except it wasn't perfect. Jordan's interest suddenly began to ebb, and quickly. It was like water draining from a tub. If she had a penis it would be going soft right now. *Shit*. It wasn't like her not to be able to keep it up. Once she started something, she was never one to give up prematurely. A clit teaser she was most definitely not. But this . . . this was weird. She couldn't explain it, had no answer for it, and it pissed her off.

"What's wrong, stud?"

"I don't know."

Panic burned in her throat. What the hell was happening to her these days? The discovery of sleeping with her first lover's daughter had thrown her world off its axis. It was unlike any reality check she'd ever known and it had put the brakes to her promiscuity in one hell of a hurry. Well, except for this little lapse with Savannah. And of course Dez, who had totally eviscerated her world, annihilating everything she thought she'd ever known about herself. *Dez*. Dez was the answer to every riddle in her life, the destination of every trip, the reward at the end of a hard day. She'd never known what any of those things were like until she'd met Dez, and no matter how much it terrified her or pissed her off, she wanted Dez still. *Needed* Dez in her life. Dez made everything in her life make sense—gave a kind of order to the positively disorderliness of her life.

"Shit, I'm so sorry, Savannah." She pulled herself out from under Savannah, trying not to be rude, but Christ, she needed to get out of there. Harsh words from Savannah were probably deserved, but the woman only smiled with regret.

"Don't be sorry. I just wish I was her."

"Huh?"

"Whoever it is you're stuck on, baby. She's one lucky woman."

Yeah, Jordan thought miserably. *Wish you'd tell* her *that*.

"I'll call you a cab," Savannah said helpfully.

CHAPTER TWENTY-FIVE

Amanda

Finally, a slow song, Amanda thought with relief and silently celebrated. Deejays never played enough slow songs. Cynically, she supposed that there were all kinds of reasons for the fast songs, like the faster people danced, the more they spent on drinks. Or perhaps the fewer slow songs, the fewer public scraps people got into over strangers asking their girlfriends or boyfriends to dance. All that mattered now was that Chantal Kreviazuk's "Feels Like Home" was playing, and she'd been waiting for this chance to slow dance with Claire for at least an hour.

She took another sip of her cocktail—she'd lost count of the number of drinks she'd consumed—and forced a degree of courage on herself that she didn't really feel. "Will you do me the honor of dancing with me?"

Claire answered with a smile and followed Amanda onto the dance floor. There was only a brief moment of awkwardness as they came together, and it wasn't long before they fit like they'd been doing this for a thousand years. As the song progressed, they moved intimately closer, swaying in perfect time, each quietly lost in the feel of being so physically close. She wondered if Claire was thinking, like her, how perfect this felt, how much like being in bed together this mimicked. A form of vertical, fully-clothed sex. Not such a bad substitute, she thought, as the song and the feel of their bodies together coalesced into a sublime sweetness, and Amanda knew she was grinning like a kid at Christmas—one who'd just gotten everything she wanted. She was too drunk and too happy to care.

"Congratulations, by the way," Claire whispered.

"For what?"

"For telling Shannon the truth. She told me you did. I'm so proud of you. How does it feel now that she knows everything?"

"It feels . . . strange. Good but strange. It feels more like I'm an adult with her and not a kid anymore. More like we're equals."

"About time you felt that way, don't you think?"

"I'm not, you know."

"What?"

Amanda looked fearlessly at Claire. "A kid."

"I know." Something in Claire's eyes told her that, indeed, she was only too aware of the fact that Amanda was a grown woman. Claire looked at her much differently now than she'd looked at her earlier in the week.

They had the kid part out of the way. Now Amanda wondered why they weren't talking about how they really felt about one another. No amount of alcohol could make her say the words, and she was afraid the words might back Claire into a corner. Claire had to ease into things, feel comfortable, come to her own conclusions. Amanda couldn't blame her for her cautious approach. Amanda also didn't want to rush into anything. She'd already made a huge mistake rushing things with Jennifer, and there was much to be said for going slow, particularly given their age difference and Claire's friendship with Shannon. She would be patient.

"How is my aunt doing after that little shocker?"

"She's doing fine. She wants you to be happy, no matter what."

"I feel terrible that I hurt her by keeping secrets. I should have told her a long time ago. I ended up making things worse by not telling her about the marriage, and then not telling her it didn't work out."

"It's all in the past now and you can start with a clean slate. Not to sound like I'm psychoanalyzing things, but I think it's time Shannon accepted that you're an adult who can make your own decisions, including your share of mistakes, and that you'll be just fine. And now you can accept your aunt as a true friend and contemporary—one who will love you no matter what."

Amanda held Claire tighter. "Thank you for saying that. She's lucky to have you for a friend. Any woman would be lucky to have you in their corner."

Claire's smile was a little roguish, and Amanda immediately loved her playfulness. "I'm pretty good in corners. Other places too."

Amanda shook her head in laughter. "I have no trouble at all believing that." She'd love to put Claire to the test one day, but for now she needed to force herself to behave and not say anything too provocative. The alcohol and the feel of Claire's breasts against her and her strong arms holding her tight were dangerously fueling Amanda's sexual attraction. And it *was* sexual attraction. She was wet, turned on. She wanted Claire, and there wasn't a damn thing she could do about it.

The song segued into another slow one, "Afternoon Delight." Claire energetically spun Amanda, then dipped her. "I haven't heard this old song in decades. Isn't it a blast?"

Yes, Amanda thought, it is, and you, my sweet Claire, are a treasure. They danced to the rest of the song in companionable silence. When it came time to return to their seats, Amanda stumbled a little. It was late and she'd had way more to drink than she was accustomed to.

"I think I need to go back to the hotel," she mumbled apologetically to the group.

Shannon, still happily handcuffed to Dani, offered to help her back safely.

"I'll go with her," Claire countered. "I think I've reached my limit too."

Shortly after, in the cab ride back, Amanda watched Claire's handsome profile in the passing lights. "I'm sorry if I made you leave prematurely."

"Trust me, I'm partied out," Claire answered around a yawn. "It was fun, but I haven't had this much excitement in a long time. My body hasn't figured out yet what hit it."

"I had fun too."

The evening had felt like a date, even more so now that they were alone in the back seat of a cab and heading to the hotel together. She slipped her hand inside Claire's, insanely happy when Claire didn't resist. Yes, this too felt familiar, tenderly holding hands after a night of fun. Amanda's head swam with visions of them going back to just one room. It wasn't a silly fantasy, because it felt absolutely like the right thing to do.

In the hall, Amanda struggled with her key card. Claire, whose hand was steadier, helped her open the door. "Will you come inside?" Amanda chanced.

A look of awkward surprise settled on Claire. "Um, I—"

Her shyness was cute, but Amanda didn't want her to feel pressured that it was a come-on. "There was one more thing I was hoping to talk to you about," she quickly amended.

"Okay."

"I'd ask if you wanted another drink but I suspect you don't."

"No. I think I've had more than enough."

"Me too." She gestured to the loveseat by the large window and waited until Claire sat down. Amanda sat beside her, wishing they could hold hands again like in the cab, but holding hands alone together in a hotel room came with a different set of expectations.

"Are you okay?" Claire asked softly.

"Yes, but I'm very worried about my aunt. When we were having our talk today, she told me that she can't have any children. I know how much she and Dani want a baby. Is it really true that she can't conceive?"

"Yes, it is. It's not very common at her age, but it's not exactly uncommon either. It's unfortunate, but they do have other options if they want to be parents. Just not biological options."

"Shit. I can't believe it's so final."

"I know. It's tough news to take. It was a real blow to her at first, but I think she's more accepting of it now. Shannon's always been a realist. It's one of the things that made her such a great nurse."

"But Dani . . . she hasn't even told her yet. I'm so scared, Claire."

"Scared of what?" she asked, such kindness and strength in her eyes and voice that Amanda immediately wanted to fall into her arms.

In the gloom, Amanda felt tears gather in the corners of her eyes, then felt them slither slowly down her face. It scared her when people's dreams came crashing to a halt. It scared her when science and medicine couldn't fix what was wrong. It scared her that Shannon might be wrong about Dani's unconditional love for her. "I guess I'm scared most that they won't be able to move past this as a couple," she said in a shaky voice. "I'm scared Shannon's marriage will end up like mine. A piece of crap."

Claire slid her hand into Amanda's and held it tightly. She brushed the tears from Amanda's cheeks in an act that resembled that of a lover. Claire didn't need to say anything; Amanda felt her comfort and strength in her touch. It wasn't long before she nestled into Claire's arms, laid her head against her chest, and let Claire's rhythmic breathing make her feel safe.

After several moments, Amanda whispered, "Thank you. I can't even remember the last time anyone's held me like that."

Claire kissed the top of her head, her arms still firmly around her. "It's just about the best thing in the world, isn't it?"

"Yes, it is. Did you have anyone in your life the last few years who did this for you?"

"Unfortunately not enough, no."

"How did you manage to get through that time?"

Claire's laugh was mournful. "Who said I managed?"

Amanda thought a while before she answered. She knew grief left an indelible print and that not everyone moved past it. Only her youth and her career ambitions had got her through her mother's death. Losing a life partner was another matter, and the reality of Claire's past slammed into her with a crushing, jarring weight. *Claire would never love you. Claire lost the only person she'll ever love.* The thought made her stop breathing for a moment and she had to clear her throat before she could speak. "You're here, aren't you?"

"Yes. I guess that's something, isn't it?"

"That's more than something." Amanda raised her head to look into Claire's eyes. "You have so much to give, so much love still in your heart, so much strength within. I can feel it. You can't give up, ever. You can't ever stop giving life everything you have to offer. There's so much living left to do."

"That sounds like good advice for you as well."

"You're right. Maybe it's something we both need to hear." Another tear was working its way loose and Amanda sucked in a ragged breath. Being this close to Claire, being held in her arms, looking into her soft brown eyes, feeling her warm breath against her—it was almost too much and yet it was not nearly enough. "I'm scared because sometimes I want so much. Like right now."

Claire seemed to know exactly what she meant, for she nodded ever so slightly. Amanda knew Claire wanted things too—things she was too scared to demand or accept. With a fingertip she touched Claire's cheek, ran it down the side of her face and to her chin, and watched as Claire closed her eyes. Her capitulation was like the sand giving way easily to rising water. With a momentum she couldn't and didn't want to stop, Amanda moved closer until her lips touched Claire's, softly, like a raindrop on glass. Claire flinched once in surprise but her eyes remained closed as Amanda kissed her again. The softness turned into something bolder, harder, like a rainstorm gathering into a torrential downpour. Claire relented further, melted into Amanda's arms as the kiss deepened. Soft warm lips gave way to hungry mouths. Amanda turned up the heat, pressed harder, opened wider, demanded more. Claire gave it, matching a fervor that never stopped being tender, and it was not unlike the thousands of kisses Amanda had enjoyed in her life—a mix of tenderness and heat and promise blending perfectly together. And yet it was not like any other kiss, not a real kiss like this, where time stood still and where no one who'd come before Claire mattered in the least. Yes, it was like every corny movie and song all rolled into one, Amanda thought with amusement. *Who knew it could be this good?*

There was no question they wanted more—their bodies were quick to betray them. Nipples hardened, hands began to move in circular patterns, pelvises pressed closer together. Screw the going slow bit, Amanda thought. Some things were meant to happen. Some things *needed* to happen.

"Wait," Claire said, breathless, and pulled away with an effort that felt like they were being wrenched apart. "Oh God. What are we doing?"

"Don't."

Claire took both of Amanda's hands in hers. "I have to stop, Amanda. *We* have to stop. Please. We can't let this happen."

"No." *No, no, no, no, no!* She was being petulant but she didn't care. Claire was lovely. Claire was everything she'd ever wanted in a woman. Claire was land after a lifetime at sea. They would be so good together, she *knew* it. And so did Claire.

Claire looked pained but uncompromising. "This is too complicated right now, okay? We need to take a deep breath and slow down. Get some perspective."

Amanda wanted to lash out, but instead she said in a steady voice, "Sometimes fear is the only thing that makes something complicated."

Claire shook her head obstinately, rose, and in an instant her long strides took her to the door. Clearly, she'd made up her mind. She could not get past the impediments in their way, would not even seriously consider trying to overcome them. And all the anger and disappointment in the world from Amanda would not change Claire's mind, she knew. She had to let her go, or at least let this moment go.

Amanda reluctantly followed, and at the door, Claire touched her face as though she could not help herself. Amanda let her tears fall on Claire's motionless fingers. *Let her see how much she means to me.*

CHAPTER TWENTY-SIX

Dani

"Big day today, little sister!"

"Not as big as tomorrow," Dani reminded her.

"Ah, yes, the countdown begins." Heather peered at her watch and grinned. "My God, in about twenty-seven hours you'll be a married woman!" Dani's frown was so deep that Heather's grin left her like an eraser across a chalk board. "Jeez kid, just because I had shitty luck at the altar doesn't mean you have anything to worry about."

Heather had a good heart, but she could be so self-absorbed at times. It wasn't uncommon for her to turn conversations toward herself. "I'm not worried about having shitty luck at the altar," Dani countered.

"Okay, what then? Cuz something's eating at you. Will you tell me?"

Dani shook her head, already regretting this conversation, but there was really no escaping it. The others hadn't arrived at the poolside cabana yet—they were probably still nursing hang-overs from last night's bachelor party. It was only noon. They'd show up eventually—or not. Shannon was busy meeting with the caterers for what seemed like the third time this week. Dani only hoped she wasn't tacking more expensive last-minute things onto the menu.

"Seriously," Heather continued. "You've seemed a little, I don't know, preoccupied this week. And I don't mean with wed-ding details. I know my little sister and I know something's going on. Wanna talk about it?"

Dani folded like a house of cards, tired of holding it all together and afraid she might blow if she didn't relieve some of the pressure. She was scared—scared beyond reason on several levels. "I guess you could say I've got a pretty big problem on my hands."

Heather perched her sunglasses on her head and stared ominously at her. She knew Dani typically underplayed prob-lems. "What is it, baby?"

All right, here goes. She took a deep breath to steel herself for the words she hadn't spoken to anyone. Admitting to failure was bitter and foreign in her mouth. Even the words seemed like a different language. "I lost my job a few weeks ago."

"What?" Shock, concern, sympathy all stormed across Heather's face. "I thought you loved it there and they loved you. You've been there, what, four or five years? I thought things were going so well? Shit, Dani. I'm so sorry. What the hell happened?"

Dani had been one of three vice presidents at a marketing firm that specialized in websites and networks for the legal pro-fession. The company had grown over a thousand percent since it began in 2001, but thanks to the downturn in the economy, growth had melted into losses and the company's CEO decided he had one too many VPs. She'd never thought it would hap-pen to her, but in the end she was just another surplus item the company could do without. She quickly explained the situation to Heather in a voice devoid of emotion. Maybe if she made it sound like she was talking about someone else, it wouldn't hurt so much.

"Well, that sure sucks the big one," Heather said, still sounding confounded. "What are you going to do?"

"I've been looking for another job, but it's looking pretty hopeless at the moment. Unfortunately, there's a lot of people out there in my situation. And when I do find something, it sure as hell won't pay as much as I've been used to."

"Yeah, I guess those days are gone. It seems it's only the bank execs who are still raking in the dough, those bastards. You've been used to a pretty good salary for a long time. Are you going to be able to make the adjustment?"

Dani shrugged. "What choice do I have? I mean, my severance and our savings will get us through a few months, but still . . . it's not looking so good."

"What about Shannon going back to work?"

"Hell no. I don't want her pregnant and having to work shifts at the hospital. I'll scrub floors before I'll let that happen."

Heather smiled sympathetically. "You know, the fancy cars and the fancy digs are nice and all, but take it from me, a crapped out Ford Focus and a two-bedroom bungalow ain't so bad. It can always be worse."

"I know, I know. And money doesn't buy happiness and all that crap."

"I'm not trying to lecture you, hon. I'm here for you, okay?"

"I know." Dani tried to wrestle down her agitation. Heather was doing her best to be supportive in the best way she knew how and it wasn't fair to lose patience with her. "It's just that, I guess you get to a point where you think your value or your worth as a human being is directly tied to how much money you make. Maybe that's been my problem all this time. My identity is cloaked in dollar bills."

"Well, that is so much bullshit. You are a wonderful woman, Dani, whether you're broke or rich. Besides, in my experience, the more money a person makes, the bigger the asshole they are anyway."

Dani let out a bitter laugh. "Yeah, well, I can tell you from *my* experience that rich is better, even if it does make you an asshole."

"Oh, screw rich. You've got everything you need. A wonderful woman you're about to marry. Your health. A sister who loves you. Wonderful friends. Hopefully a kid soon."

"I know, and I do appreciate everything I have, believe me."

"Then listen to me." Heather looked pointedly at her. "Don't think I don't know why all this money crap bothers you so much. It's mom and dad, isn't it?"

"Screw them. You said as much yourself this week."

"Yes, I did say that, but the problem is that you don't actually believe it."

"What are you talking about? They're assholes. I'm not disagreeing with that."

"Verbally, yes, but your actions sometimes say otherwise. I know about the car you tried to buy them a couple of years ago."

Dani rolled her eyes as she remembered offering to buy her parents a brand-new Chevy SUV to replace their ancient, crapped out Suburban that her father kept limping along year after year. It seemed like a no-brainer that her parents would accept her generous gift. Who'd turn down a brand-new car, after all? Her parents, that's who. Said they would be too embarrassed to drive around town in something new. More like too embarrassed to admit their city slicker lesbian daughter had bought it for them. It hurt Dani's feelings that they would take nothing from her. They wouldn't even accept an all-expenses paid invitation to the wedding. The rejection still hurt.

"I don't want to talk about them," Dani snapped.

"Well, we're going to talk about them, because they seem to be at the root of so much shit in our lives." Anger was turning Heather's face hot pink. "It's damn well time you take a page out of my book and quit trying to prove anything to them. Or worrying about what they think. They don't deserve that kind of respect, trust me."

"I don't respect them, okay? It's not about that. They've treated us both like crap all our lives, okay? You'd have to be blind not to see that. We never lived up to their ideals and expectations. I know all that."

"You're right, and we never will, no matter what. It's too late for them. Always has been. There's no do-overs with them."

It was true. Her parents were in their late sixties now and as firmly entrenched as ever in their strict religious beliefs, their right-wing politics and their narrow views. They would never admit they'd been wrong about Dani and Heather, would never choose to see the good in them, would never forge relationships with them. It didn't take a genius to figure out that Dani's feelings of worthlessness most of her life had fueled her need to spend money. She'd spent a ton of money the last few years trying to prove herself to Shannon, to friends, colleagues, pretty much to everyone. Yes, the estrangement was largely her parents' fault, yet Dani's persistence—the fighter within—was why she'd never truly given up on them and why she refused to lay all her problems at their feet. Maybe a tiny sliver of religion had taken root in her all those years ago, the part about redemption and believing people could be forgiven their sins and could start over again. If God could still love her, why couldn't her parents and her younger brother and sister?

Dani sighed. She didn't have all the answers. "I'm not disagreeing with you. In fact, the way you feel about them and having written them off years ago was probably the best thing you could have done for yourself."

"Oh, there is no probably about it. And it's the best thing you could do too."

"I'm sure you're right. Trust me, I'm not going out of my way ever again to please them. The next move will have to be theirs."

"Yeah, well, they'll be dead in their graves before that ever happens."

"Wow, you're awfully bitter."

"What, you're just figuring that out now? They deserted me when I was young and got pregnant by a married man. They condemned me when I needed them most. I can't forget that. Or forgive it."

All this talk about family was wearing on Dani. It was only early afternoon and in a couple of hours she and Shannon had to host a cocktail reception for their two dozen or so wedding guests who were flying in today. Then after dinner was the wedding rehearsal with the wedding party. She was exhausted by the thought of it all. "Look, I'm sorry we got into all this. I know the odds are slim to none that the rest of our family is going to suddenly turn into decent human beings, and I promise I'm not going to hold my breath waiting for it to happen, okay?"

"Promise?"

Dani rolled her eyes. "Yes. And now I think I'm going to go have a little nap before the festivities start up again."

"Okay. Hey, one more thing." Heather clutched her arm before she could leave. "Shannon seems to be acting awfully unconcerned about your job loss. Is she okay with it?"

Dani's stomach bottomed out at the thought of the talk she still needed to have with Shannon. She winced painfully. "She doesn't know yet."

"What? Are you kidding me?"

"Sorry, I'm all talked out for now, okay?" Dani mumbled. She didn't want to deal with this subject right now. "Later."

"What do you mean later? You're just going to walk away without telling me why you haven't told the woman you're marrying tomorrow that you lost your job?"

"Yes," Dani said simply and turned away. It was her and Shannon's business, and besides, there was nothing Heather could say to her that she hadn't already told herself.

CHAPTER TWENTY-SEVEN

Jordan

She couldn't believe she'd been lured by the old habit last night of going home with a stranger. Couldn't believe it'd been so easy, so natural. *Well, years of practice, that's why*! She'd followed the same pattern for so long, it had become second nature. There was nothing wrong with Savannah—she seemed like a nice woman—and there was nothing wrong with meeting new friends. But she knew with certainty she would never go home with a stranger again like that, and this time she meant it. Yes, it was a quick antidote to loneliness, but it was no substitute for companionship, for someone who understood you and connected with you. Dez or no Dez in her life, she was finished with that behavior.

As she wandered alone among The Canal Shops in The Venetian Hotel, it occurred to her how much had changed for her over the past week. She'd gone from screwing the daughter of her first lover to stumbling across Dez and falling in love, to swearing to herself she'd never again be promiscuous. It was almost like the beginning and the end of a novel with no middle part. Well, the middle part for her had been falling for Dez, but that part of her week now seemed like it had come and gone in a blink of an eye. She was a changed woman. Transformed. Krissy had started it and Dez had sealed it. The funny part was, it didn't even feel so strange; it felt right. She had a feeling she'd be used to the new Jordan in no time.

She stopped to stare at the indoor canal, the ostentation of the marble floor and walls, the massive skylight mural, the Gucci, Cartier, Prada shops. It was blissful ignorance, all this extravagance. An entertaining distraction for the masses. She'd loved all this ostentation at one time; it was why she'd come to live part time in the city. But the truth was, no matter what her surroundings, she was lonely. Had been most of her life. Her parents, both successful lawyers, were almost never around when she was growing up. Oh, she and her brother were well provided for. There'd been nannies, private schools, every material need looked after. But there'd never been much love, only a learned sense of entitlement—an expectation that the world was her oyster. Her life had been one giant buffet of self gluttony, yet there was something supremely dissatisfying about all that selfish gorging. Stuffed full but empty inside.

She watched the couples in the gondolas. Some of them seemed almost embarrassed to have so many people staring at them, to have their romantic moment on public display. Never in a million years would she have done something as goofy as ride around an indoor moat in a little boat, a gondolier singing romantic Italian songs. But now it held a certain fascinating appeal, being wrapped so obliviously in a romantic crucible that you didn't care what sort of spectacle you made. She could picture herself and Dez in one of the little boats, laughing at themselves, laughing at the strangers and at the fakeness of it all, taking none of it seriously because they had their love for each other to take seriously.

All these years Jordan had ignored the fact that she was

lonely. She had done a good job convincing herself that she enjoyed her time alone, that she was fulfilled and living life exactly as she wanted. She'd simply extended the lessons she'd learned in childhood, and it was a good life, really. An expensive condo in Chicago, one in Las Vegas, a career in real estate that easily made her a cool million a year in commissions. She could travel whenever she wanted, buy whatever she wanted, could even eat as much as she wanted and never had to worry about her figure. Life had been pretty damned good to Jordan Scott.

Except now that she was beginning to peel back the gilt veneer, there wasn't a lot about her life that truly made her happy. The condos were lovely but they were devoid of everything that made a house a home. Travel was exhausting. The money was nice, but she had everything she needed twice over. And the women—the women made her feel good for the short term. Sometimes for days, but more likely only for a few hours or even minutes. She'd had so many lovers. Hundreds. Hell, maybe even a thousand by now. So many that they all blurred together, like the lines dividing a well-traveled highway. There had been times at parties where women had come up to her, talked to her like they knew her intimately, started reminiscing about a date they'd had, and Jordan didn't even remember them, let alone anything about the time she'd spent with them. It was embarrassing. Repulsive, actually.

Being with Dez was no comparison. Dez made her realize what happiness was. *Real* happiness. Happiness at just being with someone. Happiness with herself, and those were things money definitely could not buy.

All right, she said to herself and took a deep, calming breath. She needed to come up with another solid plan to convince Dez to give her another chance. The flowers hadn't worked. Neither had the couple of notes she'd slipped under her door. She wouldn't keep after Dez if the cold shoulder was the constant result. She had more self-respect than that. But maybe, with one last genuine effort, Dez would come around.

She walked into a shop of specialized collectors' memorabilia from the entertainment and sports world. There was a blackjack tabletop autographed by the stars of the original *Ocean's Eleven* film, as well as one autographed by the stars from the remake. There were autographed Beatles albums, same with Elvis and Sinatra. She remembered Dez saying something about being a huge Ella Fitzgerald fan, how inspired she'd been by Ella, who'd also been her grandmother's favorite singer. Maybe there was something special here from Ella she could give to Dez.

After a few more minutes of browsing, she spotted exactly what she was looking for. Two framed concert tickets autographed by the First Lady of Song. Jordan peered closer. The tickets were from Carnegie Hall, July 5, 1973. *Yeah.* She smiled to herself. *This will do nicely.* She didn't even blink at the fifteen hundred dollar price tag.

An hour later in her room, she wrapped the framed tickets and scrawled a note. She would hire a messenger to take the package to Dez's room.

Dez,

I know how much Ella meant to you and I couldn't think of a better way to honor the inspiration she gave you. Please come to the wedding tomorrow evening. You don't have to sing, just dance with me. One dance. I miss you. You have touched me in ways I can't even begin to describe. But if you give me another chance, I would love to be able to tell you in person.

Jordan

CHAPTER TWENTY-EIGHT

Shannon

All week the wedding's approach had seemed surreal. Meeting with the caterers, the decorators, fine-tuning the plans, and even the silly but amazingly fun bachelor party hadn't really driven home the fact that tomorrow she and Dani would actually be *married*. For months now it had seemed more abstract than real, like it was all happening to someone else, but now that more than two dozen of their closest friends—their wedding guests—were finally here, Shannon began to feel the heft of the approaching day. She was happy, of course she was, and thoughts of the big day should have been making her light-headed with joy, giddy, excited. And she was all of those things, except . . .

She watched Dani across the room twirling a glass of wine in her hand as she talked with Janet, a friend from college, and Janet's husband Greg. Dani looked like she had not a care in the world—and why would she? She was not weighed down by the terrible knowledge that they couldn't have a baby. That was

Shannon's burden to bear, and she could not continue to bear it alone much longer. It was the secret weighing her down, not the approach of the wedding. Keeping a secret of such importance from her partner was like an albatross around her neck. It was choking her, and even now it was as though she were underwater and had to fight for air.

Panic rose cruelly in her throat. She didn't want to lose Dani. She didn't want to let their dreams slip through her fingers, but she didn't know how to stop the slow trickle that could easily turn into a rushing cascade if she were not careful. She looked to Amanda standing alone, leaning against a wall, an untouched glass of champagne clutched tightly in her hand. Claire stood a short distance away, a mirror image of Amanda. The two were the only ones who knew what she was dealing with, and Shannon walked toward their general direction. Maybe they could give her some solace. Or at least a momentary distraction.

She reached Amanda first and smiled. "It's great to see everyone, isn't it? Have you talked to Beth and Stan yet?" The older couple, long-time family friends, were Amanda's godparents.

"Yes, I talked to them earlier. They look great."

"And Joan. Oh, my God, did you hear her daughter's just been accepted at Yale?"

"Yes, she was only too happy to tell me all about it, ad nauseum."

"All right. Wanna tell me why you're so grumpy?"

"I'm not grumpy." She stared morosely into her champagne as though it might contain something toxic.

It was entirely possible that her niece was simply hung over from the party last night—the party where she seemed to have had such a good time. Or she was just suffering from a little letdown from all the excitement, but something was definitely bugging her. "I guess this little reception isn't quite as exciting as last night's party, eh?"

Amanda sighed impatiently. "The reception is fine."

Shannon regarded her niece curiously. Until this week, she'd never seen her so emotional—so out of sorts, so uncharacteristically up and down. Maybe it was the stress of school. Or money worries. Their heart-to-heart discussion had gone pretty smoothly. The failed marriage she was understandably sad about, but surely she'd made great strides in coming to terms with that by now. Unless it was being around a wedding celebration that was making her so sad.

"Will you tell me what's wrong?" she whispered urgently. Amanda cast such a doleful look that it nearly broke Shannon's heart. "Please? I want to help. Is it being around all this wedding stuff that's making you sad?"

"No, it's not the wedding. And there's nothing you can help me with, Aunt Shannon." With that uncompromising statement Amanda slunk away. She was being stubborn or cowardly, Shannon couldn't decide which. It hurt that Amanda would not confide in her now, especially when they seemed to have grown close again. She considered going after Amanda but decided against it. She had enough of her own issues to worry about at the moment, with not much emotional energy left to spare.

Claire, she realized then, had been furtively watching their little exchange. Maybe *she* had a clue about what was going on with Amanda. They seemed awfully close lately. Perhaps Claire was in a better position to help get Amanda out of her funk.

"Claire. Is there something going on around here that I don't know about?"

"What do you mean?"

Shannon's patience was beginning to fray. Why was everyone in such denial? Or were they trying to spare her from something? "Everyone's acting weird this week. You. Amanda. Jordan. Dani too, for that matter." She sighed irritably, remembering the credit card fiasco. "I guess I have to include myself in that analysis, but you know the reason why."

"I think it's normal for everyone to be a little on edge before a wedding. I wouldn't worry too much."

"Christ, it's supposed to be a happy time, yet everyone's acting like they have the weight of the world on their shoulders."

Claire shrugged but she wouldn't look at Shannon. "Okay,

I don't know then."

This was the polar opposite of the stalwart and wise Claire she'd come to rely on. Claire was always a source of sensibleness, of strength, of objective and intelligent reasoning. She was always the steady one, even in her grief, and being out of answers was simply not like her.

"Are you okay?"

Claire shrugged again. "Sure. Why wouldn't I be?"

Ah, the defensive rhetorical question. Well, Claire, you're obviously not all right, Shannon wanted to say, but she was not sure how deep she wanted to go with the subject. Her well for dealing with people's problems was pretty dry right now, as long as she and Dani had this mountain between them they had yet to scale. It occurred to her that Claire's angst was perhaps in some way tied to Amanda's, which was a troubling prospect. Either that or it was a coincidence that they were both wound up tight and having some sort of weird Mexican standoff, when just last night they seemed so happy and such good friends. She remembered them dancing together. Close together. Almost like two people who were dating. Or wanted to date. Okay, like two people who wanted to jump each other's bones. *Oh my God! No!*

"C-Claire," she stammered, "you two aren't . . . you know. Are you?" She knew her face showed her worry, maybe even her distaste. *Jesus, Claire and Amanda together would be incestuous, wouldn't it? And kinda gross. Hell, Amanda's my little Amanda, and Claire's my best friend . . . No, it couldn't be.* Her imagination was running away on her, making something out of nothing. She downed the rest of her champagne in one gulp, studying her best friend from behind the rim of her glass.

Claire's face slowly collapsed. Her eyes darted about as though she were a drowning person looking for a life preserver, and to Shannon it confirmed that there was indeed *something* going on between the two of them. Then Claire gathered herself, pulled on the mask. She was in control again, looking at Shannon like she was entirely on the wrong track.

Claire patted Shannon's arm reassuringly, dismissively.

"There's nothing for you to worry about. Everything's under control."

Okay, whatever. She was playing the doctor role with her, and Shannon was so *not* in the mood for that kind of officiousness. She retreated. If anything was going on between Claire and Amanda—and it was a huge *if*—she was not up to dealing with it now.

Shoving the disturbing thoughts to the far recesses of her mind, she sought out Dani, stepped beside her, and let her partner's arm slip protectively around her waist. She needed Dani's comfort, her solidness. She *needed* Dani. She would love this woman, always. They belonged together, whether they had ten babies or no babies, and there was no secret they could not wrestle into submission. She would fight for Dani and for their life together. She hoped Dani would do the same.

CHAPTER TWENTY-NINE

Claire

The sex had been mind blowing. Sensational. Delicious. Fantastic. Extraordinary. There simply weren't enough superlatives. Last night's dream had by far been the best sex dream Claire had ever had, and if sex were ever actually like it in real life, she'd never get out of bed. Job be damned and everything else. She'd commit her life to having as much sex as she could. With Amanda. And there lay the problem—Amanda had been the star of her explosive wet dream.

Much as she wanted to, it was impossible to completely ignore Amanda tonight—it was the wedding rehearsal after all—but she rationed herself from looking at her too often or from acting with anything more than appropriate politeness. Moderation was the key. Like little sips of wine, she would only look briefly and intermittently at Amanda, because being in the same room with her brought the dream storming back, blazing a fiery trail through her body all over again, quickening her pulse, making her sweat, giving her that tingly sensation in the pit of her stomach. It was overload. *Damn dream anyway. Jesus, am I fifteen years old or what?*

The kiss had been the culprit. And the fact that it happened to be the best kiss Claire'd ever had. Not surprising that it had filtered into her dream afterward. Filtered in and taken over, pushing her mind into new territory, with a beautiful, naked Amanda doing impossibly sensual things to her with her hands and her mouth. She'd awakened sometime in the early morning, incredibly turned on, unable and unwilling to banish the dream. She finished herself off, willingly conjuring up images of Amanda and what Amanda could do to her. Using Amanda in this way to satisfy herself was far worse than the unwanted innocent dream. She selfishly made Fantasy Amanda do all the things she ached to have done to her, until she attained an explosive orgasm. Like paint peeling off a wall, the orgasm ripped her insides into blissful shreds.

The room was closing in on Claire and she needed to escape. She walked to the hotel's indoor lion sanctuary a short distance away, her breath coming quickly as if she'd sprinted there instead of walked. People lined the thick glass walls, watching and pointing at the majestic golden creatures lounging on the fake rocks, and the anonymity of the crowd was Claire's sanctuary. She liked the female lions. Or lionesses, she supposed. They were hunters, so graceful and sleek, built for stealth and strength. But as fascinating as they were to watch, nothing could stop her from thinking about last night's dream and the kiss that had preceded it.

Kissing Amanda had been a selfish thing to do, and if she could take that kiss back, she would. The fact that it would have been impossible to stop it was not something she was willing to accept. She was in a mood to punish herself. Of course she and Amanda were attracted to one another. So what? Attractions happened between people all the time. It didn't mean you had to act on them. To throw your life all to hell because of an impulse. She was stronger than that. Better than that. She *would* be better than that.

"Hey."

The soft voice at her side shocked her into the present. It was Amanda.

Claire swallowed, her pulse kicking into high gear again. "Hi."

"We should talk."

No, no we shouldn't. "Why?"

"Because we can't leave things like they are."

There was only another day to get through—the wedding day—and then this whole week would be over. She wanted to plead with Amanda to let it go, to leave things alone. But the young woman had that solemn, galvanized look in her eyes, like she wasn't letting anything go until it was resolved. And resolved now. *Shit.*

Claire sighed and reluctantly gave in to the inevitable, gazing at the lions as she spoke softly. "We shouldn't have kissed."

"Why not?"

"Because it was wrong."

"Why?" Amanda pleaded impatiently. "Why was it wrong? We're both adults. Single adults who don't have to answer to anyone. We're allowed to make our own choices, Claire."

"There's more to it than that." She looked at Amanda and saw fresh tears in the corners of her eyes. She wanted to soften the blow but didn't know how. "You're twenty-one years younger than me. It would never work."

Amanda laughed acidly. "Please. So what if you grew up in an era of rotary telephones and typewriters, and I didn't. What the hell does that honestly have to do with anything?"

"It's more than being from two different eras. Jesus, Amanda, you don't know what it's like to wake up with stiff knees every day. Or to forget something and wonder if that's the start of—of getting old and forgetful. Or to feel like your best years are behind you and that you're too old to start over. You have no idea how *any* of that feels."

"There's a lot of things I don't have firsthand knowledge of. So what? Aren't there more important things than worrying about our differences? Like how we connect. How we communicate. How we *feel* when we're together. Don't those things count for anything?"

"Of course they do, but do you think I want you taking care of me someday when you're still in your prime?" That was the crux of it all. She'd had to take care of Ann in her dying months, even though Ann was only four years older. Claire knew what it was like to give every ounce of yourself physically and emotionally to someone who was ill, and she did not want to put Amanda or anyone else through that. "There's more," she said in a quavering voice, "than just the present to think about."

"Oh, Claire." Amanda moved closer, clutched Claire's hand protectively. "I think you're getting way ahead of yourself, okay?"

Ahead of herself or not, it was called life. It was called being responsible, selfless, practical. Of course, Amanda was too young and optimistic to think of dark things like illness and old age, but Claire had seen those things before. Had *lived* them. She shook her head, momentarily unable to speak.

"I just want us to have some time to explore our feelings without fear," Amanda whispered pleadingly. "We can go slow. As slow as you want."

"No, it's impossible," she answered forcefully. "For one thing, Shannon would never understand or approve."

"Shannon wants me to be happy. And she wants you to be happy too."

"Yeah, but not with each other."

"How do you know?"

Christ, was this nightmare never going to end? "Because I know her and she wouldn't. Why can't you take no for an answer?"

"Because in this case, no doesn't make any sense to me. It's all based on fear."

Fear! What the hell did Amanda know about fear? She hadn't seen death in her lover's eyes. She hadn't faced the prospect of a lifetime alone. No. Amanda had no right to be so judgmental, to take things so lightly, like it was a simple math problem that could be solved. "All right, then how about this. I've had my kick at the can. I've had my happily-ever-after. It's over now. That's it for me."

Disbelief was written all over Amanda's face. "So you're just going to give up on life?"

Cranky and pushed to her limit, Claire dug in her heels. "Maybe I am."

The tears that had threatened earlier rushed down Amanda's cheeks. Claire hated hurting her like this. But maybe it was better to hurt her now rather than later, when they were more invested.

"I'm sorry," was all Claire could manage, knowing the words were hollow and useless, but needed to be said anyway. The only thing to be thankful for was that they'd only had sex in her dreams.

Without a word, Amanda turned and dissolved into the crowd. Claire watched her disappear. Knowing she'd done the right thing was poor consolation at the moment.

CHAPTER THIRTY

Dani

Shannon had been clearly preoccupied throughout the rehearsal, and it worried Dani. Three times she'd had to be reminded of the lines to their vows, when Dani knew for a fact she'd committed them to memory. They both had.

In their room, their obligations for the evening finally over, Dani joined her on the sofa. She took a deep breath, then tentatively took Shannon's hand. "What's wrong, love?"

"Wrong? What do you mean?"

She wasn't fooling Dani. There was panic in her eyes. And something grave. No, it wasn't about florists delivering the wrong flowers or the rings getting lost or some other wedding detail gone awry. Dani's stomach tightened. Had she found out she'd lost her job? Had Heather let it slip?

She wanted to know and yet didn't want to know what was troubling Shannon. She was scared, but Shannon looked downright miserable. If this was finally going to be the epic unveiling of her secret, then so be it. It was the right thing to do anyway—clearing the air before the wedding. And if it meant there was not going to be a wedding tomorrow . . . *Shit*. With all her being, Dani did not want that to happen. They couldn't turn back now. Everything was bought and paid for, the guests were all here and eagerly anticipating the wedding. They were locked and loaded, and all that was left was to pull the trigger on this thing and get married. As a business executive, Dani's job was all about guiding projects to their fruition. For a project to die on the vine—a project that had been heavily invested in—was disaster. No. Whatever the consequences of this long overdue talk, it could *not* be the cancellation of the wedding. That was her bottom line. She'd already suffered the indignity of losing her job; she would not suffer the indignity of being stood up at the altar.

Dani licked her lips, swallowed her fear. "We can talk about anything, I promise."

Shannon looked so tortured that Dani immediately wrapped her in a tight hug. Something was horribly wrong and horribly frightening. It couldn't be the job thing. This was something much bigger. Oh God, Dani thought, trying hard not to let her panic show.

"Are you sick?" she finally blurted out.

"Not exactly," Shannon whimpered into her shoulder.

"What do you mean? What's wrong?"

It took another minute or two, during which Dani thought she might die from the stress of the situation, before Shannon pulled away and looked tearfully into her eyes. "I'm so sorry, sweetheart."

Oh God, this must be bad! She swallowed hard. "So sorry for what? For God's sake, take a deep breath and just tell me, okay?"

"There's something I should have told you a few weeks ago. I know I should have, and there really is no excuse, but—"

Dani tuned out her partner's ramblings, a little relieved that whatever this secret was, it had nothing to do with her jobless state. It was something Shannon hadn't told her; something about Shannon. And now she was talking about doctors and tests. "What? Is there something wrong with you?"

Shannon nodded, sobbed a few more tears. "A baby. I can't have a baby."

"You can't what?"

"I'm so sorry Dani. I've had every test possible and they all come back the same. I'm infertile. There's no possibility of a baby."

The words crackled in the air. Dani's lungs were on fire. She couldn't breathe, couldn't talk, couldn't even cry. Her dream had just been snatched away, and she had not even seen the thief creeping up on it. She sank back into the sofa, stunned, scared. Having a baby, something they'd discussed for three years, had seemed like fruit dangling from a tree just beyond their reach but there for the taking whenever they were ready. Like buying a house or a car or planning a vacation, they'd taken it for granted, as though it were their right to have a baby whenever they chose to. They were ready now. And yet the decision had been taken out of their hands. No amount of money or negotiation or praying was going to change it.

Dani began to cry into her hands. It was another grave, soul-destroying disappointment. Parenthood was something she would never have now, never accomplish, the way her parents and siblings had so easily done. Her hysterectomy a few years ago hadn't entirely snuffed out her hopes for a baby, because she was so sure Shannon would be able to bear children. They'd not been in a hurry because they had wanted to buy a house, be financially secure first. Even with Dani's job down the drain, Shannon's biological clock was ticking and they could not put it off any longer. But they *had* put it off too long, and now the window was closed.

Shannon put her arm around her and pulled her close. They cried together. For the moment, Dani was too numb to be angry. Anger would come, it would rush into the void that was in her soul, but not yet. Right now she wanted to feel sorry for herself, wanted to beat herself up a little. *You're not good enough to be a parent.* Smack! *You're a loser. No job, no baby.* Smack! *You can't do anything right.* Smack!

"Please say something," Shannon finally said. "You can be angry at me, I deserve it."

"I'm not angry with you."

"I should have at least told you sooner."

"Yes, you should have." Dani's anger threatened to burble up and she had to bite down on the inside of her cheek to stop it. How could she condemn Shannon for keeping a secret, when she too had been keeping one?

"I didn't want to ruin the wedding. I didn't want to crush your hopes."

"I know." And Dani did know. They were the same reasons why she'd kept her own secret. Each of them had been shouldering such a heavy burden when they should have been there for one another, sharing the load. "Shit." This was a hell of a way to start their marriage.

"I'll understand if you want to, you know . . ." Shannon sniffled, still teary, unable to say the words.

"If I want to what?"

"You know, postpone things."

Postpone the wedding? Panic and disbelief gripped her. "Is that what you want?"

Shannon's eyes flashed wide. "No! Of course not."

Calm down, she commanded herself. There was not going to be a wedding postponement or any high drama tomorrow. Unless Shannon couldn't forgive her for losing her job and not telling her about it. There was still that little matter to clear up. *Oh, well. What the hell!* She was all in, the cards dealt. Go big or go bust, those were her choices now. "There's something I need to tell you too."

"Okay." Shannon looked relieved to have the attention shift away from her.

"You're going to be mad at me for this."

"I am? Oh God, what did you do?"

"Who said I did anything?"

Shannon's face paled. "You didn't have an affair, did you?"

"What? That's a hell of a thing to say!"

"Shit. Sorry. But I mean, what am I supposed to think when you tell me I'm going to be mad at you?"

"Well, it sure as hell wasn't having an affair! Jesus, give me some credit, would you?"

"Okay, okay, I'm sorry."

Dani pouted as Shannon took her hand and soothed her with affection and reassurance. Dani was being petulant, feeling far less than perfect. But at least she'd never had an affair, and so she clung to that with righteous indignation. "You know I would never do anything like that to you for God's sake."

"I know, I know. I didn't mean it, it just came out. Please tell me what's going on."

It was so damned hard admitting her failure to the person she loved the most, the person whose respect and trust she most desired. But the moment was here, they were both raw and open from Shannon's news, and she could not go back now. "I lost my job."

"You what?"

Was she really going to have to repeat it? "For Christ's sake, you heard what I said!"

Shannon's mouth dropped open and her cheeks flared red like she'd been slapped. "Oh my God, you lost your job?"

"Do you want me to shout it down the hall? YES, DANI BERRINGER IS UNEMPLOYED!"

"Jesus, honey, don't get pissed off at me! I'm just trying to process this!"

Dani took deep gulps of air, like a drowning person bobbing in the water. "I'm sorry. I didn't mean to yell. Christ."

"When did this happen?"

"Seven weeks ago. With the economic downturn, they decided they had too many managers and they let me go."

Shannon tried to hide her shock but not well enough. Dani could see it wasn't easy for her. She looked like she was trying to catch falling snowflakes, except that they were falling faster than she could collect them. "God, what are we going to do?"

"I've been looking for another job, but managers and lower level executives are a dime a dozen right now. We'll be okay for a few months, then . . . I don't know. We'll cross that bridge when we come to it."

"Why didn't you tell me about this when it happened?" Shannon's words stung, even though her tone wasn't critical.

"I guess for the same reasons you didn't tell me about the baby. I didn't want to hurt you. I didn't want you to worry. I just wanted to get through this damned wedding and then deal with it."

Shannon scrubbed at her cheeks worriedly. "We didn't need to have such a lavish wedding. We could have changed it, canceled it. *Something*."

"I know, but I always wanted a fancy wedding, you know that. It was so close, and we couldn't have gotten our money back on most of it anyway."

"Shit, Dani. Being together is what's important, not a lavish wedding. I never wanted any of this."

"Well I did, okay? You can blame it on me, spending money like a drunken sailor, as usual. It was me being irresponsible with money." They'd had this same argument many times before, with Dani always promising to cut back on her spending. Well, now she would finally be forced to, and so the argument was moot.

"Honey, I don't want to fight. Please. It's the last thing we need."

Dani closed her eyes and felt the sting of exhaustion and sorrow behind her eyelids. Everything was up in smoke, it seemed. Their entire future was being rewritten, authored by circumstance and not choice. Somehow, they were going to have to pick their way through this new landscape. The first thing she was going to have to come to terms with was her pride. *Stupid, stupid pride*! She could see now how it had cost her. By keeping her job loss from Shannon, she had sacrificed Shannon's trust, love and support in order for this lavish wedding to go ahead. That same overblown pride of hers was partly responsible for Shannon keeping her own secret, because Shannon hadn't wanted to crush her hopes, hadn't wanted to ruin the wedding for Dani's sake. And that was the thing. So much of what they'd done the last few years revolved around what Dani wanted, around Dani's moods. Moving downtown, living lavishly, having a stay-at-home wife, a baby. Somehow it had all become about Dani needing to prove things to people. Well, that shit was going to have to change. And now!

Dani threw her head back against the sofa and stared at the ceiling. It was going to be a long damned night. And there were going to be more tears.

CHAPTER THIRTY-ONE

Shannon

Thank God for makeup, because Shannon knew she looked like hell. Staying up most of the night had ravaged her. So had shedding the emotional load they'd both been carrying around for weeks. The weariness in her face and body was a small price to pay for her new sense of freedom and the relief. They would work this out, *were* working it out, still had one another. They were bonded together for better or worse, stronger than ever. And while their problems were a long way from being solved, at least they were tackling them together now. She shot a wink at Dani, her rock, who stood at her side, holding her hand and smiling at her.

It was with this newfound lightness in her step that she waited with her betrothed to make their grand entrance into the small chapel. They had chosen a nontraditional walk up the aisle, side by side, and they would dance, not walk. No one was giving them away. They were giving themselves to each other and entering this marriage together, happily. Yes, breaking tradition, breaking free from the shackles of customs and expectations was the perfect way to start off their marriage. Queen's "You're My Best Friend" was blasting through the speakers. She'd already glimpsed Amanda, Heather, Claire and Jordan each dance their way up the aisle. Now it was their turn.

She appraised Dani in her black tux—handsome and strong, a little worse for lack of sleep like herself, but she was happy. Dani winked back at her, squeezed her hand, and they grinned stupidly at one another, as if to say, *wow, are we really doing this? Did we really make it through the rainstorm of tears together?* Yes they were and they did, and it felt absolutely right.

They shoved open the double doors to the hotel's small chapel, waited until all eyes were on them like a spotlight. Hand in hand, they started down the aisle, dancing and twirling one another as the song rolled over them and carried them joyously to the altar, as if on a wave. Dani dipped her at their destination and Shannon, in her flowing white bridal gown, laughed and curtseyed at her handsome tuxedoed bride. Their guests clapped their approval. The wedding officiant, who was nondenominational, waited for the commotion to die down before she smiled indulgently at them.

"We are gathered today, friends and loved ones, to celebrate the union of Danielle Berringer and Shannon McCarthy. And while their union may not *yet* be legal in most of our country—and I emphasize the word yet—their love, their commitment, and their pride in that love and commitment is no less profound or meaningful than a husband and a wife's. If anything, their willingness to overcome the obstacles of joining in marriage only signifies that they are perhaps more committed and more earnest in their love than most."

The words and the audience's applause swelled Shannon's heart. She loved the fact that they were pioneers in this relatively new territory of gay marriage. They were at the forefront of history in the making, helping draw maps in this uncharted territory, and it was thrilling to be a part of it.

The officiant faced Dani first. "Repeat after me. I, Danielle Berringer, take you, Shannon McCarthy."

Dani repeated the words, staring deeply into Shannon's eyes. There was a little nervous twitch to her mouth, but her gaze exuded love and confidence.

"To be my wife, my best friend, my partner, my lover, to love and cherish and help you in any way I can. To forsake all others and to be faithful and loyal only to you, for as long as we both shall live."

Dani repeated the words, then took the ring from Jordan that she would place on Shannon's finger. Her hand shook a little but her voice was sure as she said, "Let this ring represent my love for you, for it has no beginning and no end. Let this ring always be a reminder to you that I am at your side, always, through all our trials and victories, and through our everyday lives, no matter what life brings us. As long as we wear these rings, my love, we will be joined through time, forever, a circle with no beginning and no end."

She slipped the ring onto Shannon's finger, and Shannon had to wipe the tear that had crested and begun to slither down her cheek. She couldn't find her voice for a moment. If she could give the timeout signal she would have, but instead she cleared her throat and smiled through her tears, finding her strength and forging on.

"I, Shannon McCarthy, take you, Danielle Berringer, to be my wife, my best friend, my partner, my lover, to love and cherish and help you in any way I can. To forsake all others and to be faithful and loyal only to you, for as long as we both shall live."

She retrieved the ring from Claire, who first pretended to search her tuxedo pockets desperately. It gave Shannon a much-needed laugh.

"This ring is the symbol of all my love and strength, my faith in you and in us, and my loyalty to you, always. This ring is the unbroken circle of my love for you." She slipped it on Dani's finger, watching the emotions dance in her eyes. She'd never felt closer to Dani, couldn't believe now that they'd each kept such an important secret from one another, couldn't believe they'd not shown more trust in themselves and in each other than that. She would never let it happen again.

The officiant smiled her permission. "Dani and Shannon, you may each kiss your bride."

Dani scooped her up, lifting her off her feet a few inches and kissed her long and hard, even playfully giving her a little tongue action. The guests whooped and hollered and whistled, and it was the most romantic kiss they'd ever shared—at least in public. When the kiss ended and they hugged tightly, Shannon whispered, "I promise I will *never* keep a secret from you again."

"Neither will I, my love. Neither will I."

"Deal." Shannon kissed her again, and when they turned to face the audience, everyone was standing and applauding.

This time the two walked slowly down the aisle to Jack Johnson's "Better Together," high-fiving as they walked arm in arm. Jordan and Heather followed, then Claire and Amanda. Jordan and Claire, the brides' two best women, wore matching black tuxedoes with pale Easter yellow bow ties and matching cummerbunds. Amanda and Heather wore knee-length tight dresses in matching yellow satin that showed off slim shoulders and sexy cleavage. They'd had a meeting and decided to pair up according to their personalities and dress, agreeing it would be too weird to see Claire and Jordan walk arm in arm together down the aisle in their tuxes and straight-backed, soft butch demeanors.

The hotel had weddings down to a science, even providing a small studio room for professional photos. While the guests retreated to a private ballroom for cocktails, the wedding party gathered for pictures. Thank God Jordan had thought to sneak in a bottle of champagne for the photo session; it would provide some much-needed lubrication.

"Jesus, I can't wait to loosen this tie," Dani complained, making like she was going to rip it off before the photos had begun.

"Don't you dare," Shannon scolded.

"I feel like a penguin."

"Me too," Jordan whined.

Claire, imperturbable as usual, seemed to be enjoying the dress code. She smiled as if to say, *What's the problem?* "You two have never looked so good, and you probably never will again, so enjoy it."

Shannon winked at her best friend, then stood on her toes to kiss Claire's cheek. It was fun to see her dressed up and finally, *finally* looking happy to be here. Whatever had been bothering her off and on all week, she seemed to have put it behind her. "You look gorgeous, my friend."

"Oh no, *you* look gorgeous! In fact, you look happier than you've looked in a long time."

"I am. Happy and so relieved and grateful for what I have."

"Good. I knew it would turn out okay."

"Do you always have to be so smart?"

Claire laughed. "What can I say. Some days I forget to take my stupid pills."

Shannon glanced in Amanda's direction. She looked tight, worried. Or maybe sad. She was such an enigma this week—happy, miserable, happy, then miserable again. "Do me a favor tonight, will you Claire?"

"Of course. Anything."

"Look after my niece."

Claire's face registered surprise. "What do you mean?"

She didn't know exactly. The words had slipped out, but they seemed appropriate. "I guess . . . I don't know. She seems a little lost to me, a little adrift. And you're always such a compass."

"No, not always. Did you forget I've been a little lost myself the last few years?"

"True, but you're a survivor. You're the most sensible, grounded, nicest, smartest, most caring woman I know. Besides my wife, of course. I like that you and Amanda are friends, but sometimes . . ." She shook her head and tried to ignore the alarm in Claire's eyes.

The two of them confused her. They seemed so close at times, other times distant or even a little pissed off at one another.

Always there was a definite spark between them, a vat full of chemistry, an unending well of emotion that neither seemed willing or able to quite bring to the surface. Well, whatever was between them, she really didn't want to examine it too closely right now. In truth, it made her uncomfortable and yet she couldn't deny it comforted her too that they should find some kind of deep friendship together. "Look, never mind. Just have some fun tonight, okay? Both of you. And that's an order."

"Yes ma'am. As your best woman, I'm beholden to follow your wishes today."

Shannon raised her eyebrows for effect but let the subject drop. They got into their poses, hamming it up, but serious too. They all looked so beautiful and vital, she wished she could freeze-frame this moment.

The champagne fountain was a huge hit. It stood eight feet high, and the champagne, lit from below by blue and red flickering lights, cascaded down in narrow waterfalls so that guests could simply slip their glass under them for a refill. Dinner, grilled salmon in cranberry sauce, was exquisite, or at least Shannon supposed so. She and Dani were interrupted so often by clanging utensils demanding a newlywed kiss that they hardly consumed any food before it was whisked away and the speeches began.

Jordan was her usual funny and sarcastic self, but tasteful, thank God, in recounting some ancient stories about Dani and about Dani and Shannon's early dating days. Everyone laughed when Jordan told them how Dani had called and asked to borrow some Gravol before her first date with Shannon, she was so nervous. And then it was a whole package of Gravol before she popped the question. Jordan said since they'd become a couple, Dani had never even glanced once at another woman. "I was such a good friend," Jordan joked, "that I even took up the slack for her! I mean, hey, isn't that what friends are for?" When the laughter died down, she looked at Dani, uncharacteristic tears in her eyes. Her voice cracked with emotion. "Seriously, buddy, I am so jealous of you, you have no idea. Some of us never find our soul mate. The road to nowhere simply runs out eventually after a million detours. And some of us do find our soul mate but the timing's all wrong. Kinda like hitting a road temporarily closed sign. But you . . . you hit the expressway to love. Happy journeys, you two."

Claire was next. Ever serious, she spoke eloquently about her long friendship with Shannon, about how Shannon had helped her through the toughest time in her life. She knew very well the gifts Shannon had to give, she said, and that made Dani a very lucky woman. Shannon felt herself blush a little as Claire described her attributes. "You've got the big things covered, you two, but don't forget the little things. Don't forget to say I love you every day, don't forget to say you're sorry, and no matter how tough times may get, don't forget to laugh with one another. Smell the roses when you can, because it matters. Enjoy one another every day, because being with the one you love matters more than anything in the world."

They toasted one another, and Shannon reached over and gave Claire's hand a squeeze. It couldn't have been easy for her; her thoughts were surely on Ann tonight. She'd never been able to have a wedding with Ann, their time together far too short. With luck, maybe one day Claire would find someone else to grow old with. She wanted that for Claire, so much.

Dani rose and took hold of the microphone. "Today, I am truly the happiest woman in the world. I thought I was on the day she said yes, but I was wrong. *Today* is the happiest day of my life." She blew a kiss at Shannon. "You know, since I popped the question eight months ago, I couldn't wait for this wedding. I wanted it to happen right away, like the day after she said yes. But I'm so glad it didn't, because I didn't realize until last night that I wasn't ready before."

She paused to collect herself, her voice tremulous. "I've learned some valuable lessons in the last twenty-four hours. Lessons that I know will make me a better person and a better partner. I learned that dreams don't die, they simply change because sometimes they have to. But you roll with it, you go forward, you adapt, you learn to make your way across the new terrain, because you have to. If you don't—if you cling to the past—your future is doomed. I know that now. But I also know that I'm lucky enough to have a partner by my side, and that I will never *ever* take that for granted." She raised her glass to Shannon. "To my beautiful bride, whose love keeps me strong and keeps me going forward. You're the wind beneath my wings. I love you."

Shannon stood, smiling through her tears, and kissed Dani. It was her turn now. She would keep it short because if she didn't, she'd end up blubbering her way through it. She thanked the guests for coming, thanked the wedding party for being so supportive and generous with their time. "But you're not off the hook after tonight," she said pointedly to Claire, Jordan, Heather and Amanda. "I'm afraid your duties continue for the rest of your lives. If Dani and I ever have a day where we're angry or upset with one another, or where we take one another for granted, or mistreat each other, I'm counting on all of you to tell us we're being stupid and to smarten up."

The four laughed and eagerly nodded their agreement.

"Good. You didn't realize you were signing a lifetime contract, did you?" Her gaze shifted to Dani. "To my partner, who has more strength and more goodness than she realizes. Luckily, I plan on reminding her every day! Dani, you are the love of my life, the person I want to grow old with, the woman who gives everything in my life meaning. Thank you for sharing the best and most rewarding years of my life with me. I love you so much."

They kissed for the millionth time today, wiped tears from each other's cheeks. When Dani took the microphone for a second time, it was to proclaim that the party was on.

Jordan, acting as emcee, cued the deejay to start the song for the bridal dance. There was a long pause, a glitch the deejay seemed befuddled about. Jordan stormed over to the deejay's corner, ready, no doubt, to give her hell. Finally, the first bars of their wedding song, "I'll Stand By You" began, but it was a karaoke version and not The Pretenders, as they'd requested.

What the hell?

CHAPTER THIRTY-TWO

Jordan

There was a hush in the room, a quiet ascendency, as though the pinnacle of some moment was about to be reached, but all Jordan wanted to do was throttle the deejay for screwing up the song. Just as she reached the deejay, a voice—deep, resonant, familiar, the kind that made your toes curl—faded in, singing the words, sending chills up and down her spine. Dez! Desperately, she scanned the darkened room. *Where is she, dammit?* The voice grew stronger; she was getting closer. And then she saw her, gliding toward the front of the room, a cordless mic in her hand. She was belting out the words now, and Jordan had an uncontrollable compulsion to cry.

God, she's beautiful. She was of course, but when she sang, she glowed with a joy that was ethereal, palpable. Even in the darkened room it was as though there were a spotlight on her, lighting her and magnifying her joy of singing, so that the light shone over everyone. Whatever that mesmerizing quality was—star power, charisma, magic fairy dust—Dez had it in spades. Dani and Shannon were the only ones immune, dancing together in their own little newly married world, but Jordan felt dizzy. She couldn't believe Dez had come after all. Was she here for her sake? Had the Ella tickets done the trick? She swallowed, nervous as hell, wanting to faint or escape somehow, and yet she would not have left the room for anything in the world.

The rest of the wedding party was being signaled to get out on the dance floor. Claire and Amanda began dancing, looking like an old married couple themselves, two-stepping in perfect time together. Heather beckoned her onto the floor. Reluctantly she followed, commanding her feet to move, nearly tripping along the way. She could not take her eyes off Dez and went through the cardboard motions of dancing with Heather.

The next song was Taylor Dayne's "I'll Always Love You." Yes, how perfect, Jordan thought. She wondered if Dez had any idea of the power she held over her, Dez the sun with the planet Jordan revolving around it. Magnetic, paralyzing, but oh, so sweet was the pull. As she watched Dani and Shannon hold each other close, she finally understood what it meant to *need* someone, to open up your entire being, to give up everything and yet gain everything at the same time. To be a part of something so much bigger. Sure it was scary, but at least she understood it now instead of wanting to heap scorn on it. No. She wanted to love Dez, wanted Dez to love her too, to give her a chance to show that she was capable of it. Worthy too. And she would not be afraid, she resolved. She was ready for this awesome, defining step.

The song ended. The deejay switched to some eighties dance music—Blondie—and Jordan made a beeline for Dez. She would not let this opportunity slip by. It was time she went after what she wanted, go in for the kill like closing a business deal. And it was the biggest deal of her life.

"Dez. You came." She tried to smile but found she was too nervous.

Dez looked equally nervous. Jordan hadn't been expecting

that. "Yes. I—Can we talk somewhere?"

Without a word Jordan took her hand and led her out of the ballroom. Silently they rode the elevator up to Jordan's room. If Dez was going to tell her to piss off for good, she wanted her heart broken in private.

"Something to drink?" Jordan asked, not sure where to start. She needed to calm her nerves.

"Do you have any wine?"

Jordan produced a bottle of merlot and proceeded to open it. She was so nervous, she felt like a kid on the first day of school, or maybe more like a teenager on a first date. Hard to believe— the slick playgirl and hotshot real estate agent who was trembling so badly that she could not open a damned bottle of wine.

Dez's warm hand fell on top of hers and gently she took the corkscrew from Jordan. "Careful with that thing or you're going to hurt yourself."

Jordan smiled dumbly and let Dez open the wine and pour them each a glass. She blinked, finding it hard to believe Dez was actually in her room with her. Alone with her. She fought the sudden urge to cry, or at the very least, to fall on her knees and give thanks. "I didn't think I'd see you again."

Dez closed her eyes, her face crumpling beneath a sledge-hammer of emotions. "Me either."

Jordan sipped her wine, took her time, forced herself to stay calm when all she really wanted to do was throw herself at Dez's feet. She had no pride to swallow when it came to this woman. "So what happened to us?"

Their glasses of wine were consumed in silence before Dez spoke. "You know, I have the original album from that concert."

"What concert?"

"Ella. The autographed tickets you gave me. Carnegie Hall, July 5, 1973, part of the Newport Jazz Festival. They made a live album out of the concert. I was just a kid then, of course. I didn't buy the album until much later."

Jordan let her ramble animatedly about her admiration for Ella Fitzgerald. Dez was obviously buying time, maybe sorting out her thoughts. But Jordan was in a hurry for the truth, whatever that might be. Was Dez going to dump her again? Give her the let's-be-friends speech? Or dare she hope for something more? She threw off her uncomfortable bow tie and opened the top two buttons of her tux shirt, impatient to close this deal. "You killed me the other night, you know. When you dumped me."

Dez nodded, clamped her eyes shut. "I know."

"I thought things were going so well between us. I thought we really liked each other. I thought . . . hell, I don't know. I really thought something good—no, great—was happening between us. And I thought you felt it too."

Dez opened her eyes slowly. There was fear there, and it was not what Jordan had expected to see. She moved closer to Dez on the sofa, placed her hand carefully over hers. "Tell me what you're so damned scared of. I want to help you, Dez. I want to help us. I want to work this out. I'm not a horrible person and I'm not going to hurt you. Ever. My God, don't you know what you've done to me?"

"I didn't want this to happen," Dez answered softly.

"Didn't want what to happen?"

"To fall in love with you." She pulled her hand away and scrubbed her eyes, but all Jordan could think was, *Hallelujah! Dez loves me.*

"I was so mad at myself for taking you home with me that night," Dez continued. "For sleeping with you. For falling for you. I knew better and yet I couldn't help myself."

"Why is it such a terrible thing? I don't understand." To Jordan it was beautiful, two people falling in love. Why was that so wrong? "Did someone you love hurt you? Is that why?"

"Please." Dez's laughter was as blunt as a hammer. "I'm not some twenty-year-old who's had her heart broken. I've been around, okay?"

Okay, I deserved that, Jordan admonished herself. Dez was not some fragile, virginal young woman, frightened that the big bad Jordan Scott was going to tear her heart to shreds. "What then?"

"You want the truth?"

"Yes."

"Okay, fine." She spoke in a tone that said, *You might be sorry you asked.* "It was a while ago. The mid-nineties. I'd had a couple of top five hits. I was packing the concert halls, I was all over the radio, the clubs, made some TV appearances. I couldn't miss. I was twenty-nine years old and I'd finally made it. Had everything I'd ever dreamed of. All the work finally paid off—singing at weddings, summer fairs, crappy bars, private parties, paying out of my own pocket to cut CDs. Begging people in the business to work with me. I'd finally made it. People *dug* my music. They wanted me, and I was making a good buck."

"Sounds perfect."

Dez went for the half-bottle of wine and refilled their glasses. "My agent talked me into moving to New York. You know . . . if you can make it there . . ."

"You can make it anywhere."

"Exactly. So I thought, why not? The pop and dance music was paying the freight, but I wanted to get into jazz, blues, soul music—the stuff I grew up with. I could remake myself in the Big Apple, stretch myself. I started playing some cool clubs, making the right connections, cut a couple of albums I was pretty proud of—not chart-toppers, but it was the kind of music *I* wanted to do. I didn't really care that much about the fame and the money, except that they allowed me the freedom to do the kind of music I really wanted to do."

"Sounds like you got exactly what you wanted."

"Yes and no. There was always pressure. My record company wanted the chart-toppers, so did my managers. People couldn't make money off my ass if I kept playing the small clubs and cutting records nobody bought. It was a constant fight." She sighed loudly, her shoulders slumped. "I made some mistakes. Big mistakes. Started drinking a lot. Got into coke. It was so easy—somebody was always handing you something. People would do anything to be your so-called friend."

"I'm no angel myself, you know. I understand. Better than

you might think." Jordan had spent too much time with the bottle occasionally, had even done her share of coke and weed in her younger days.

"I'm sorry but it's not a contest, okay? I'm not trying to compare our misdeeds and I'm not looking for sympathy or understanding. I'm trying to explain."

Ouch! "All right."

"Sorry I bit your head off," Dez mumbled. "I don't—"

"It's okay. Please. Tell me the rest."

"I stumbled through a few years like this in New York. There were women too—lots of women, faces I don't even remember."

Jordan knew about that too, but she kept her mouth closed.

"One night—it was May 3, 2001. I picked up this woman, Tammy, in a bar after I'd done a show and went home with her. She was bad news, I knew that, but I wasn't very discriminating back then. I knew she'd do some drugs with me, we'd have a good time for a couple of days. She was exactly the kind of woman I'd pick up—it's not like they'd ever go to the press or to anyone that mattered with stories about what we'd done together. Who would believe them? They had no credibility, so they were safe. In that sense, anyway."

A growing knot formed in Jordan's stomach. "Go on."

"We drank vodka, snorted coke, had some forgettable sex. Then we smoked some heroin—her drug of choice, not mine. I fell asleep. When I woke up I found her dead."

"Oh my God. That's terrible."

"I panicked. Ran out, called my agent. He cleaned up my mess, but it scared the living hell out of me. I went into rehab, then I went underground. Spent a year back home in Georgia. Couch surfed after that with friends in California. I had to start over again, my career was trashed. People in the business knew I was damaged goods, and this was before the Lindsay Lohan era of third and fourth chances. I played small gigs, wrote songs, made money singing backup vocals for people like Madonna, Cher. It was Cher who helped get me this offer to open in Vegas a few months ago for Smokey. I've been very careful in the years since." She held her hands out, palms up in surrender. "So. That's what happened to the great Dez Adams."

"Wow, rough ride. I'm so sorry. I had no idea, but I knew from the minute I met you that you were a survivor. I could tell."

"What happened to that girl Tammy could have happened to me too. If I hadn't made the changes I did—rehab, getting the hell out of New York . . ." She shook her head. "I almost destroyed myself there."

"Thank you for sharing this with me, Dez." Jordan took her hand and gave it a squeeze. It was a sad story with a happy ending, but she was still puzzled. "What made you run away from me?"

"Confusion. I don't know. Before you, I hadn't spent a night with a stranger since 2001."

"You were afraid I was going to get you into drugs again?"

"Maybe. I don't do risky behavior anymore for exactly that reason—any kind of risky behavior. I don't go to parties, I don't pick up strangers. I drink modestly now, but no drugs stronger than aspirin. I was upset with myself for bringing you to my room for a one-night stand, even though I was—am—incredibly attracted to you."

"But I'm not a druggie, surely you realized that after we began spending time together. I wasn't going to pull you into that world." Dez's reasons for dumping her still weren't making a lot of sense.

"I did realize that. I could see that you were a woman of substance, but I was afraid of starting this risky behavior again, doing one-night stands, that kind of thing. It's like when a recovering drug addict takes a pain pill. Just one little itty-bitty pain pill. It's not like it's coke or heroin, right? So how bad can one little pill be? It isn't bad, except it can start you down a road that you don't want to visit again. With you, at first, I was afraid of that. And then . . . ."

"And then the fear became something else?"

"Yes. I realized how lovely you are, Jordan. How special you are, how much I wanted to be with you." Her eyes began to moisten and her voice grew thick with emotion. "We were having so much fun, but we could really talk too. I really connected with you. Like no one I'd ever connected with before. I feel like I've known you all my life."

Jordan couldn't keep from smiling. So Dez had felt all those things too. She wanted to dance a little jig.

"And then I got scared again," Dez continued. "Scared you'd find out about my past or figure it out for yourself—you were already asking a lot of questions and I didn't want to lie to you. I was afraid once you knew the truth about me, you'd dump me."

"So you did the old preemptive strike thing. Dump me before I dump you." It was a tactic Jordan had used many times herself. Better to hurt someone early on, before it hurt them too much. Or before they hurt you. But Dez was wrong. Jordan wouldn't have hurt her.

"Yes."

"Oh, Dez. Don't you know that I'm in love with you? Don't you know that nothing about your past would ever scare me away? Don't you know you can trust me more than that? Jesus, I want to know every little thing about you."

Dez began to sob—real sobs that came from deep inside. Her body shook, and Jordan clasped her in a hug. She rocked her gently. "It's okay, honey. I'm here and I'm not going away."

"I don't deserve it," Dez mumbled into her shoulder. "I don't deserve you and I don't deserve another chance."

If Jordan's love for Dez could grow more, it did now. Exponentially. "Promise me you won't shut me out again, okay? Please?"

"I won't, I promise."

Jordan smiled through tears she hadn't realized were in her eyes. "We have a lot of catching up to do."

Dez pulled her head up, nuzzled Jordan's neck. "Tonight . . . will you just hold me?"

Jordan laughed. "I thought you were going to ask me to do

something kinky, or at least to make love to you all night long."

"Oh, there'll be time for that," she purred. "Later."

"Good because I'm going to hold you to that."

"I'm counting on it."

CHAPTER THIRTY-THREE

Amanda

The party was in full throttle, the guests dancing wildly to Lady Gaga. Shannon had already shed her sexy garter belt—Dani having removed it with her teeth in front of a cheering crowd that raucously urged her to go further and further. The event was cheesey and campy but worth a good laugh. Unsurprisingly, the music and alcohol were quickly stripping away everyone's sense of decorum. Heather was dancing dirty with the burly young bartender. Dani must have thought she'd suddenly transformed into a break dancer, the way she was spinning on her back on the floor like a top. Shannon stood over her, giving her a little show beneath her dress that bordered on obscene. The guy who'd won the contest for Shannon's garter belt had it around his neck like a choker and he was dancing like a 1980s robot. *Jesus, I hope nobody gets hurt tonight!*

Amanda's wedding had not been a public celebration like this, just a quick trip to city hall with their two best friends, then a nice dinner out. She'd never had dreams of a fancy wedding, thank goodness, because she could never afford one anyway. But she did desire something a little more public, a little more celebratory than her lame excuse for a wedding with Jennifer. If there ever was a next time for her, she would do things differently. She would do *everything* differently!

Claire materialized by her side. "Is there something in that champagne fountain I should have tested at a lab?"

"Yes, but I doubt you'd find anything. It's that crazy phenomenon unique to Vegas."

"Ah! The old what-happens-in-Vegas-stays-in-Vegas. I've been warned about that."

"Yes. A license to make a fool of yourself." It was nice to share a laugh with Claire again. The tension between them since that kiss had been driving her nuts. The kiss—she had not been able to stop thinking about it. She only wished Claire did not regret it, but that was a wish that was not going to be fulfilled. Claire obviously did regret it. Very much. "Claire? Have I been making a fool of myself with you this week?"

Clearly surprised by the question, Claire verbally fumbled for a moment. "No. No, you haven't." She sighed quietly, but if she was frustrated, she didn't let it show. "I've been . . . confused this week. I don't know what to think, what to do. One minute I want to run away and ignore all of this, and the next . . ." She looked helplessly at Amanda.

The music switched to a slow song. Amanda grasped Claire's hand, giving her no option but to follow her out to the dance floor. If they were going to have a heart-to-heart, at least they could dance at the same time, because if Amanda were honest with herself, she wanted, *needed* to touch Claire right now. Words alone were not enough.

They danced to an Anita Baker song, neither speaking. Amanda inhaled the scent that was Claire, brushed her cheek against Claire's soft skin, felt the wisps of Claire's short hair against her cheek. She tingled where Claire's hand perched at the small of her back, and she considered how different her feelings were for Claire than they'd been for Jennifer. With her ex, it had strictly been a chemical reaction—lust and combustible feelings that resulted in a lot of sex or fighting, and not much companionship in between. But this! This was a perfect balance of companionship, friendship, sexual and physical intensity—an intimate connection that seemed to transcend all boundaries. When she was with Claire, the past, present and future all collided into the same spectrum. It was as though Claire had always been a part of her life, always with her, to the point where she would sometimes refer to something in her life from years ago as if Claire already knew, and she'd have to stop herself and fill in the blanks for Claire. It was a strange and yet totally familiar sensation. Instantly she understood Dani and Shannon's wedding vows about no beginning and no end, because that was exactly how it felt with Claire.

"I want us to figure this out," Amanda whispered, near tears. She was not above begging. "You're too important to me, and I don't want to let you go. Please."

Claire pulled back enough to look into her eyes. "You're important to me too. I'm just . . . I'm all over the map with my feelings, and it's not like me. I always know exactly what I'm feeling. I always own my feelings, even when it's sadness or grief or futility. But this week, with you, it's like I don't recognize myself anymore. I'm a different person."

"Is that a bad thing?"

Claire considered for a long moment. "No. It's not a bad thing. I've felt happier this week than I've felt in years. Younger, lighter, freer somehow. Like a weight's been lifted."

"Okay, that's good then, right?"

"Except it scares the hell out of me."

"Why, because these feelings are so new to you?"

"Not really. It scares me because you are . . . you."

"Huh?"

"Shannon's niece. And the age difference, and—"

"Okay, wait. All I'm hearing are negatives. And frankly I'm sick of it. I'm sick of you treating me like I'm some kind of pox on your life, treating me like I'm a kid, like I'm a different species than you. I am not trying to wreck your life, Claire Cooper."

Claire stared at her in shock, wordless, as the song segued into Lady Antebellum's "Need You Now."

"I'm a woman, Claire. Like you. Everything else is just a stupid excuse."

Claire had the wisdom to keep quiet and not dispute her. They danced to the remainder of the song in silence—not an angry silence; more like a respectful truce.

"Okay," Claire finally said after the song ended. The music grew loud again and she yelled over the noise, "You want to talk about it all, then okay, let's talk."

Finally, Amanda thought, twisting her mouth into a wry smile. "I think that's the first thing you've said in the last couple of days that I agree with."

Shannon stepped up to them before they could make their escape. "Oh no, you two, you're not going anywhere yet. I'm about to toss my bouquet." She smiled wickedly at Amanda, as if dangling something covetous. "Got your catching mitt with you?"

Amanda frowned. "If catching that thing means I'm the next to get married, no thanks. Been there, done that, don't need to do it again." It was the first time she'd ever joked about her failed marriage, and it felt kind of good.

"When did you become such a cynic? You were always my sweet little sunny Amanda, innocent to the world. Damn, I miss her."

Had she really been sweet and sunny and innocent? Years ago maybe, but she had not been the mythical creature her aunt was making her out to be, at least not for many years. She stole a glance at Claire and made a face as if to say, *Family can be such a pain in the ass sometimes*.

Obediently, Amanda and Claire joined the small throng of women clustered behind Shannon, waiting like a pool of sharks to be fed. Well, they could have the bouquet and the stupid symbolic meaning that went with it. If she ever got married again, and it was a big *if* at this point, things were going to be a lot different. She would not rush into anything again. A long courtship, like Dani's and Shannon's, was exactly the right way to go about it. *That and picking the right person next time!*

She tried to hide behind Claire a little, but since they were the tallest, there wasn't much hiding to be had. The bouquet breezed through the air, smacked her on the shoulder and dropped at her feet. She stood looking at it like it was a snake that might bite her, until the others told her it was hers and that she had to pick it up. She shot an accusing glare at her aunt, who only smiled victoriously.

"All right," Claire said firmly. "How about a drink in the bar so we can talk?"

"How about a drink in my room where we can talk privately?"

Claire didn't look very happy about the suggestion but she relented with a short nod.

A few minutes later in her room, Amanda poured them each a glass of wine. They sat respectfully on the sofa, separated by at least of foot of precious real estate. Amanda didn't want to spook Claire. She could and would behave herself, even though she wanted to feel Claire's lips on hers again, feel Claire's mouth greedily pressing against hers. She couldn't help but remember the last time they were together on this couch, kissing like a couple of teenagers who wanted more but didn't dare. She would love to move onto Claire's lap, pull her face to hers, kiss her madly, and run her hands along those strong shoulders. But she didn't dare.

"So," Amanda began, growing bolder. "Tell me this. When we're together, does it feel to you like our age difference is some huge gulf between us? That we can't relate to one another?"

"No. But I know that you're so much younger, that you haven't had the same experiences—"

"I asked how you felt, not what you know."

Claire nodded to acknowledge the point.

"How do you *feel* when we spend time together?"

The worried frown between Claire's eyes flattened and disappeared. Her face softened. Her eyes too, and it told Amanda all she needed to know. Claire's spontaneous smile lifted Amanda's heart. "Like the happiest woman in the world."

"I feel the same way too," Amanda added quietly, deciding to take a chance. "With you, I feel like I'm with the woman I'm meant to be with." She swallowed. "And that's never happened to me before."

Claire grew nervous but she didn't try to talk Amanda out of her feelings, thankfully. "There's Shannon," she said, but the warning sounded lame. She was weakening.

"No. No one else belongs here with us. This is about you and me and no one else."

"Okay. You're right."

Amanda slid closer and reached for Claire's hand. "For once, I want you to feel and not think."

Claire's eyes fluttered shut. Amanda moved closer still, so that her shoulder touched Claire's. The contact sent a noticeable shiver through Claire—Amanda could feel it. She put her mouth to Claire's ear, brushed the lobe with her lips, and whispered, "I want to touch you. So much. Everywhere. All night long. I want you, Claire. Goddamnit, I want you like I've never wanted anyone before. And if it doesn't *feel* right, you can stop it anytime you want. But I don't want you to think about anything. Okay? Just let me do the things I so want to do."

Claire nodded. She seemed paralyzed but in a pleasurable way. Her eyes remained closed as Amanda's lips moved to hers. She kissed her softly, lengthened the kiss, and Claire responded instantly. Her arms slipped around Amanda, pulling her close, and soon they were both breathing hard, both pressing their mouths and bodies hard into one another, as if by doing so they could become one.

"Make love to me, Claire. Make love to me right now." It was as though she'd never spoken words more important in her life. Making love with Claire was all that mattered now, all she needed—the culmination of her life to this point.

Claire answered with her actions. She stood, held her hand out, and guided Amanda to the king-sized bed. Amanda sat on it and Claire knelt at her feet. Softly Claire began kissing her throat, her chest, the point at her cleavage where the dress ended. Claire inhaled her, tightened her hands at her waist. Amanda was happy they didn't speak; she wanted them both to feel one another with every part of their bodies. The anticipation of Claire inside her made her squeeze her legs together. *Yes!* She wanted Claire inside her, knew it would feel like a bird coming home to nest. Emotionally, Claire already resided in her, and now she needed her physically inside her to consummate their relationship—to close the circle.

No beginning and no end.

CHAPTER THIRTY-FOUR

Claire

Feeling and not thinking wasn't so tough after all. Amanda helped make it that way. She made it so easy to let her senses take over, and God, did it feel good! The creamy satin of her dress as she slowly slipped it from her body, the lightly perfumed scent of her skin with its buttery softness that age had not yet encroached upon. Claire's lips, as they caressed her shoulders, felt the warmth of her desire. The pulse at her throat was like a tiny life of its own in Claire's mouth. The urgent moan that escaped Amanda's mouth quickened Claire's pace, like a starter's pistol signaling the beginning of a race.

Making love was absolutely the most perfect thing to do right now, no question. She was anxious to suck Amanda's nipples, to push her mouth between Amanda's legs and make her come, to feel Amanda's fingers bring her own desire to fruition. She wanted to lie on top of Amanda, press her nakedness against Amanda's, pulsate against her, unite their skin, their breasts, mingle the liquid between their legs. But she also wanted to go slow, to stretch it out all night, to taste and touch every part of Amanda until all those tastes and touches became second nature to her—a part of her.

She shed her tuxedo jacket, let Amanda pull her tie loose and toss it to the floor. She enclosed her fingers over Amanda's as they methodically released each button of her shirt.

Shirt, bra, pants, underwear in a pile on the floor, they lay on the bed together, touching softly, exploring patiently. Claire closed her eyes, melted an inch at a time with every kiss Amanda planted on her neck, shoulders, chest. No. She needed to take Amanda first, to erase the strands of thoughts and memories of Ann that were trying to edge into her consciousness. She needed to own this beauty beside her if only for a few moments—to consume and assimilate, absorb and consolidate. Become one with her.

She moved onto Amanda, smiled into her eyes, kissed her lips ever so gently. Her fingers found a breast, circled the hardening nipple, thumbed it to a stiffer peak. Amanda moaned into her mouth, arched against her. Claire dipped her head, sucked on that nipple and then the other as Amanda undulated rhythmically beneath her. Claire's mouth continued to work Amanda's nipples until the movements beneath her became more frenzied and irregular. Amanda's moans quickly grew more insistent.

"Oh, God, I'm going to come just from this. Oh my God—" She bucked against Claire and cried out. Her body trembled and Claire tightened her hold on her until she stilled.

"Oh, God," Amanda said in astonishment, still gasping for breath. "I can't believe that happened, just from my breasts. That's never happened before."

Claire nuzzled her neck. "I can't wait to see how else I can make you come."

"Oh, I can't wait either." Amanda's eyes twinkled. "And I'm more than up to the challenge."

"Be careful you don't bite off more than you can chew."

"Oh, I plan on doing some biting. And some chewing!"

Claire stifled her with more kisses, pressed her body into her. Amanda felt slender beneath her, but strong. Very strong. She was sure the younger woman would be able to take anything she could dish out and then some. If anything, it would be Claire biting off more than she could chew.

She moved lower, lingeringly touching her breasts to Amanda's stomach before moving further south. She wanted her first touch of Amanda down there to be with her tongue, not her fingers. She needed to taste Amanda's desire, have it dissolve on her tongue like a holy host. She needed to possess her with her mouth. Amanda's thighs were already quivering in anticipation when Claire's mouth claimed her.

"Oh, Claire."

Hearing her name on Amanda's lips in breathless capitulation gave her a jolt of satisfaction. *Oh, Claire*. The words repeated in her head; it was like being welcomed home. And it was home, Amanda's sex seeming so familiar to her, so right, so wonderful. She breathed her in, instantly intoxicated, and with her tongue explored every contour and every texture, stroked her until Amanda's fingers were in her hair pulling her hard against her, urging her on. Her tongue worked in tiny circles, flicked lightly, then hard, fast and faster yet, the salt of Amanda's desire mixing with her own saliva. Thank God it was all coming back to her. She was inordinately pleased she was giving Amanda so much pleasure. She didn't want to stop. She wanted to pleasure Amanda all night long like this, tasting her, pushing her over the edge, letting Amanda's fingers dig into her scalp, pulling at her. Amanda wanted her. Only *she* could satisfy Amanda right now. It was heavenly.

"I need you inside," Amanda urged roughly.

Yes. She needed to be inside her too when she climaxed, needed to feel with her mouth and fingers Amanda's shudders break through her body, like turbulent waves crashing to shore. The warmth and wetness that greeted her fingers were divine. Heat and velvet. She danced inside Amanda, matching her fingers' rhythm with her tongue. Within minutes Amanda was writhing wildly, crying out, shuddering and bucking beneath her. She was hot lava spilling over, igniting Claire's own desire. She wanted Amanda to possess her as she had just possessed Amanda.

"Come here," Amanda murmured.

They kissed deeply, Amanda clutching her tightly to her chest. There were tears on Amanda's cheeks.

"You okay?"

"Yes." Amanda nodded happily through her tears. "You make me so happy. You make me want you so much. So, so much. You make me want everything."

Yes, and I want you too, my sweet girl. But she would not think about the incredible happiness in her heart and body right now. It was new terrain, or least terrain she had not visited in a long while, and she was afraid to feel too much right now. Everything in moderation had been her motto all her life. But there was no moderation in making love with Amanda. No moderation in her bursting heart right now either.

"I need to make love to you," Amanda whispered urgently. "I won't be happy until you're happy."

There was that damned word again, happy. Well, defining happy and accepting being happy could wait. Satisfied, content, pleasured, turned on, needing release, needing Amanda's touch . . . those she could let herself be immersed in. Those things were safe.

Amanda's touches were bold, confident, full of tenderness. Claire closed her eyes to the waves of pleasure that were ceaseless and only grew in intensity. She had not known there was such want, such red-hot desire within her, nor that Amanda was the only person who could feed those cravings. But she knew now, and with Amanda's mouth on her and fingers inside her, Claire was falling through time and space, her mind separating from the fierce pleasure ripping through her body and floating on nothingness. When orgasm came, she felt connected again, like all the pieces of the puzzle had converged within her. Amanda brought the pieces of her together. Amanda made her *feel* again.

Afterward they lay silently wrapped in one another's arms,

and Claire's mind began to solidify and form thoughts again. It occurred to her that this was like wedding sex, this consummation of their desire and feelings for one another. She had never had a wedding night, but Amanda had. Amanda had married someone and had shared a wedding night with another woman, and the knowledge saddened her a little.

"Are you okay?" Amanda asked, as if sensing Claire's unease.

She tightened her arms around Amanda. "Yes, I'm fine."

"You sure? I mean, I know this is a big step for you."

She meant Ann. Yes, making love with someone who wasn't Ann was a huge step, not counting the brief tryst she'd had at the medical conference last year. This was the first time someone had truly competed with Ann for her love, for her body, for her soul. She didn't yet understand what that meant for her. Did it erase her love for Ann? Was there only room for one love—one lover—in her life, in her heart, forever? Could she even begin to think of starting over with someone else? Those, she supposed, were the real issues, and not Amanda's age difference or her relation to Shannon. Amanda was no kid; she was a woman. A woman who loved women, a woman whose entire future was still ahead of her, an intelligent and kind woman who was falling for Claire. She was offering the gift of herself to Claire.

Claire kissed the top of Amanda's head. "I'm just sleepy, that's all."

They slept soundly, pressed against one another, and when they awoke early they made love again, much more familiar this time with each other's bodies. There was no denying the love in Amanda's eyes and the love Claire conveyed in her caresses and strokes. This was no transient affair, and the prospect of what might lay ahead frightened Claire. She had stepped onto a path from which it would be very difficult to turn back.

Over room service breakfast, Claire summoned her courage and, in a less certain voice, told Amanda that she was not ready to move forward with their relationship in a public way.

Amanda, hurt, said, "You mean we're supposed to sneak

around or something?"

"No." Claire hesitated, not at all sure what she meant, only that she wasn't ready to announce their relationship to the world. She wanted to take things slowly, a step at a time.

"We can talk to my aunt together. She might need a little time to get used to the idea, but I know she'll be supportive of us."

Shannon was only a small part of the issue. "No," Claire repeated. "It's more than Shannon." It was about her whole life and the need to go slow.

"Okay." Amanda's tone softened and she snuggled closer to Claire. "I'm not trying to rush you. I don't want you to be uncomfortable. In fact, I want you to be as insanely happy and sure about this as I am."

"You do make me happy." But the real question was, was she ready to *allow* herself to be truly happy?

"I do make you happy, but at the same time I don't. You feel guilty for feeling happy, don't you?"

"I don't know. I guess I need some time to figure it out. To figure out how to be happy. I'm out of practice."

Amanda sighed miserably. In her silence, she seemed resigned to the fact that Claire's fears were once again pushing them apart.

"I'm sorry," Claire said feebly. It was all she could think to say, knowing full well it was not enough. She simply wasn't capable of making any promises, commitments, right now. Amanda would have to patient. Or not.

CHAPTER THIRTY-FIVE

Jordan

It was a rewarding kind of exhaustion—staying up late talking from their hearts, then holding one another through what remained of the night. They made love well after the sun came up with an energy that surprised them both. Yielding was more like being conquered, touches were rough and demanding, hurried. There was a possessiveness and wildness and urgency to their lovemaking, as if they were truly, finally, laying claim to one another, and with a permanence this time. A trail of tiny bruises was left behind, their exhaustion now bone weary. They lay in each other's arms, limp but completely satiated.

"I don't think I could ever get enough of you," Jordan admitted, and it was the absolute truth. She would never tire of Dez. "You're so beautiful."

"You're beautiful too, and I don't want you to ever get enough of me."

"Ah-ha, so you will be complicit in me keeping you in bed

all day."

"Is there a reason we have to get up?"

"No. Well, I guess I should say goodbye to the others. They're heading back to Chicago today."

"Speaking of Chicago, I have a question for you." Dez traced a finger along the inside of Jordan's palm. "How come no woman ever captured you before now?"

That was easy. "I never wanted to be captured. I never thought being captured was something I'd ever want."

"And now?"

Jordan grinned at her lover. "Now I wouldn't trade it for the world."

"I'm a very lucky woman that you decided it was worth being captured."

"We're both lucky." Jordan thought back to her morning with Krissy last weekend and how that had changed everything. She told Dez the story, admitted her shame and how the event turned out to be a catalyst to changing her ways.

"Sometimes," Dez said, "it takes something ugly to make us wake up and change our lives. I certainly know all about that."

"But the important thing is reaching the destination, not in how you get there."

"Yes." Dez smiled. "Not only are you beautiful and a wonderful lover, but you're wise too."

Jordan laughed. "I don't think I've ever been called wise before."

Dez raised herself up on one elbow, a tiny frown surfacing. "I guess we need to talk logistics, huh?"

"I have a two-bedroom condo here in town. I don't have to leave anytime soon."

"That's good to know, but the problem is, I do."

Jordan's stomach turned over. "What do you mean?"

"Another week. I'm supposed to do a nine-week tour across Europe—France and Germany. Amsterdam too."

"Shit." Jordan had not expected this, but she supposed she should have, given Dez's line of work. She'd had the unreasonable fantasy that they'd hang out in Vegas for weeks or months, Dez singing, Jordan going to her concerts and conducting her real estate business from here. She'd envisioned cooking for Dez, running a bath for her after her shows, making love to her half the night, waking up together followed by lazy mornings by the pool. She'd not been expecting reality to encroach on their lives so soon. "Nine weeks?"

"Afraid so, darling. If I could get out of it I would, but I signed a contract."

Jordan believed her—the part about wanting to get out of it, but she was still scared. She didn't want to lose Dez all over again. "I feel like I just found you and now you're leaving."

"I'm not going anywhere here, where it counts." Dez pressed Jordan's hand to her chest.

"Promise?"

"Yes. In fact, why don't you come with me?"

"Can't. I've got too much business on the go right now." Deals would fall through if she left now. Important deals that she'd been working on for months.

"We'll find a way to work this out, I promise."

Jordan couldn't quite stop herself from thinking the worst. Thinking that if she lost Dez, she'd never be able to find this kind of love again. That she'd walk through empty rooms, a shadow of herself, looking for Dez and never being satisfied with anyone else. She'd be a ghost. She wasn't yet used to how much she needed Dez.

Dez wiped a tear from Jordan's cheek. "It's okay, honey. We'll make it through this as long as you believe in me. In us. I love you and I'm not going to do anything to jeopardize that."

"I do believe in you and in us. I guess I'm thinking that somehow I'm destined to get hurt, and that I deserve it, because of the crap I've put other women through."

"My grandma always told me you can never be truly happy as long as you think you don't deserve it. We can never feel guilty for being happy, okay? So get that other nonsense out of your head."

Jordan leaned over and kissed her. "How about you help me take my mind off all those other things?"

"I'd love to, baby. But there is one more thing I want you to think about first. Actually, two things. I want you to at least come over to Europe and join me on the tour for a week or two. And then I want you and me to sit down and figure out a plan where we can be together and both do the work we love. Can you do that?"

Jordan laughed, relief like a bolt of sunshine parting the clouds in her heart. "Yes to both. But can we think about those a little later? There's something I want to do first."

Dez rolled onto her back. "I was hoping you'd say that."

CHAPTER THIRTY-SIX

Dani

They were both famished, not waiting for Heather before starting breakfast. It was nothing new for her to be late.

"So," Dani said to Shannon, swallowing another bite of scrambled egg. "How does it feel to be married, my love?"

"Wonderful! Like everything I thought it would feel like and more."

"The legal piece of paper would be nice. That's the only thing that's missing as far as I'm concerned."

"I know. But we'll get that piece of paper in Canada this summer, and then as soon as we can in Illinois. They've got to get on the right side of history one of these years."

She wondered how many other gay couples were getting married in Canada or in one of the few states that allowed it. She wondered if, once it ever became legal across the land, there would be a stampede of gay couples to the altar. Jordan was someone who'd never given a rat's ass about a legal marriage being available to her, but now, Dani wondered with amusement, perhaps Jordan's thoughts *would* turn to marriage. She'd noticed Jordan and Dez reunite at the wedding reception, and she couldn't be happier for Jordan.

"I guess you noticed Jordan's in love with Dez Adams?" She hadn't had a chance to discuss it with Shannon until now.

Shannon shook her head, smiling. "Oh yeah, how could you not? You could practically see the sparks flying between them last night. I'm shocked that Jordan actually had it in her."

"I am too a little. But I think all her smart-ass remarks about love were really just a cover. She either never thought it would happen to her, or she never thought she'd be able to do it."

"Well, she'll be eating crow now."

"Or eating something." Dani grinned and raised her eyebrows suggestively at Shannon.

Heather sauntered up to their table, a small parcel tucked under her arm, and took a seat. "What'd I interrupt?"

"Nothing, just a little gossip," Dani replied.

"What? Who got laid last night?"

"Besides you?" Dani quipped.

"Yes, besides me."

Dani shook her head and laughed. "The young bartender?"

Heather frowned. "I don't kiss and tell, okay?"

"Yeah, whatever."

Shannon nodded at the package Heather had set down on the table. "What've you got?"

It wasn't large but there was something heavy and ominous about it. It was addressed to Dani and Shannon. "When I went by the front desk they asked me to give it to you. It came last night."

There was no return address on the package. Dani set it aside, figuring it was probably a stray wedding gift. "Sorry we started without you, Heather. We were starving."

"No problem. My stomach isn't up to eating right now but I would absolutely murder someone for a cup of coffee."

"Feeling a little hung over this morning?"

Heather stuck out her tongue. "What do you think, Einstein?"

"I'll bet you're a little sore too. Gets a little harder to do the limbo every year, huh?" Dani teased.

"I should hope you two are a little sore. I'm actually surprised you're here. I figured honeymoon sex would keep you in that room till it was time to head to the airport."

Shannon winked at Dani before she answered. "Honestly, we were too tired for sex. This getting married thing is downright exhausting."

Heather laughed, then squawked in pain. "Damn, it hurts to laugh. Hey, trust me, you aren't the first newlyweds in the world too tired to do it after the wedding."

An older Latina waitress came by with a pot of coffee. Heather practically tackled her. "Oh, thank God! I'm going to die if I don't have coffee right this minute."

"Honey, the only thing that sells as well as alcohol in this place is coffee," the waitress answered.

"Yeah, well, I can believe that. So . . ." Heather turned her attention back to Dani and Shannon, the cup of coffee cradled like gold between her hands. "How does it feel to be Mrs. and Mrs. . . . Are you going to hyphenate your names or what?"

"We're keeping our own names for now." Dani glanced at the shiny band of gold on her hand. She hoped she never got used to the delight of seeing it there. Already it felt like it'd been there for years. "It feels great to be married. Should have done it a long time ago."

"Well, our damned laws haven't exactly been making it easy for you. Hey, why don't you open that package? Looks like it's probably a gift or something."

As Dani opened the package, a note slipped out. From the Desk of Mary Sedgewick, it said in italic script. Her youngest sister. Casting the note aside, she lifted out a Bible wrapped in white tissue, white hand-tooled leather with gold lettering.

"For fuck's sake! Mary's sent us a Bible. How wonderful. Even less useful than the third cappuccino maker we got." Would her family never learn?

"Calm down," Heather said. "It's just a Bible. I mean, think about it, what else would Mary give you as a wedding present? A dildo?"

"That is so not funny. She knows how I feel about religion, especially the kind that thinks we're sinners for loving each other. Sending me a Bible is an insult. It's bullshit."

After a moment, Shannon said, "Heather's right. We should give Mary the benefit of the doubt. I'm sure she thought she was being kind."

Heather reached for the Bible Dani had angrily thumped down on the table and examined it closer. "Hey, this is handmade. With your name *and* Shannon's stamped on it. It's a wedding edition. Look, there's a nice page in here to list all the wedding day details—the names of the wedding party, your birthdates, even a family tree. Jesus, I think she was serious about this gift." Heather shook her head. "I'll be damned. You could just about knock me down with a feather right now."

"Let's read the note," Shannon suggested.

Haltingly, Dani took the slip of paper and read it out loud.

Dear Dani,
I know we've had our differences in the past—

"No kidding," Dani interjected.

—and for that I'm sorry. I have always believed that marriage is between a man and a woman. We were raised to think that, but obviously you came to a different conclusion at some point in your life. I too can make my own conclusions, and while I don't profess to know what the answer is on marriage, I know that God loves us all equally. God would not have created the institution of marriage if it was not meant for all of us to enjoy. Please accept this gift from me as a reminder that I will always love you and that I am trying hard to understand and accept.
Love,
Mary

"Holy shit," Heather said. "I sure didn't see this coming. Hell, maybe in another year she'll be grand marshal of the gay pride parade or something!"

Shannon snapped, "It really was a nice thing for her to do, and I don't think you guys should make fun of it."

Dani sighed, leaned back in her chair. She refused to get her hopes up when it came to the rest of her family; they'd let her down so many times before. But what the hell. If Mary was suddenly turning into a real person, then good for her. She'd always been a smart girl, so perhaps it wasn't all that surprising that she was warming to Dani's homosexuality. And Shannon was right; they shouldn't be making fun of her.

"Maybe I'll actually get a Christmas card in the mail from her this year," Heather mocked, refusing to give it up. "Unless her Christian generosity only extends to you."

Dani slid the note and the Bible back into the torn package. "I don't know what to say. I'm not exactly going to roll out the welcome mat to her, but hey, people can change I guess. And if she's changed, then I'm happy for her."

Shannon looked at her meaningfully. "People are meant to change. It's when they refuse to change that they make a royal mess of their lives and their relationships."

Dani could agree with that. She knew what was important, had come to accept that their lives had to change now. Financially the landscape had altered, plans of parenthood were gone too—at least for the time being. But they were together and life went on. She could either seize the changes and make the best of them, or get left behind and continually grieve for what was lost. "You're right darling. Here's to changing."

They clinked coffee cups.

Nostalgically, Dani glanced around her surroundings, thought about all the visits she'd made to Vegas over the years, the money she'd spent at the casinos—money she'd taken for granted. Ah, well. She'd never really expected the fun would last forever—not with the Bible-thumping, God-will-strike-you-down kind of upbringing she'd had. God was a punishing God,

she'd been made to believe, and so a part of her was always waiting for the other shoe to drop, for her ship to run aground.

As if reading her thoughts, Shannon squeezed her thigh in
reassurance. "We're going to be just fine, you know."

"I know. It's going to be different, that's all."

"Different is okay with me, as long as we're together."

CHAPTER THIRTY-SEVEN

Claire (Chicago)

Claire gazed out the plane's tiny window, wishing she could get off at the next nearest cloud. Someone had asked her once if she felt close to Ann when she was up in the air like this, in the fluffy clouds and sunshine. Closer to heaven. No, she had answered. She felt closest to Ann when she closed her eyes at night, right before sleep claimed her, and in mornings after she'd dreamed of Ann.

Amanda was sitting a few rows ahead of her. She couldn't see her, and it was just as well. Amanda had given her an ultimatum this morning. She didn't want a small part of Claire, and she certainly didn't want a guilty or reticent Claire. No. If and when Claire was ready to jump with both feet, she could come to her, but it was ultimately Claire's decision.

The internal struggling had instantly begun. Her mind wouldn't stop churning with all the possibilities and angles, as though she were trying to solve a complex math problem.

Amanda was a lovely woman. Warm, kind, intelligent, fun. Sexy as hell. She involuntarily squeezed her thighs together as she remembered the body she'd brought to orgasm many times with her mouth and hands last night and this morning, the feel of Amanda's soft skin, the smell of her. Amanda giving her the most delicious, forceful orgasms she'd ever had. *Oh, God!* She was warm and wet all of a sudden, a hot flash of fresh desire. But panic was dry in her mouth. She'd never come that hard, that intensely with Ann before, not even in the early days of their relationship. Sex between them had always been loving and tender and fulfilling. But with Amanda it had been electric, all-consuming, thrilling beyond imagination. Every cell in her body, in her mind, had been engaged and set on fire. Amanda was the match to her wick. She wanted her with a hunger she'd not known before, and it scared the hell out of her. What if it was too much, too overwhelming? Was it possible to self-combust from too much pleasure? And what if Amanda woke up one day, decided she didn't want to be with someone two decades older? Was Claire capable of being everything she needed? Was she being selfish giving in to this hunger, this need for Amanda? What of her loyalty to Ann, gone only three years? How could she not help but compare Amanda to Ann, and . . . Oh, Lord, how wrong that would be! It would not be a fair comparison at all. There was Shannon to consider too; she surely would not approve, and their friendship would suffer.

She closed her eyes, wanting to wipe the slate of her mind clean, even if just for a day or two. It was all too much to think about. She couldn't wait to get back to the world of delivery rooms, menopause, ovarian cysts, STDs, pregnancies, her dog, her house, her books. The world she'd made for herself the last few years. There was comfort in routine, and yes, comfort in pulling the blankets over her head and disappearing.

It was still dark the next morning when she went to work. The hospital never slept, but her office was dark and empty—just the way she wanted it this morning. She'd go over the reports and charts of everything she'd missed over the past week, check all her messages, though she knew Maria would have alerted her if anything serious had come up. Her reading glasses perched on her nose and a cup of coffee steaming away on her desk, she flipped on her computer and got started. Like magic, the immersion in work erased thoughts of Amanda and the week in Vegas.

Maria rushed in shortly before eight, squealing excitedly as she gave Claire a welcome back hug. "I've been dying to hear how your week went, and if you make me wait another minute, I might have to have a hissy fit."

Claire smiled. "Give me a break. You've never had a hissy fit in your life."

"Well," she answered sheepishly. "Maybe once or twice. You look great by the way! Tanned, fit, relaxed. Vegas sure seems to have agreed with you."

Claire tried to stop from visibly wincing but failed.

Maria's unspoken questions shot at her like daggers. "Oh, I get it. You're going to use the old what-happens-in-Vegas-stays-in-Vegas routine to keep from telling me about your week. That is not fair! Come on!"

Claire hated that stupid phrase about Vegas. It didn't apply to her at all. Or did it? Was Amanda some kind of sexual escapade she was supposed to chalk up to losing her head in Vegas? A sexual detour, like the nice woman at the conference last year? She felt warmth rushing to her cheeks, and with it, guilt.

Maria flopped down into one of the cozy office chairs, draping her legs over the arm. "I know. You had some wild affair out there that you don't want to fess up to!"

"Please." She knew her face wasn't lying, knew it for a fact when Maria's smart-ass grin dissolved.

"Oh, shit. What happened?"

Claire felt close to tears suddenly. Confessing the events of the week had been the last thing on her mind this morning. In fact, she'd unequivocally decided that she would *not* tell Maria a single thing about Amanda. It was no one's business, and no one else would understand anyway. Except emotions now thundered through her chest and pounded wildly in her ears, and Maria was studying her with a mix of apprehension and empathy.

She tried to lie. "It was fine. Fun. The wedding was great. You know, everything you'd expect of a Vegas wedding."

"Oh, no. Wait a minute. I know there's more to it than that. Something's upset you. Or scared the crap out of you. What are you not telling me?"

Claire weakly waved her hand in dismissal because she couldn't find her voice.

"I've worked with you for six years, Claire. I know you better than anyone else, except maybe Shannon. Something happened last week, and you can't just blow me off. I'm worried about you. I want to help."

You can't help me, she ached to say. No one could help her; only she could solve her problems. When it came down to it, people made their own decisions, failed or succeeded, went about their lives, lived with the consequences. The responsibility of her dilemma was hers alone.

"I know what you're thinking." Maria leaned closer in the chair, her posture erect and poised for confrontation. "That I won't understand. That you're perfectly fine being the lone wolf you are. That you can deal with whatever happened by yourself, the way you deal with everything. Alone."

Claire spun around. "What's wrong with that? What's wrong with trying to solve your own problems? Jesus, people are always looking for someone else to solve their problems. Well, it's my life, and I know you don't approve of how I live it, but that's too damned bad."

"Whoa! Who said anything about approval or disapproval?"

"You think I should be dating, out having fun instead of moping around, pining for Ann. It's what you all think. That I stopped living my life the day Ann died."

Maria looked horrified. "Claire, your friends want you to be happy, that's all. We worry that, you know, that a part of you has given up on life."

"Why, because I'm not out trying to get laid every weekend?"

"Of course not. You're blowing this way out of proportion. Will you tell me why you're so sensitive suddenly about dating and getting *laid*, as you put it? Did you meet someone?"

She wished Maria would stop nagging her. Well-meaning or not, she was tired of people telling her she should be with someone, that she needed to get on with her life, like there was some simple recipe or how-to manual she should be following, and that dating would make her feel better. "We have our first patient in thirty minutes."

"You're evading."

"So what if I am. Isn't there something you should be doing?"

"Yes there is, and it's getting to the bottom of whatever is going on here."

Claire rolled her eyes. "I'm not in the mood for this."

They'd worked together so long they were like an old married couple, which meant Maria was not to be derailed. "You met someone there, I know it. And you're confused and upset."

"Now why would you think I met someone?"

"Because it's the only thing that would put you in this state. Something . . . no, *someone*, has sent you completely off the rails. And now you're feeling guilty and upset."

"Guilty? Hell, I'm single. Free as a bird. I can do anything I want, see anyone I want. You've told me that yourself a hundred times."

"That's true in theory. Except you're not like that. Nothing is that simple with you. You'll torment yourself over this, act like it's some medical condition you have to research the hell out of first before you commit to a treatment."

"Jesus, you make me sound like a pompous ass. Or a coward, maybe."

"Hardly." Maria reached across the space where Claire leaned against her desk and touched her arm. "You're warm, kind, the smartest woman I've ever met. But you're cautious. Overly cautious. And sometimes you overthink things."

She didn't want to prolong this argument, didn't want to debate the quirks of her personality. "Look, I know you're trying to help, and I appreciate it, but—"

"Will you tell me about her?"

Claire sucked in her breath. The pain in her stomach was sharp. Biting. She reached into the pocket of her lab coat for the small bottle of antacids, popped a couple in her mouth. Would it be so bad to talk to someone about Amanda? To unburden this guilt and apprehension a little? There was no one else, not really. She certainly couldn't talk to Shannon about this.

She pulled the matching chair closer to Maria's. Slowly, calmly, and in halting sentences, she unloaded on her. She left out Amanda's name and the fact that she was Shannon's niece, but she recited their age difference, their immediate and deep connection, their mutual attraction, and finally, confessed that they'd slept together.

Maria listened in stunned silence until Claire finished. "Wow. That's wonderful! Seriously. I'm so happy for you. But you're not going to let her slip away, are you?"

"It's complicated."

"Complicated, shmomplicated. What the hell isn't in life?"

"True. But I don't know if I'm ready for this."

"Oh, you're ready, trust me. I can tell you really care about this woman, the way you talk about her, the way she's got you in this state. There's a lot of love still left in that heart of yours if you'd just open it up a crack. Are you falling in love with her?"

Claire sighed miserably. "I think so."

"Then allow yourself to explore things further. You know, make sure it wasn't just the sunshine and alcohol and all those crazy wedding bells down there."

Claire smiled. "It wasn't."

"Then don't let this opportunity slip away."

She thought of Amanda, wondered what she was doing right now. Probably getting ready for a class, or maybe preparing for final exams. Maybe she was just getting out of bed, and Claire smiled as she remembered her tousled morning hair, the sleepy but peaceful look in her eyes. No, she didn't want Amanda to slip away from her, to disappear, to become just a memory. Maybe this was indeed her shot at happiness, her shot at a future. Again. She supposed there was nothing to say you couldn't start over in life. Like halftime in football—two separate games in one.

"What would Ann think of her?"

The question shocked her back to reality. God, she hadn't thought of that. It took her a moment to coalesce her thoughts enough to answer. "She'd like her. She'd like her intelligence, her warmth, her humor. She'd say she was worldly and very mature for her age. And she'd definitely think she was hot."

"She sounds perfect."

Yes, Amanda did sound perfect. But their timing wasn't so perfect. In fact, it wasn't good at all. "It might be too soon for this, that's all. I still miss Ann."

"Of course you do. You'll always miss Ann. She shared your life for a long time. But I don't think she'd want that to hold you back forever. I think she'd want you to keep her in your heart, to keep the memories, but she'd want you to be happy, to live your life."

"I know. She'd probably kick my butt right now if she could."

Maria laughed. She'd known Ann long enough to know that was true. "God, you deserve some happiness, Claire. And you deserve to have someone love you. A future is the best gift you can give yourself."

Claire shrugged, relenting a little. Maria had a good point, but there was still the matter of Shannon. "I hope everyone else agrees, but I'm not so sure."

"Well, the only person who has to approve of it is you." Maria leapt up suddenly. "Crap, our first patient is due any minute. It's great to have you back. And it's great to see you happy. Or at least, starting to be happy. Just keep it up, will you?"

"You know something? You're a lot smarter sometimes than

you look," Claire teased.

"So are you."

Later in bed, Tucker snoring away at her feet, Claire stared into the blackness that was the ceiling and thought about Ann, remembered the good times they'd had, but also the harder times. They were together the years Claire worked obsessively hard at her career. There were times when she worked fourteen-hour days, six days a week. Times they hardly saw one another, times when they let their relationship survive on autopilot. And when Ann was so sick, their focus had been on her health and comfort and not on their relationship. Ann's death had forced her to slow down and begin the process of taking stock of her life and of what was important. Her period of introspection had included a heavy dose of guilt for all the years she'd spent working instead of spending quality time with Ann. Doubts had crept in, doubts about how healthy their relationship truly was when they'd spent so little time nourishing it. She remembered wishing, and then later promising herself, that she would do things differently if given a do-over some day. Work wasn't her entire life anymore like it had been. She tried to do a better job of listening to people now, to place more value in the simple things, like a good meal, walking the dog, or moments with friends. Since Ann, she tried to live in the now. It was a good thing, being present in the present, but at the same time, she had refused to allow herself to consider what the future might look like. Especially a future that involved someone other than Ann.

Ann's death had been a life-changing event for her. So too had meeting Amanda. Claire was fresher, more alive, more hopeful now than she'd been in many years. She had begun thinking about the future again, thinking, for the first time in three years, that maybe she wouldn't have to go through the rest of her life alone. For a week, the albatross of her loneliness had evaporated from around her neck, invigorating her, making her feel free and unencumbered for the first time in many years. Amanda had given her a glimpse of the future. And so much more.

She closed her eyes and pictured Amanda. Amanda smiling, laughing, looking at her with love in her eyes. It was the future being dangled in front of her, and like a drowning person seconds from being rescued, it was her choice to either grab the life ring or sink below the surface.

She missed Amanda. Deeply. She also missed the woman she had been last week—the woman who had been happy, free. The woman who was falling in love.

CHAPTER THIRTY-EIGHT

Shannon

"Can you believe a week ago now we were dancing at our wedding?"

"Ah," Dani sighed happily, joining Shannon on the sofa. She handed her a glass of red wine. "To a week of wedded bliss."

They toasted. Shannon sipped tentatively from her glass. "Hey, not bad for an eight-dollar bottle." They'd drink nothing more expensive than that now unless it was for something very special.

"Guess we should have waited for Claire before we opened it."

"She should be along any minute."

Claire had phoned hours ago asking to come over and have a chat with them. It sounded serious, and more than a little mysterious.

"Think she'll mind a cheap bottle?" Dani asked.

"She knows we're cutting back. Besides, I get the feeling she has something important on her mind. She won't care about the wine."

"Hmm, it does sound serious. You don't think she's going to tell us she's moving away or something like that, do you?"

Shannon's stomach dropped. "Shit, I hadn't even thought of that."

"Sorry, I'm sure that's not the case. Claire's rooted to this place, and God knows she's devoted to her patients. Hey, maybe she's going to take a six-month trip around the world."

"Yeah, right. Vegas was the first vacation she's had since Ann got sick. I doubt she's about to go on another one so soon."

"True. I can't really see her taking a long vacation anywhere, though she did seem to have a good time in Vegas."

Moments later Claire walked through their door, her eyes shadowed with fatigue and her smile nervous and wary.

"Everything okay?" Shannon asked as she poured her a glass of wine. It sure didn't look like things were okay in Claire's world.

"More or less."

"Busy week at work catching up?"

"Yes. Every day has been a twelve-hour marathon." She accepted the glass of wine and took a small sip. "Thanks. I think I need this."

"Come on in here and get comfortable."

Dani welcomed her with a hug.

"Nice fire," Claire commented.

"Yeah," Dani answered wistfully. "I'm going to miss this fireplace. And the killer view, of course."

"Are you putting it up for sale?"

"Probably," Shannon said. "But we're hoping we won't have to. We're going to wait a couple more months before we decide and see what happens."

"That's probably wise."

"I talked to human resources at the hospital yesterday."

Claire's eyes brightened. "Really? You're coming back to work?"

"If they'll have me." She exchanged a look with Dani. They'd had a couple of arguments about it over the past week. Dani didn't want her to go back to work, at least not full time, but Shannon didn't see any other choice. Besides, she wanted to go back. She felt useless sitting around the condo all day, especially now that there would be no baby to plan for and conceive. She was a nurse, and the hospital was where she belonged. Dani relented after finally seeing that it made sense on several levels. They could sure use the money and it would make Shannon happy.

"Oh, they'll have you, trust me," Claire said confidently. She looked questioningly at Dani. "How are you with that?"

"Fine." She wasn't totally fine about it yet, but she would be. Dani was quickly learning pragmatism.

"So," Shannon ventured. "What about you? Everything okay with you?"

"Yes and no."

Claire could be stubbornly difficult to elicit information from sometimes and often needed help in that department. "Well, you seemed very happy in Vegas, but also kind of . . . I don't know. Stressed sometimes. Like something was bothering you."

Claire nodded, stared into her glass, her hands cupped tightly around it. "I haven't been a very happy person the last three years. I hadn't realized quite how much until now."

"Perfectly understandable. What you went through with Ann's illness, and then her death . . ." Shannon glanced at Dani. "I don't know how I would survive all that if the same thing happened to us."

"You do survive. At least most people do. But I'm tired of being one of the walking wounded." She looked at Shannon. There was pleading in her eyes. "I realized last week that I want to live again. I mean really *live*. I want to be happy again. I don't want to just exist or survive anymore. I'm tired of that, to be honest."

Thank God. So that's what all this drama is about? "I'm so glad you've come to that realization. You deserve to be happy and to have a future. I hate seeing you alone, and I can't tell you how long I've waited for you to say those words."

"We've all been worried about you the last three years," Dani added solemnly. "You know that we would do anything for you."

Claire stood and began pacing, not looking at them. "There's something else I need to tell you guys, and I'm scared as hell, because I love you both and I'm selfish enough to want your continued love and friendship."

"You have it," Shannon said flatly. There was nothing Claire could tell her that would ever change her mind on that score.

"I hope so, but . . . crap, I don't know."

Shannon rapidly grew more worried. "Claire, we love you. There isn't anything you could tell us that would change that. You have to know that by now."

Claire stopped her pacing and looked at her with such distress that it made Shannon's heart skip a beat. She looked like she'd done something terrible, something criminal. Something that her friends might not be able to forgive her for.

"Please tell us what's wrong," Shannon urged softly. The suspense was nearly killing her.

Claire paced some more before she turned to them, her jaw trembling. "I'm in love with someone. And I want to be with her. And I want you to try and understand."

Shannon expelled the breath she hadn't realized she'd been holding. She was relieved as hell. "Well, that's great news! I mean, that's—"

"No." Claire held up her hand ominously. "Wait. There's more."

"Okay." *Shit*. So it *was* some kind of bad news after all.

Claire sat down, this time across from them, and Shannon was grateful the pacing had stopped. It did little to unravel the knot in her stomach, however.

Claire took a deep breath, closed her eyes briefly, then spoke firmly. "I'm in love with Amanda. I mean, she and I . . . are . . .

you know."

"What?" Shannon's head spun with the news. Her heart had stopped. "Amanda? *My* Amanda?"

Claire swallowed nervously, but her voice remained firm and her eyes resolute. "Yes."

Shannon might as well have been slapped. Her head back against the sofa, she closed her eyes and replayed Claire's words in her mind, slowly grasping their meaning. *My best friend is in love with my niece? What the hell? How is that even possible?*

"Will you say something? Please?"

Shannon shook her head. *I can't.*

Dani cleared her throat and took over. "Are you sure about this Claire?"

"Yes, I am."

"And Amanda. Is it mutual?"

"Yes."

Curiosity was beginning to take root in Shannon's mind. Anger too. The questions began flying out of her with rapidfire speed. "When did all this start?"

"In Vegas."

"How? I mean, for God's sake, we were only there a week. And before that you hadn't seen Amanda in years, right?"

"Yes, that's right."

"But how—?"

Claire shrugged. She was amazingly calm, the way Shannon had seen her give a patient bad news. "We got to know each other really well in Vegas. We spent a lot of time together there. And we realized how much we clicked. How much we liked each other and enjoyed spending time together."

There was the trip to the desert they'd been alone for. Had they had dates or something right under everyone's noses? Shannon's memory searched through every moment she'd seen them together. They hadn't acted like they were an item. Nothing to indicate that they'd taken that kind of an interest in one another. They got along well, obviously liked each other, though it was true there were some moments when they'd acted a little strange.

In a quavering voice, Shannon finally said, "I don't understand this. I trusted you with her."

Claire's eyes moistened. "I—We didn't do anything wrong."

Shannon shook her head, hot angry tears streaming from her eyes. "She was vulnerable, Claire. She just came out of a bad relationship, for God's sake! How could you take advantage of her like that? You're almost twice her age!"

Dani clutched her hand for support, whispered it was okay, but Shannon brushed her off. She was not ready to be pacified. "No, I need to hear this."

Claire bowed her head. "I'm sorry. I didn't plan for it to happen. Neither did she."

"Did you sleep with her?" Shannon demanded brusquely.

When Claire raised her eyes, they were devoid of their earlier determination. She looked weak, wounded. "Yes," she whispered.

"Oh my God!" Shannon felt sick to her stomach. How could Claire, the person she trusted most in this world next to Dani, do something so hurtful? So betraying? So disloyal? How could she *fuck* the young woman who was like a daughter to her? "How could you?" she demanded.

"Wait," Dani interjected. "Can't we talk about this calmly?"

"I think I should leave," Claire offered.

"Yes," Shannon said. "I think that would be a marvelous idea."

"I'm sorry," Claire said quietly at the door, "but she makes me happy."

Shannon could not look at her. She turned away. She could not fathom how or why this could happen. Her best friend and her niece. Sleeping together! Claire old enough to be her mother. And Claire knowing Amanda was her closest family member. It was incestuous. Disloyal. Sick. Hurtful beyond words.

"I think you're overreacting," Dani said quietly after Claire was gone.

"Don't."

"Amanda is not a child. If she wants to sleep with Claire or anyone else—"

"Don't even talk to me about them sleeping together!"

Dani sighed in exasperation. "I'm sorry, but would you rather not know the truth? Would you rather they lied or kept it from you? Jesus, Amanda is family and so is Claire. We don't turn our backs on family."

"Amanda's vulnerable right now. She doesn't know what she's doing. She needs our protection."

"What do you mean vulnerable?"

"She has a bad history with women!"

"Now wait. A bad history with *one* woman," Dani corrected. "She's a grown woman. And she doesn't need anyone's protection."

"She's going through a divorce!"

"Yes, to someone she was married to for all of about five minutes, and who she's been separated from for over a year."

"Look, I don't want to argue about this. It hurts, okay?"

"No, we need to talk about this. I don't want to stand by and watch you throw your friendship with Claire away. And don't you think Amanda is going to be hurt over this? If she's in love with Claire, your disapproval is going to hurt her very much."

Shannon needed time to process this. It still felt like a punch to the stomach.

Dani pressed her into her arms and held her tightly. "It's not about you, my love. They didn't do this to hurt you, okay? They're just two people trying to find some happiness in this world. It shouldn't be wrong to try to do that."

"But . . ." Shannon gulped back the tears. "If it was anyone but Amanda and Claire."

"I know, but it isn't. It's two of your favorite people in the world. And they both love you. You have to believe that. It can't be easy for them right now either."

She was still angry, still hurt, but Dani's sensitivity and

wisdom made her smile inside. The tough businesswoman who was a caring, sympathetic marshmallow inside. It was one of the reasons she loved her so much. "I'm sorry, but I need some time with this okay?"

Dani would give her time, but not too much, she knew. Each understood that supporting one another and giving unconditional love also meant acting as one another's conscience, shoulder to cry on, and butt kicker, all in one. Dani would help her through this; no more carrying burdens alone.

CHAPTER THIRTY-NINE

Amanda

Amanda tried hard to keep her eyes from glancing at the door, but it was often an exercise in futility. She'd mostly given up expecting Claire to call or walk through her apartment door, yet she continued to hope it might miraculously happen. And while she'd decided she couldn't let it continue to monopolize her thoughts, there were still reflexive moments like this when she glanced at the door expecting—hoping—Claire would materialize. Claire loved her. Claire would do the right thing and give them a chance. She *had* to. Wouldn't she?

Amanda hurriedly drained her coffee cup and set it in the sink. She dared not be late for her first walking tour of the season, at least not for such a sorry reason as daydreaming about Claire.

The El train traffic was fairly light. It was early April—too soon for tourists to be out in droves, but hopefully there'd be enough of them to make the tour worthwhile. She loved conducting the walking architecture tours downtown; she could talk about the old buildings all day. And while it didn't much matter whether there were three people or thirty on her tour, she found that the greater the number of questions and interest shown, the more she got excited about it.

Two weeks had gone by since the wedding, three since she met Claire at the airport in Vegas. In some ways it seemed like yesterday, and in other ways, it was as though months had gone by. Being away from Claire seemed to consume disproportionate chunks of time—time that was wasted, as far as Amanda was concerned. But Claire needed space and some time, and she had agreed to give it to her without realizing how wrenchingly difficult it would be.

She was still reeling from the conversation at lunch with her aunt yesterday. Anxiety churned anew in her stomach. Shannon confessed that Claire had come over and told them what had happened between them in Vegas. The news hadn't pleased Shannon, which was totally predictable. She was being overprotective, hurt beyond reason, but she seemed to recognize that her reaction was her own problem and she was trying to come to terms with it. She hadn't seen it coming, but then, none of them had, Amanda assured her. She told Shannon that she and Claire certainly hadn't gone looking to get involved and hadn't fallen into it without giving it a lot of thought. It hadn't been an easy decision, she said.

"Are you in love with her?" Shannon asked after much hesitation.

Amanda simply nodded, afraid if she tried to speak, her voice would desert her.

Shannon frowned. "She said she was in love with you too."

Amanda exploded in a smile. Hearing someone else say Claire was in love with her made her giddy inside. She wanted to leap up and do a fist pump. *Yes! Claire loves me!*

"Well, you don't have to look so happy about it."

Amanda's excitement evaporated, but only a little. "I won't be miserable about it, if that's what you're suggesting."

Clearly, her dating Claire was torturing her aunt. Her emotions paraded across her face—anger, disappointment, fear, concern, puzzlement. Finally Shannon sighed, and her small, conciliatory smile was her white flag. "You're right. Love is not something that should make you miserable. I'm sorry."

"Good, because I'm happy with Claire. Incredibly so."

"Are you scared about it? After what happened with Jennifer?"

"No. Claire is not Jennifer, and I'm not the person I was two years ago."

The inquisition ended there. Shannon went on to express her worry that she didn't know how to act around the two of them, that it would take some getting used to but that she really did want them to be happy. "It just means I have twice the worry now, since I worry about both of you so much."

Amanda promised it would be okay, that they would all figure it out together and do whatever it took to make sure everyone was comfortable. What she hadn't been able to confess to her aunt was whether she and Claire were even an item anymore, because she simply didn't know. This self-imposed blackout in communicating with Claire was killing her. While it thrilled her that Claire had spoken to Shannon about their love for one another, she had no idea how Claire felt now. For all she knew, Claire was going to tell her she needed another six months to get her head around this. Or that she couldn't bring herself to try a relationship with her after all.

Distractedly, Amanda approached the small cluster of people she pegged as her clients. The fact that most of them were clutching the brochure for the tour was her first clue. "Good morning," she said with her customary cheery smile, forcing her attention on her work.

They greeted her eagerly. After introductions she began explaining the history of the great fire of 1871 and the massive rebuilding. She led them across Adams Street to her first showing—Berghoffs, which was one of the first buildings constructed after the fire. It was only four stories high because there were no elevators, she explained. To illustrate the construction differences after elevators made their appearance right before the turn of the twentieth century, she pointed to the Marquette Building, a national historic site built in 1895 and one of the city's first skyscrapers at sixteen stories. She talked about the history of the building and how it was constructed as she led the small group into its lobby. The rotunda was spectacular with bright mosaic murals depicting the early settlers, solid bronze grillwork and mahogany sheathed walls. The floor was marble. It really was a thing of beauty and the group was awed.

Several minutes later they were standing outside the neo-gothic Fisher Building, now a twenty-story luxury apartment building. Amanda was pointing to the various terra-cotta carvings of aquatic life on the façade when she did a double take at the figure hovering on the sidewalk a few yards away. It was Claire, trying to be unobtrusive, yet clearly she was following Amanda's group from a distance. Amanda's heart beat in double time, somewhere in her throat. Claire, realizing she'd been caught, smiled shyly and gave a hasty half wave.

"I'll be right back," she told her group before striding boldly up to Claire. "Well. It's you."

"Yes, it's me. Can we talk?"

Alternately pleased Claire was back in her life and annoyed it took her two weeks, Amanda hedged. "It would seem I'm a little busy right now."

"I know, I'm sorry. Shannon told me you would be conducting this tour here this morning and I didn't know what time you'd be back at your apartment."

"I'll be home in a couple of hours."

"Good. I'll meet you there with some take-out hot and sour soup. Would that be all right?"

"Okay." Tingling with anticipation, not all of it in a good way, she watched Claire leave. She hoped Claire was going to tell her what she wanted to hear. Hoped they would spend the afternoon in bed together. If that wasn't to be the case, well, she'd have to figure out how to deal with it and how to say good-bye.

Her heart heavy with that thought, she walked slowly back to her tour group.

The hot and sour soup was good, but Amanda barely ate it, she was so nervous. When she could stand the suspense no longer, she looked directly at Claire and asked her to break it to her, one way or another.

"You think I'm going to break your heart, don't you?" Claire asked.

"It's my worst fear. Jennifer could never truly break my heart, but you could."

Claire reached across the small kitchen table and squeezed her hand reassuringly. "I would never hurt you."

"Then make me the happiest woman in Chicago."

Claire's smile deepened, making her easily look ten years younger. "I would like nothing better. I love you, Amanda Malden. I want us to be together, no matter what the obstacles. But I need to be sure that I'm enough for you."

Relief flowed from her body in one giant exhale. *Oh, thank God!* Hearing that Claire loved her and wanted to be with her was the very pinnacle of her life so far, as though all her other pinnacles had simply been foothills and not mountains. Tears brimmed in her eyes. "Oh, God, yes, you're more than enough for me. I was so afraid I'd lost you."

"You haven't. And you won't."

A shred of doubt lingered. "What about Shannon? I know she's trying to accept us as a couple, but what if she can't?"

"She will. Besides, I'm in love with you, not her. You're my priority."

Amanda swallowed hard. She'd not let herself imagine the words Claire was now saying, but she had one more question. "Your past. Ann. Are you sure you're ready to be with me?"

A shadow of pain fell across Claire's face, but only for a moment. "Yes, I'm ready. I'll always keep Ann in my heart, but I don't want to be alone anymore. I don't want to live my life in the past. I want a future, and I want that future to be with you. I need you."

"You're really sure?"

"Yes. You know, I used to think the lesson in Ann's death was the appreciation for how lucky I'd been to have her. And I was. But now I realize the real lesson is how fleeting time is. I don't want to lose any more of it."

In seconds Amanda was in Claire's lap and in her arms, kissing her and insanely happy.

"Wait," Claire blurted out. "I'm not too late, am I?"

"What?"

"You haven't gone off and started dating some other Ms. Right while you were waiting for me, have you?"

Amanda feigned shock. "How did you know I had three dates with three different women last week?"

Claire's face fell for a moment until she realized Amanda was kidding. "Crap, you almost had me there."

Amanda kissed her lips playfully and giggled. "There's only one place I want you."

"Oh, yeah? Where's that?"

"My bedroom."

Claire moaned lightly. "I thought you'd never ask."

Amanda giggled again and couldn't resist lengthening the joke. "You're much easier than those other women I was dating last week."

"Well, you know what they say about us gynecologists."

"No, what do they say?" she growled playfully against Claire's throat.

"That we can't get enough pussy."

Amanda laughed so hard, she nearly fell out of Claire's lap. She knew Claire was teasing, and she loved her surprising sense of ribald humor. "Well, then, I sure wouldn't want to keep you waiting. And I plan to give you more than you can handle."

Moments later they were in the rumpled bed, Amanda planted between Claire's legs, her tongue stroking Claire's erect clitoris, Claire's urgent moans and insistent hands quickening her tempo. She loved how vulnerable Claire was when she came, how exposed and open her need was, and how utterly satisfied she was when she cried out and shook in orgasm. Amanda held her quaking body, stroked her face and told her how much she loved her. Claire began crying softly, crying tears of joy, she assured Amanda.

"You make me so incredibly happy, Amanda. Happier than I ever thought I'd be. Happier than I ever thought I deserved. God, I love you so much."

"Funny. You just took the identical words out of my mouth."

"We seem to do that a lot, don't we?"

"Yes. Is that what happens when two people are meant for one another?"

"Yes, I suppose it does." Claire's fluttering fingers parted Amanda's thighs. "There's something else two people do when they're meant for one another."

Amanda grinned, unable to contain her delight. "I see, and what would that be?"

"This for starters." Claire's fingers began dancing in light circles on her engorged flesh. "And then this." A finger slipped inside, then another.

"Oh, God." Amanda's breathing quickened, her clit suddenly stiff and begging for attention. "If you keep doing that . . . Oh, God."

Claire's mouth found a nipple and latched on. If sex was this good between them now, Amanda thought, imagine how good it would be in a few more months. It was her last thought before she completely melted into a shattering orgasm.

EPILOGUE

Six months later~Dani

It was uncharacteristically warm for late September, but with the sun angled low and the leaves on the trees beginning to turn, there was no ignoring the fact that summer was over. That was fine with Dani because she liked winter, but today she was pleased the weather was cooperating for their picnic at Grant Park to celebrate their six-month anniversary.

There'd been no criticism when they'd announced they wanted to celebrate quietly and cheaply with a picnic instead of at some expensive restaurant. Their friends understood. Their cutbacks had been fairly severe, though they'd managed to hold onto the condo. Shannon was back working full time at the same hospital Claire worked at, while Dani had secured a part-time teaching job at the Kellogg School of Management. They could both walk to work, even meet for lunch sometimes at the nearby Corner Bakery café.

Dani had to admit that life was pretty good. Different, but

good. A year ago, she'd have thought they'd be pregnant by now and still living high on Dani's inflated salary. Truth was, she was okay with the changes. She felt better about herself and their relationship now. The baby part of it . . . well, that was still upsetting, but she'd not given up hope that they might one day adopt or look into a surrogate.

Shannon smiled at her as she flattened the blanket on the grass. Grant Park was busy but they'd managed to find a spot big enough for the six of them. "Penny for your thoughts?"

"Nothing really. Just thinking how happy I am with the way things turned out."

"Even though some of it wasn't what you were expecting?"

"No, but that's okay. The six months being married to you has been even better than I expected." Her gold wedding band flashed in the sunshine. They'd flown to Toronto, Canada, three months ago and made it official.

Shannon kissed her on the lips. "You're right about that, my love. It's been the best six months ever!"

"You're a lot happier now that you're back to work, aren't you?"

"Yes. I hate to say it, but I'm really not cut out to be the stay-at-home type."

Dani laughed. "So if we ever have a kid, guess I'll be the stay-at-home mom, right?"

"Would that be so bad?"

"Actually no, it wouldn't." It surprised Dani how well she'd adjusted to working part time and fixing dinner most nights, as well as doing all the grocery shopping and bill paying. She'd never dreamed she might be the domestic type, but she was adjusting quite well to it.

"Ah, there you guys are!" Amanda, holding Claire's hand, sauntered up to them.

Shannon leaped up to hug them both. Dani did the same.

"Have a seat," Shannon said. "Jordan and Dez should be here any minute."

Amanda and Claire certainly looked happy these days.

Tanned, constantly grinning, their eyes almost never leaving one another, they seemed deeply in love. Claire looked younger and more energetic than Dani ever remembered her looking, and Amanda was so relaxed these days, so happy. They touched all the time, did the little things for one another. They were good for each other.

"No Tucker today?" Dani asked.

"No," Claire said. "Unless you wanted all the food eaten before we get to it. Labradors and picnics aren't a very good match."

"You're right, what was I thinking. Are we still on for the big move next weekend?" She was scheduled to help Amanda move in with Claire, and frankly, it was about time they made their living arrangement official.

"You bet." Amanda grinned. "So long as Claire doesn't change her mind before then."

Claire pretended to ponder, her fingers rubbing her chin contemplatively. "Hmm. I'm still not sure if I can live with her standards. Things like insisting the toothpaste tube be squeezed from the bottom, picking up my dirty clothes from the floor. It's going to be tough."

"Somehow I think you'll be able to handle it, honey. Along with all those massages you're going to get, and the other . . . pleasing things your body will enjoy."

Shannon cleared her throat. "All right you two. Enough of the sex talk." She was smiling when she said it.

Amanda giggled. "Who said anything about sex? Maybe I was talking about tickles and kisses and warm snuggles."

"Oh, I see. No premarital sex, is that it?" Shannon said.

Dani cringed inside, hoping the word *marital* wasn't presumptuous. It wouldn't surprise her if Claire popped the question one of these days, especially now that it looked like Amanda's divorce would be going through soon. The thought of the two of them getting married thrilled her. It would officially bond them all as family.

"That's right," Claire said. "We're having about the same

kind of premarital sex as you two had!"

Shannon began to blush. "Oh my God. In that case, it's a wonder you even got out of bed to come over here."

Claire and Amanda shared a private look and a smile, making it obvious that Shannon had hit a bull's-eye. It was true, if they were having as much sex as Dani and Shannon, well, that was a hell of a lot!

"Did someone say the word *sex*?" It was Jordan calling out, approaching with Dez in tow. "Cuz if that's the case, please, don't stop."

Claire threw her head back and laughed. "Figures your finely tuned ears would pick up on that word from a distance."

"I'm just pleased everyone's getting some," Jordan added. "The more the better."

Everyone exchanged hugs. It was the first time they had all been together in one place since the wedding.

"It's so good to see you," Dani said to her oldest and best friend. "More to the point, it's so good to see you happy."

Jordan clasped her arm around Dez's waist. "I have this woman to thank for that."

Shannon surveyed the group, a smile splitting her face. "It's so great to see everyone so happy. It's like some kind of a dream come true."

"We all have your wedding to thank for bringing us to this point," Amanda said. She shook her head in wonder. "Imagine if you'd never had your wedding in Vegas and invited us all along."

"Let's not even think about that," Dani said.

What Amanda said was exactly right. Their friends' happiness was evidence of the good things they had inadvertently brought to others' lives. You couldn't often see how you affected other peoples' lives in your day-to-day living. It was a wonderful feeling of accomplishment, knowing her and Shannon's happiness with each other had brought that same kind of happiness to the people who mattered most to them. It was the best wedding present they could ever have hoped for.

Shannon reached into a cooler and pulled out a frosted bottle of nonalcoholic bubbly. "What we need, ladies, is a toast."

"Here, here," Jordan echoed.

Plastic cups filled, each woman took a turn offering a toast to Shannon and Dani, then to one another.

Dani winked before sipping from her cup. "Let's hope there are more weddings in the future for our little group."

Claire laughed, her eyes twinkling. "To the best wedding party ever! And may our work as bridesmaids and, er, brides, never be done!"

Publications from

Bella Books, Inc.

Women. Books. Even Better Together.

P.O. Box 10543
Tallahassee, FL 32302
Phone: 800-729-4992
www.bellabooks.com

BLIND BET by Tracey Richardson. The stakes are high when Ellen Turcotte and Courtney Langford meet at the blackjack tables. Lady Luck has been smiling on Courtney but Ellen is a wild card she may not be able to handle.
978-1-59493-211-3 $14.95

JUKEBOX by Gina Daggett. Debutantes in love. With each other. Two young women chafe at the constraints of parents and society with a friendship that could be more, if they can break free. Gina Daggett is best known as "Lipstick" of the columnist duo Lipstick & Dipstick.   978-1-59493-212-0 $14.95

SHADOW POINT by Amy Briant. Madison McPeake has just been not-quite fired, told her brother is dead and discovered she has to pick up a five-year-old niece she's never met. After she makes it to Shadow Point it seems like someone—or something—doesn't want her to leave. Romance sizzles in this ghost story from Amy Briant.   978-1-59493-216-8 $14.95

DEVIL'S ROCK by Gerri Hill. Deputy Andrea Sullivan and Agent Cameron Ross vow to bring a killer to justice. The killer has other plans. Gerri Hill pens another intriguing blend of mystery and romance in this page-turning thriller.
978-1-59493-218-2 $14.95

SOMETHING TO BELIEVE by Robbi McCoy. When Lauren and Cassie meet on a once-in-a-lifetime river journey through China their feelings are innocent...at first. Ten years later, nothing—and everything—has changed. From Golden Crown winner Robbi McCoy.   978-1-59493-214-4 $14.95

LEAVING L.A. by Kate Christie. Eleanor Chapin is on the way to the rest of her life when Tessa Flanagan offers her a lucrative summer job caring for Tessa's daughter Laya. It's only temporary and everyone expects Eleanor to be leaving L.A . . .   978-1-59493-221-2 $14.95

WILDFIRE by Lynn James. From the moment botanist Devon McKinney meets ranger Elaine Thomas the chemistry is undeniable. Sharing—and protecting—a mountain for the length of their short assignments leads to unexpected passion in this sizzling romance by newcomer Lynn James.

978-1-59493-191-8 $14.95

WEDDING BELL BLUES by Julia Watts. She'll do anything to save what's left of her family. Anything. It didn't seem like a bad plan . . . at first. Hailed by readers as Lammy-winner Julia Watts' funniest novel.

978-1-59493-199-4 $14.95

WHISPERS IN THE WIND by Frankie J. Jones. It began as a camping trip, then a simple hike. Dixon Hayes and Elizabeth Colter uncover an intriguing cave on their hike, changing their world, perhaps irrevocably.

978-1-59493-037-9 $14.95

ELENA UNDONE by Nicole Conn. The risks. The passion. The devastating choices. The ultimate rewards. Nicole Conn rocked the lesbian cinema world with *Claire of the Moon* and has rocked it again with *Elena Undone*. This is the book that tells it all . . .   978-1-59493-254-0 $14.95

FAÇADES by Alex Marcoux. Everything Anastasia ever wanted—she has it. Sidney is the woman who helped her get it. But keeping it will require a price—the unnamed passion that simmers between them.

978-1-59493-239-7 $14.95

HUNTING THE WITCH by Ellen Hart. The woman she loves—used to love—offers her help, and Jane Lawless finds it hard to say no. She needs TLC for recent injuries and who better than a doctor? But Julia's jittery demeanor awakens Jane's curiosity. And Jane has never been able to resist a mystery. Number 9 in series and Lammy-winner.   978-1-59493-206-9 $14.95

2ND FIDDLE by Kate Calloway. Cassidy James's first case left her with a broken heart. At least this new case is fighting the good fight, and she can throw all her passion and energy into it.   978-1-59493-200-7 $14.95

MAKING UP FOR LOST TIME by Karin Kallmaker. Take one Next Home Network Star and add one Little White Lie to equal mayhem in little Mendocino and a recipe for sizzling romance. This lighthearted, steamy story is a feast for the senses in a kitchen that is way too hot.

978-1-931513-61-6 $14.95

SUBSTITUTE FOR LOVE by Karin Kallmaker. No substitutes, ever again! But then Holly's heart, body and soul are captured by Reyna . . . Reyna with no last name and a secret life that hides a terrible bargain, one written in family blood.   978-1-931513-62-3 $14.95

DEADLY INTERSECTIONS by Ann Roberts. Everyone is lying, including her own father and her girlfriend. Leaving matters to the professionals is supposed to be easier! Third in series with PAID IN FULL and WHITE OFFERINGS.   978-1-59493-224-3 $14.95

WHEN AN ECHO RETURNS by Linda Kay Silva. The bayou where Echo Branson found her sanity has been swept clean by a hurricane—or at least they thought. Then an evil washed up by the storm comes looking for them all, one-by-one. Second in series.   978-1-59493-225-0 $14.95

LESSONS IN MURDER by Claire McNab. There's a corpse in the school with a neat hole in the head and a Black & Decker drill alongside. Which teacher should Inspector Carol Ashton suspect? Unfortunately, the alluring Sybil Quade is at the top of the list. First in this highly lauded series.
                                                        978-1-931513-65-4 $14.95

THE WILD ONE by Lyn Denison. Rachel Weston is busy keeping home and head together after the death of her husband. Her kids need her and what she doesn't need is the confusion that Quinn Farrelly creates in her body and heart.   978-0-9677753-4-0 $14.95

CALM BEFORE THE STORM by Peggy J. Herring. Colonel Marcel Robicheaux doesn't tell and so far no one official has asked, but the amorous pursuit by Jordan McGowen has her worried for both her career and her honor.   978-0-9677753-1-9 $14.95

THE GRASS WIDOW by Nanci Little. Aidan Blackstone is nineteen, unmarried and pregnant, and has no reason to think that the year 1876 won't be her last. Joss Bodett has lost her family but desperately clings to their land. A richly told story of frontier survival that picks up with the generation of women where Patience and Sarah left off.   978-1-59493-189-5 $14.95

SMOKEY O by Celia Cohen. Insult "Mac" MacDonnell and insult the entire Delaware Blue Diamond team. Smokey O'Neill has just insulted Mac, and then finds she's been traded to Delaware. The games are not limited to the baseball field!   978-1-59493-198-7 $12.95

WICKED GAMES by Ellen Hart. Never have mysteries and secrets been closer to home in this eighth installment of this award-winning lesbian mystery series. Jane Lawless's neighbors bring puzzles and peril—and that's just the beginning.   978-1-59493-185-7 $14.95

NOT EVERY RIVER by Robbi McCoy. It's the hottest city in the U.S., and it's not just the weather that's heating up. For Kim and Randi are forced to question everything they thought they knew about themselves before they can risk their fiery hearts on the biggest gamble of all.
                                                        978-1-59493-182-6 $14.95